KILL the BEAST

A TALE OF
EVERYONE'S FAVORITE GUY

KILL THE BEAST

A TALE OF
EVERYONE'S FAVORITE GUY

BY SERENA VALENTINO

DISNEP • HYPERION

LOS ANGELES • NEW YORK

Adapted in part from Disney's *Beauty and the Beast*

Text copyright © 2024 by Disney Enterprises, Inc.
All rights reserved. Published by Disney • Hyperion, an imprint of
Buena Vista Books, Inc. No part of this book may be reproduced or
transmitted in any form or by any means, electronic or mechanical,
including photocopying, recording, or by any information storage
and retrieval system, without written permission from the publisher.
For information address Disney • Hyperion, 77 West 66th Street,
New York, New York 10023.

First Edition, July 2024
10 9 8 7 6 5 4 3 2 1
FAC-004510-24144
Printed in the United States of America

This book is set in 13-point Garamond 3 LT Pro.
Designed by Phil T. Buchanan

Library of Congress Cataloging-in-Publication Control Number:
2024931169

ISBN 978-1-368-07659-3

Reinforced binding

Visit www.DisneyBooks.com

Dedicated with love to my amazingly sweet and supportive readers. I appreciate you with my entire heart. Thank you.

FROM THE BOOK OF FAIRY TALES

You may think you know Gaston's story. You may even remember the intrepid self-proclaimed hero blustering his way through the Beast's saga, flexing his muscles and jutting out his cleft chin as he sang his own praises, like he was the king of Buttchinland. But sometimes there is more than one villain in a fairy tale. And make no mistake about it, both Gaston and the Beast were the villains of this story, even if the Beast eventually redeemed himself.

Some even say *we* are the true villains lurking in these pages, pulling the strings of fate and weaving these tales to fit our own design. The meddling, scheming, fiendish witches of all these tales: the Odd Sisters. And they may be right.

Being the authors of the Book of Fairy Tales, we can say with magical authority this is a book like no other. It's fluid and as ever changing as the fates of those whose stories we've chronicled have shifted. And though the events that shaped Gaston's life and his eventual demise happened long ago, our narrative reflects everything that happened before his time, and what's happened since. You may wonder how that is possible. It's simple: we see things much more clearly from our new home in the Underworld with Hades. We see everything. Past, present, and future.

If you've read the Beast's legend in the Book of Fairy Tales, you know why we helped to curse him. He was a selfish, vain, and cruel man who broke our daughter Circe's heart. We say daughter because that is what she is, but long ago, at the time of these events, we lied to our daughter and told her she was our sister. Our little sister, who we would do anything to protect, including befriending Gaston so we might get our revenge on the beast prince. And though you may think you know the part Gaston played in these events, there is always more than one version of a story. This is Gaston's.

Whether this is a story of redemption or not is up to you. It is the tale of two young boys who loved each other like brothers and who would forever change each other's lives.

CHAPTER I

BLOOD BROTHERS

Gaston grew up in a picturesque kingdom, its castle perched atop a towering rocky island that was connected to its lands by a long stone bridge. It was a beautiful and architecturally unique castle composed of many levels—each level with its own landing and garden. The castle spires, and there were many, resembled pointed witches' caps that pierced the sky majestically. Gaston had the run of this castle and the grounds surrounding it, and together with the prince of this kingdom he spent his days exploring every inch of the castle and the kingdom's vast forests.

Gaston and the prince had been the best of friends

since they were first old enough to explore. Their mothers were very close and fancied the idea of their sons growing up together, and so they did. They were wild, adventurous, rough-and-tumble young boys, constantly seeking excitement, and they never had to look too hard to find it. The pair always found a way to create their own fun.

They made games of finding the oldest trees and the most overgrown paths. They found abandoned outbuildings that were in disrepair and hollowed-out oaks that led to underground tunnels, and they discovered an ancient and crumbling graveyard that seemed to have been there long before the prince's family ruled in this land. Some days they would spend hours riding their horses, jumping creeks and fences, daring each other to ride out as far as they could away from the prince's kingdom so they could explore strange lands they had only learned about through stories in books they found in the castle library. And some days they would stay close to home, poring over those stories and dreaming of what their lives would be like when they were old enough to do whatever they liked.

One of their favorite bits of mischief when in the castle was sneaking into the library to find all manner of books, including those on the history of the Many Kingdoms. These books were filled with lavish illustrations of beings that hadn't been seen in hundreds of years, like the great Tree Lords who once ruled over all the lands that the Many Kingdoms were now built upon. Little did they know not too long after, the Tree Lords would emerge again, awaking from their long slumber to take their place in the world once more.

The castle librarian, Monsieur Biblio, was a peevish and stuffy man who was rather particular about books never leaving the library, even though by rights the books belonged to the prince—or at least would belong to him one day. Monsieur Biblio guarded the books like a greedy dragon protecting his treasure, sometimes even snarling and grumbling if he found that one was missing. Both the boys agreed Monsieur Biblio looked more like a mole than a dragon. He was a squat man with a very round bald head and small eyes that were magnified by his thick glasses. Gaston and the prince liked making a game of sneaking into the *Dragon's Den*, as they called it, daring each other to creep in while Monsieur Biblio was attending to his duties. Sometimes the prince would go in under the pretense of asking Monsieur Biblio a question, usually on a topic they knew the librarian was especially interested in and could talk about at great length. The boys had observed Monsieur Biblio was particularly intrigued by the history and construction of the various castles in the Many Kingdoms. And he was notably drawn to the diverse protocols in each of these castles' households. But his special interest, what occupied his time most, was learning about the keepers of books who came before him and how they ran their libraries. The average person, through no fault of their own, might not realize the royal librarian's province went well beyond the safekeeping of the royal tomes. The castle librarian was also the most knowledgeable about the house, its possessions, and those who have lived within its walls over the ages. They were also historians. So all the prince would have to do was ask Monsieur Biblio a question about the house, or who was featured in a particular portrait, and Monsieur

Biblio would blather on about it endlessly. This would give Gaston the opportunity to sneak in and slip some books into his knapsack. Afterward, the boys would laugh, pleased they had outwitted stuffy old Monsieur Biblio again, and take their ill-gotten treasures to their tree house, where they wouldn't be disturbed.

Gaston and the prince loved almost nothing more than getting their hands on magnificent books filled with exciting tales of adventures. Gaston loved looking at the drawings while the prince read their histories aloud. They'd sometimes spend hours with one of Monsieur Biblio's precious tomes, tucked away in the tree house Gaston's father had built for them, not far from the cottage where Gaston lived with his father. His father was the only grown-up who knew about their secret tree house—as those who lived in the castle rarely visited the cottage—and he promised he would never tell. The hideaway was everything the boys could wish for, with its large round windows and a trapdoor they could close when they were inside. It was tucked high up in the strong branches of a massive and venerable oak, and at night the boys felt they were among the stars. They had cushions to sit upon and stacks of the books from the library to enjoy, surrounded by the interesting things they found on their adventures. It was their secret place. A world where only the boys and their stories existed.

"What book are you reading for us tonight? Is it about dragons?" asked Gaston, tossing their wooden swords and shields into a corner of the tree house.

They were dressed in their knights' outfits from their adventure earlier in the day. They had been running around the catacombs deep beneath the castle, searching for dragons. Of course, they didn't find any real dragons, but they had the grandest of times slaying the dragons in their imaginations.

After a day of dragon slaying, they made themselves comfortable, lying back together on a mountain of cushions they had taken from the castle and deciding to fall into the pages of one of their favorite books. Luckily, no one seemed to notice the various things that went missing from the castle that ended up in their tree house. (Except, that is, for the books they spirited away from the library.)

"It's another story about the Dead Woods," said the prince, holding an old, thick book called the Book of Fairy Tales.

"Those are my favorites! I hope there's a battle with all those dead soldiers!"

"There is! It's about Sir Jacob, remember him? This story is about his life before he died and how he came to serve the Queens of the Dead."

"Oh wow! I always wondered how he ended up there." Gaston imagined what Sir Jacob must have looked like when he was alive. He hoped there would be a good description of him. Gaston loved the Book of Fairy Tales. It had everything he enjoyed most: exciting stories steeped in the history of the Many Kingdoms. And of course it didn't hurt there were many tales involving dragons, gigantic talking trees, undead soldiers, witches, and magic.

"Do you think we could go to the Dead Woods one day, Kingsley?"

"Not unless you want to become one of Jacob's undead soldiers," said the prince with a laugh. "But we can go to Morningstar Kingdom. It's a long ride, but not so far we wouldn't be able to go there and back before dinner if we left early enough."

"Do you think our papas would let us?"

"Let's not give them a chance to say no." Gaston loved this about his friend. The prince was always willing to go on an adventure, without a care for the rules. If he had been the sort of prince who followed the rules, they wouldn't be friends, and they wouldn't get to go on so many capers. They wouldn't have all the treasures they had collected on their many adventures.

Some of their treasures were seemingly mundane, like interesting-looking pinecones, or brightly colored rocks, or acorns with strange symbols carved into them. They also had crows' feathers, and broken pieces of headstones from the cemetery, and small bones they found on the forest floor. No matter how small, each treasure told a different story, a reminder of the adventure they had that day. But their most valued treasure was the little hunting knife they used to cut the palms of their hands so they could become brothers. There wasn't anything magic in this, of course; neither of them knew of such things except from the fairy stories the prince read aloud on occasion. They just wanted to be brothers, and this was the closest thing to being actual brothers they could think of.

Being blood brothers.

If it were up to Gaston and the prince, they would stay in their tree house all day and well into the night if they could, poring over their most-loved books and discussing the fantastic tales they discovered. And sometimes they would, until Gaston's father called up to them to remind the prince he was due home for dinner, or for his lessons with his tutor, Mr. Willowstick. Gaston would usually accompany the prince back to the castle, where they would part ways, the prince going to the dining hall and Gaston going to visit Mrs. Potts down in the kitchen or her sitting room. When dinner was over, they would both run off on another adventure, their pockets stuffed with goodies Mrs. Potts gave them.

One of their other most loved pastimes was sneaking around parts of the castle that were forbidden. Telling either of them something wasn't allowed was like giving them a direct order to seek that thing out and discover its secrets. They spent countless hours wandering the catacombs under the castle and exploring its many secret passageways.

They had even found hidden panels leading to passageways between the castle walls that took them directly to the kitchens in the basement, which weren't actually a secret at all but rather well-known to the staff, being a more direct passage for the servants so they might bring meals to the dining hall and attend to their other duties without disturbing the royal family. But the boys had invented other reasons for these secret passageways, wild tales that fueled their imaginations, giving them endless hours of fun. They both loved hiding behind the secret doors and popping out when they heard someone on the other side to give the unlucky passerby a fright, though taking special care not to do this to Mr. Cogsworth. Neither of the boys wanted to give Mr. Cogsworth a reason to be cross with them. Or more precisely, even more reasons to be cross with Gaston, because Mr. Cogsworth seemed always to be in a state of disapproval where Gaston was concerned.

This wasn't so with the head housekeeper, Mrs. Potts, or the majority of the other servants; they all seemed to love Gaston and were happy to let the boys have their fun, even letting Gaston and the prince believe they had made a new discovery when they'd pop into the kitchen unexpectedly, pretending to be ghouls and then begging for treats, which Mrs. Potts always had on hand when the boys came bounding into her sitting room or kitchens.

Almost all the servants treated Gaston and the prince like they were brothers. Not that they *were* brothers, mind you, but they were around the same age, and being such good friends, they were always in each other's company. And they had declared they were blood brothers, after all, and who was to tell them otherwise?

Gaston's father, Grosvenor, was the king's groundskeeper and royal huntsman. It was his job to oversee the grooms who cared for the horses and the dogs, and to supervise those who cared for the grounds and forest that surrounded the castle. But most importantly, he arranged the royal hunts for the king and his various royal guests.

And though Gaston had the run of the castle upstairs and down, in the evenings he would go home to the stone cottage he lived in on the grounds with his father, away from the bustle of the castle, just as his father preferred. Grosvenor hadn't always been content to be tucked away in his cottage; he used to be very social with the other staff. But these days he preferred his own company to anyone else's—that is, except for Gaston, whom he loved heartily.

Gaston loved his father, too, but life with him could get lonely in their cottage in the woods. Grosvenor was a good man who took pride in his work and made it his business to pass his craft on to his son. He was a kind and loving father, but Gaston sensed there was a deep wound within his father's heart, a secret wound his father protected that sometimes caused him great melancholy. Grosvenor would sit for hours outside their cottage and just gaze at the starlit sky. Gaston was always welcome to join his father in the chair right next to his, and they would on occasion sit together in silence watching the stars blink against the dark curtain of night. Gaston knew who haunted his father's thoughts: his mother.

Gaston's mother, Rose, died when he was very young. He had no real memories of her, just the stories the servants and his father told him, and it seemed she had been loved by everyone who knew her. And though she had been very friendly with the other servants, she had been particularly close with Mrs. Potts. The two had become fast friends when they came to work in the castle as young parlor maids. Together they rose in the ranks, Mrs. Potts becoming head housekeeper and Rose becoming lady's maid and companion to the queen. The two ladies were always in each other's company when they weren't attending to their duties and stood for each other when they eventually got married. In those days, Grosvenor and Rose would take their meals in the big house (which is what they called the castle) with the other servants, and together they shared the stories of their days, laughing and sometimes staying up until all hours enjoying each other's company. And so it was, until Rose died.

According to Mrs. Potts, no one had an unkind word for Rose, and everyone in the house, upstairs and down, was heartbroken when she died. The queen was said to be in a tragic state of grief when Rose was taken from them so unexpectedly, and insisted Rose be buried on the estate so the queen might visit her friend's resting place, often bringing flowers to her grave with her own hands. No one would tell Gaston how his mother died, and he knew it was tragic because it was always talked about in hushed tones, with stricken facial expressions. But the one thing Gaston was almost sure of: his father's face bore the scars from whatever happened that night, and he knew they were nothing compared to the scars on his father's heart. So Gaston understood why his father sometimes wouldn't speak for hours and why he liked the isolation of his little stone cottage in the woods.

With Gaston's mother gone, the other grown-ups in his life rallied around him. Though Gaston's father's responsibilities to the crown were great, and he often slipped into silent melancholia without warning, he would always make time for Gaston, taking special care to show his son everything he would need to know so that one day Gaston could take his place as the royal huntsman. It was a good position, especially for someone who loved to be out of doors hunting and adventuring. And though Gaston shared that love with his father, and respected him and his position, Gaston wanted more. He wanted to learn to read and to write, and he wanted to learn about the world and its stories. He wanted the same education the prince received. He was happy when the prince read him stories, but he wanted to read them for himself. When he shared this with his friend, the prince insisted Gaston sit with him in the lessons, but his tutor, Mr. Willowstick, refused, saying Gaston would only be a distraction. And when Gaston asked his father if he could attend the village school, his father said he saw no reason since Gaston had so much to learn to become the royal huntsman. Eventually, Gaston gave up asking his father if he could attend school and learned what he could from the books he and the prince enjoyed together, but it always made him feel like he was missing something.

And it was yet another example of how he wasn't truly the prince's equal, no matter how the prince insisted he was.

Since Rose's death, Mrs. Potts had taken a special interest in Gaston. Mrs. Potts adored him and was always there to offer advice or a scolding wag of her finger, depending on the situation. Gaston was welcome to pop into Mrs. Potts's sitting room, where she spent much of her time completing her various duties. When she wasn't in her sitting room, she was overseeing the kitchen staff and the maids, or keeping Chef Bouche company while doing a little baking of her own, which was one of her cherished pastimes.

Mr. Cogsworth, who was rather stuffier, didn't approve of Gaston having the run of the castle. More times than not if he was tutting or grumbling it was about Gaston, especially when he and the prince would run into the castle after one of their adventures with muddy boots. Cogsworth never missed an opportunity to remind Gaston he shouldn't enter through the front door but rather around back where the servants entered the castle. The prince would always wave Mr.

Cogsworth off, saying that sort of thing didn't matter, but it was Cogsworth's job, after all, to keep up the standards of the house, and one of those standards was making sure Gaston knew his place. Or at least, that was how Mr. Cogsworth saw it. Gaston was a servant's son, after all, and servants entered the castle around back. And though the king and queen didn't seem to mind their son's friendship with the Gaston, Mr. Cogsworth made it clear he felt it was a friendship that could not endure into adulthood. There were stories, of course, of aristocrats and their servants crossing the great divide and becoming true friends, but they were rare. And even though there had already been such a miraculous friendship in their own household between the queen and Gaston's mother, Rose, Mr. Cogsworth still frowned upon such things.

When Rose was still alive, the queen insisted after Gaston's birth that he would be cared for in the castle nursery during the day, rather than Rose finding someone from the village to watch him while she attended to her other duties. The queen herself was expecting a child of her own soon, and the two women loved the idea of their children growing up together. Mr. Cogsworth didn't approve of any of this course. He was a fan of the old ways, you see, and wasn't what one would call a modernist, but there was little he could say when it was what the queen desired.

Mr. Cogsworth's rather stodgy ways inspired many discussions over the years between him and Mrs. Potts, rather *loud* discussions, which would often send the other servants scattering in every direction, especially when Mrs. Potts started throwing teacups in frustration.

On one particular day, when the boys were both around seven years old, Cogsworth and Mrs. Potts had driven everyone out of the kitchen with one of their arguments. She had been in the kitchen going over the menu with Chef Bouche while doing a little baking of her own when Mr. Cogsworth came stomping and grumbling into the kitchen. Mrs. Potts spent most of her time in the kitchen when she wasn't in her sitting room tending to her other duties. She liked the company of Chef Bouche and the kitchen maids, and the hustle of the footmen running in and out and cracking their jokes. She even enjoyed when Mr. Cogsworth would come in for a little chat or cup of tea, but she could tell by the look on his face that day the major-domo wasn't in good spirits.

"I don't know how many times I've had to tell that boy Gaston to go through the servants' entrance! You should see the mud he tracked into the vestibule. As if we all didn't have enough work preparing for the king and queen's return from their travels."

Mr. Cogsworth's mustache was twitching with frustration, and Mrs. Potts shook her head and sighed while she continued making her cookies. Strictly speaking, baking was not one of Mrs. Potts's duties. She was the head housekeeper. She was second in command to Mr. Cogsworth, but it was more of a partnership, or at least that was how she saw it. The fact was, she enjoyed baking, and rather than adding to Chef Bouche's duties by asking him to bake extra treats for the prince, Gaston, and her own children, of which she had many, she did it herself, because she loved almost nothing more than indulging children.

"And I suppose the prince didn't track in any of

this mud." Mrs. Potts brushed away a strand of hair that had managed to make its way from under her cap as she stamped dough with a large cookie cutter in the shape of a pirate ship, raising an eyebrow at Mr. Cogsworth.

"He's the prince. He can track whatever he wants wherever he wants. Gaston is the son of a servant!" Cogsworth always took this stance. In his eyes, the prince could never do wrong. Gaston, on the other hand, was another story.

"Why do you always have to put the poor lad in his place like that, Mr. Cogsworth? Have one of the cookies I've baked for the boys, perhaps that will make you less grumpy," she said, grinning at him.

"It's refreshing to hear you think Gaston has a place at all, Mrs. Potts! You treat those boys like they are brothers. You're not doing Gaston any favors, you realize, treating him like he's the prince's equal."

"They love each other like brothers, Mr. Cogsworth, and why shouldn't they? You couldn't pry those boys apart if you tried."

"Don't I know it! And how do you think that

will go when they're both grown and Gaston is the groundskeeper here?" said Mr. Cogsworth. Mrs. Potts supposed he might have been right in different circumstances, with different boys. But she knew them better than Mr. Cogsworth did. She knew their hearts.

"Gaston will be the royal huntsman, Mr. Cogsworth, and the king and queen don't seem to mind their friendship, so I don't see why you should."

"The king and queen are too busy to notice." The comment took Mrs. Potts by surprise. That kind of thing was never spoken out loud, even if from the servants' perspective it did seem to be the case. The king and queen were often away, and when they were at the castle, they were too busy to spend time with their son. But Mrs. Potts knew the queen loved her son and took a special interest in Gaston and was pleased the two of them were friends.

"Well, I say leave it alone, Mr. Cogsworth. Just let them be. Think about how lonely the prince would be without Gaston. Think of the trouble he would get into without Gaston's friendship, especially with the likes of you telling him he can do and say what he pleases. So what if they remain friends when they grow up? What harm will it do? You know how close the queen was to Gaston's mother. She loved her like a sister."

"No matter how well the queen loved Rose, she was still the queen's servant, and Rose knew her place. Even I, the majordomo of this great and respected house, know my place. And as such, it's up to me to keep a watchful eye on the prince," he said with hands on hips, blustering and posturing. Mrs. Potts knew when Mr. Cogsworth put his hands on his hips, he was staunchly ensconced in stubbornness. There was no shaking his resolve.

"Well, you keep your eye on him your way, and I will do the same in mine," she said, handing a baking sheet covered with pirate-shaped cookies to one of the kitchen maids to take to the oven.

"By passing them sweets and treating them both like little princes, no doubt," Mr. Cogsworth grumbled.

"So what if I do! Now, off with you! You'd better get upstairs and make sure all is ready for the king and queen's return. I have enough on my plate managing their welcome home feast with Chef Bouche without you coming in here and scaring everyone out of the kitchen." Mrs. Potts could hear her voice rising like a teakettle about to boil. And it was no wonder, with Mr. Cogsworth prattling on and being, in her opinion, a considerable snob.

"Well then, if you see the prince, do tell them I expect him downstairs to greet his parents when they arrive, *without* Gaston in tow!"

"Ticktock, Mr. Cogsworth! The king and queen will be here before you know it!" said Mrs. Potts, pointing to the clock.

With a twitch of his mustache, Mr. Cogsworth turned on his heel and left the kitchen. Like a general at war he looked, on his way to secure the battlements. When he was gone, Mrs. Potts could hear the sounds of giggling and shuffling feet from behind the hidden panel that led to the passageway connecting the kitchen to the dining room. She wondered how much of the conversation they had heard.

"You can come out now, boys, he's gone," she said, smiling at them as they came out from behind the hidden wall panel. "I suppose you heard everything he said? Well, for the record, I love you both the same. Don't listen to stuffy old Mr. Cogsworth. Don't give him a second thought, do you understand?" She glanced at Gaston, who seemed a little sad. It broke her heart to see him disheartened, and she always did her best to bring him out of such moods. It was a promise she made herself when Gaston's mother died, that she would look after him like he was one of her own.

"I wouldn't mind if Gaston were my brother," said the prince, beaming and proud as he stood next to his friend. What a pair they made, both covered in mud from their adventures. Each of them so devoted to the other.

"I know you wouldn't mind, dear, you're a sweet boy," Mrs. Potts said, smiling at the prince. "And I suppose you were playing knights in the woods? Killing some creature or another, perhaps a mud monster?"

"Everyone knows there's no such thing as mud monsters, Mrs. Potts! No, we were hunting dragons in the—"

"Gaston, shh!" said the prince, elbowing him in the ribs. "Don't give away all our secrets." The prince often made Mrs. Potts laugh. The idea that they could keep anything from her was comical.

"You don't think I know everything you boys get up to? Never mind; you heard Mr. Cogsworth—get yourself upstairs and ready to greet your parents. I won't have you covered in mud when they arrive. Here . . ." She handed them each a cookie topped with a dollop of something ill-favored that looked like it might be frosting.

"What's this gray stuff?" asked Gaston, eyeing the cookie and sniffing it suspiciously.

"Try it, dear. It's just crumbled cookies mixed in with pudding and cream. I promise it's delicious," she said, piling more frosting into pudding bowls in anticipation of them wanting more.

The prince munched his cookie, seeming to agree with Mrs. Potts's description, and happily took the bowl Mrs. Potts offered him.

"Come on, Gaston, have some, it really is delicious." The prince scooped a dollop of gray stuff out of the bowl with his finger and nudged Gaston with his elbow. "And then we can go back to our tree house," he added, smiling.

"I'm going to keep Gaston here with me for a spot of tea, dear. You go now and get ready for your parents' arrival." Mrs. Potts, who, unlike Mr. Cogsworth, never stood on ceremony, didn't bother to call the prince by his royal title. The prince didn't seem to mind, but he did look grumpy that Mrs. Potts didn't let him get away with sneaking off with Gaston to their tree house rather than making himself presentable for his parents. "Here, take these," she said, giving him a pile of cookies wrapped in cloth and a kiss on the cheek to take with him. After the prince slipped out of the room, Mrs. Potts put her hand on Gaston's. It was clear something was bothering him.

"What's wrong, dear?"

"I wish we were brothers," he said with a big sigh.

"You are brothers in your heart, dear. And that means even more than sharing parents," she said, nudging his chin gently with her hand so his eyes would meet hers.

"But what if Mr. Cogsworth is right? What if the prince doesn't want to be my friend when we're older?"

"I know in my heart he will, dear. I promise you. Come on, cheer up. I've sent a message to your father saying you two are to join us in the servants' hall for dinner this evening," she said, noticing Chef Bouche was walking toward them.

"Really? Is that allowed?" asked Gaston.

"Of course it's allowed, my boy!" said Chef Bouche. "And we will have a magnificent feast to celebrate. It's been far too many years since your father joined us for dinner." He patted Gaston on the shoulder.

"But won't Mr. Cogsworth mind?" Gaston asked.

"You leave Mr. Cogsworth to me, dear," Mrs. Potts replied. "Dinner won't be until late this evening after we've served upstairs dinner. Here . . ." She handed him a plate of sandwiches. "Have these with your tea before you go. I won't have you going hungry waiting so long before dinner."

"Thank you, Mrs. Potts," Gaston said, wondering what he had done to deserve such luck.

After his tea and sandwiches Gaston went through

the passageway between the walls of the castle. He imagined he would find the prince there waiting for him, deciding he would skip greeting his parents. Gaston had even put some of the sandwiches aside should his friend want something to eat before being made to eat the fancy food they served in the dining room. To Gaston's disappointment the prince wasn't waiting for him in the passageway, but he reasoned his friend had actually done what he was told and was now getting ready for his parents' homecoming. So Gaston finished off the sandwiches himself as he made his way through the passageway.

He wished the prince was with him. They loved these secret places, and knew them all by heart. He chose the path leading to a tunnel taking him down to the grounds without having to cross the bridge. He made his way through the forest, which was rather beautiful that time of the day. It was the moment when night and day met, turning the sky orange and making the trees and buildings look like black paper cutouts. The cemetery looked like the pages of a pop-up book he remembered from when he and the prince were young children together in the day nursery. It didn't seem real, with its tombstones, mausoleums, and gnarled trees silhouetted against the too-perfect sky. It didn't seem real that this was where his mother was laid to rest. His mother was nothing more than stories to him. Like a character in a book, or one of the fairy tales the prince read to him. He supposed he loved her, as much as anyone could love someone they didn't know, but he wished more than anything that he had known her, not only for his sake but for his father's, because Gaston knew his father loved and missed her with all his heart. As he stood there watching day turn into night, looking at the changes of light, and shadows of the tree branches stretch across the cemetery, he wondered how life would have been if his mother had lived. Or what it would have been like if he and the prince were truly brothers. He thought about this as he continued walking home through the forest he knew well until finally he arrived at the stone cottage where he lived with his father.

It was a nice cottage, really. Larger than most

cottages on the estate. His father had said they were given such a grand quarters because of how well loved his mother was before her passing, but it seemed to Gaston (even at such a young age) that his father never truly saw his own worth. Even though his father was the *best* at everything. He was the best hunter, stalker, and tracker. He knew the names of all the trees, flowers, and bushes. He knew which plants, mushrooms, and berries were poisonous and which could be eaten, and he knew the names of all the creatures, including the different species of birds that resided in the vast forest, of which he was the caretaker. And he knew how to care for sick animals, for which Gaston felt a particular pride, because he was in awe of his father's extensive knowledge and experience when it came to animal care. He had even been known to bring home a wounded creature on occasion, nursing it back to health, or staying up all night with the grooms caring for a sick or injured horse or dog. Gaston thought his father was a great man. But he didn't think his father had a sense of his own greatness. He didn't realize he was the best. But then again, if he had, he wouldn't be the same person. And Gaston loved his father just the way he was.

When Gaston got to the cottage, he saw smoke billowing from the stone chimney. His father was probably sitting by the fire, already comfortable in his favorite chair. Gaston had been hoping he would get there before his father so he wouldn't have had time to settle in for the night. His father worked hard, and when he came home he was happy to be there, happy to just sit by the fire and relax. Gaston wondered how happy he would be to learn he was making a trip to the castle this evening.

"So I hear we're having dinner in the big house tonight. Is this your doing? Did you wrangle an invitation from Mrs. Potts?" said his father when Gaston walked into their cottage. As Gaston suspected, his father was already sitting next to the large stone fireplace in his favorite wooden chair, his hand dangling down to absentmindedly pet their tortoiseshell cat, who was resting on her cushion next Gaston's father.

"No, Papa, she just told me about it," said Gaston, noticing the cat slowly blinking her large yellow eyes at him. "I see you've come back home," he said, kneeling down to giving her chin a scratch. "What have you been up to while away so long, I wonder?"

"Oh, you know how she is. She's like you, Gaston, always off on her adventures. And just like you, I never worry she won't come home, no matter how long she's away," Gaston's father said with a smile. "Now, I suppose we both have to bathe and dress properly for this grand event?"

"It's not an event, Papa. It's just dinner with the inside staff," said Gaston, hoping his father wouldn't grumble his way into refusing Mrs. Potts's invitation.

"I'd rather eat dinner in my own home, Gaston. I'm comfortable here. But I suppose it's lonely just having the company of your old papa every evening?"

"I wouldn't say that."

"Perhaps not to me, but I'm guessing you've said so to Mrs. Potts."

"It won't be so bad, will it, Papa? I hear you used to eat dinner in the big house all the time when Mama was alive. And I know you like Mr. and Mrs. Potts."

"That I do, son. All right, then. Who am I

kidding, anyway? There is no way I am going to turn down Mrs. Potts's invitation. She would blow her top." He laughed his deep, warm laugh. "And I suppose you and the prince were in the kitchens today. Mrs. Potts has enough on her hands, with all her work and her own children running underfoot, without you and the prince pestering her for treats."

"She doesn't mind."

"I don't believe she does. She's always had a big heart, that Mrs. Potts. Well, we'd better smarten ourselves up, then, shouldn't we? And we mustn't be late for dinner. We don't want to give old Mr. Cogsworth a reason to twitch his mustache at us, now do we?" Grosvenor said, making Gaston laugh.

"You're right, I've already had enough mustache twitching for one day."

CHAPTER II

BE OUR GUESTS

Both Gaston and his father looked smashing in what Gaston's father called their Sunday best. The other servants would still be in their uniforms, of course— which was rather fancy attire, all things considered, being uniforms of servants in a royal household. And Gaston's father knew it wouldn't be appropriate to wear his outdoor clothing to dinner, so he decided to put on his best suit, and told Gaston to do the same. They were a handsome pair, the two of them entering the servants' hall together. Both of them with their dark hair, and blue eyes, and strong features. Gaston looked like a miniature version of his father, all except

37

for the long scar that ran diagonally across his father's face. But that scar did nothing to diminish Grosvenor's good looks. It was almost as if it made him more handsome. And in Gaston's eyes, it most certainly made him seem strong and brave, and rather mysterious as well, since his father would never speak about how the scar came about.

When Gaston and his father entered the servants' hall, everyone was making their way to their seats at the long wooden dining table in the center of the room. Mrs. Potts spotted Gaston's father right away and wrapped her arms around him tightly. Grosvenor laughed and squeezed her back heartily. Mrs. Potts looked tiny wrapped in the huge man's arms, and everyone could see she had the sparkle of tears welling up in her eyes, so overjoyed he accepted her invitation.

"I'm so happy you've come, Grosvenor! It's been far too long since you've joined us for dinner. I never get to see you these days—but I do keep up on how you're doing from Gaston, of course," she said, smiling at the boy.

"I hope he isn't bothering you, Mrs. Potts," he said, tussling Gaston's dark hair.

"Are you kidding, Grosvenor? Mrs. Potts dotes on the boy!" It was Mr. Potts, patting his dear friend on the back and laughing. "This is like old times, seeing you here with us," he added, pulling out a chair for his friend to take a seat.

"Gaston, why don't you go into the kitchen?" said Mrs. Potts. "I put together a hamper for you to take home after dinner. Go on and take a peek at the good-ies Chef Bouche and I packed for you and your papa, while we grown-ups catch up."

Gaston's father watched as his son ran off to the kitchen excitedly. It made him smile to see Gaston so happy, to be so at home among the other servants. There had been a time when he felt the same, and it felt good to be with them again. He wasn't sure why he had waited so long to be among them again. Why he hid himself away in his own little world. He knew all too well how it started. He couldn't bear being in the castle, or seeing their faces. It all reminded him of

Rose, how much he missed her, and he hated seeing his own pain reflected in their grief-stricken faces. But it had been nearly eight years now, surely that was time enough. If not for his own sake, then for Gaston's. It was time to be among his friends again.

"You're too sweet, Mrs. Potts. I just hope Gaston isn't getting any ideas."

"Gaston is always full of ideas, Grosvenor, and they are usually brilliant." she said, looking perplexed.

"No, that's not what I mean Mrs. Potts. I was referring to ideas above his station. He spends all his time with the prince, and now dinner with the inside staff . . . I just don't know."

"Stuff and nonsense! You're the king's huntsman, you arrange the royal hunts, you're the head of the outside staff, that means something. There's no reason you shouldn't eat with us," said Mrs. Potts.

"You're the Mr. Cogsworth of the outdoor staff, Grosvenor. You're senior staff," Mr. Potts added, then cringed as he seemed to regret comparing him to Mr. Cogsworth. "Well, you know what I mean, anyway."

"Still, Mr. Cogsworth won't like it," said Grosvenor.

"It doesn't matter what he likes. You know Mr. Cogsworth, he'll never catch up with the times," said Mrs. Potts.

"Speaking of which, isn't it time to serve dinner?" said Mr. Cogsworth from the servants' hall doorway where he had been standing quietly listening to the conversation without their notice. At once everyone at the table stood up at attention, as was the custom when he came into the room.

"Good evening, Mr. Cogsworth," said Grosvenor, waiting with everyone else for the majordomo to take his seat before he sat down again. Everyone looked nervous, waiting to see if Mr. Cogsworth had heard Mrs. Potts and how he might react. But he just sat in silent disapproval. The fact was, Grosvenor had every right to be there, even if it wasn't customary for the outside staff to join the inside staff at meals. There had been reason for him to join when Rose was alive, as she was a senior member of staff. But there was nothing Mr. Cogsworth could do about it then, and very little he could do about it now Mrs. Potts had issued an official invitation. As far as she and most of the other staff were concerned, Grosvenor was family, and they were happy to have him back again.

"Yes, well, now that Mr. Cogsworth has joined us we can start dinner. Lumiere, would you do the honors?" asked Mrs. Potts.

Lumiere, taking Mrs. Potts's cue, went off into the kitchen. A few moments later a legion of kitchen maids in smart black-and-white uniforms came into the servants' hall carrying delicious and magnificent food in massive serving dishes. Chef Bouche, at the instruction of Mrs. Potts, had provided a splendid meal for the servants that night, and Lumiere, as if he was presenting the meal upstairs for the royal family, announced all the dishes as they came out of the kitchen. The aroma of their feast filled the room from the moment the maids set the dishes on the table. There wasn't usually so much fanfare during the servents' dinner, but everyone was so pleased to have Gaston and his father join them that evening they had decided among them to make it a special occasion.

At the center of the table was a large of tureen filled with boeuf Bourguignon, and next to it were

a lovely Duck Pâté en Croûte; a miraculous-looking
chicken confit; a large bowl of potatoes with salted
pork, onions, mushrooms, and cheese; an enormous,
colorful ratatouille; freshly baked bread; savory cheese
pastry puffs; and, of course, heaps of chocolate mousse
with a rich whipped cream for dessert.

Gaston and his father were seated near Mr. and
Mrs. Potts, at the other end of the table from Mr.
Cogsworth. Aside from the glowering majordomo,
they were a merry party, composed of the senior members of staff: Lumiere, the castle maître d'; Plumette,
the head housemaid; and Chef Bouche.

"It's so wonderful to have you here, Monsieur
Grosvenor! It has been far too long since we have had
your delightful company. We of course hear of your
adventures from young Gaston, but it is so nice to
see you looking so well, and among us here tonight,
isn't that so, Mr. Cogsworth?" said Lumiere, taking
delight, as he always did, in making Mr. Cogsworth
grumble.

"Well, I think it's magnificent," said Plumette putting her hand on Lumiere's. "It has been far too long

since you've eaten with us. Of course, we understand why you stayed away—"

"No need to go into all of that," said Mr. Cogsworth, clearing his throat and tugging at the lapels of his coat with a violent twitch.

Lumiere gave Mr. Cogsworth the side-eye as he stood up and theatrically clapped his hands three times to summon the footmen who were standing by.

"And now, for a finishing touch to our scrumptious feast Chef Bouche has so expertly prepared for us, I picked something special—oh, it's splendid, a simply divine libation to celebrate the return of Monsieur Grosvenor! I can say without any hesitation whatsoever we will all enjoy it immensely!" said Lumiere as the footmen came into the servants' hall with lovely sparking glasses on silver trays.

"As we won't be bothering you or the maids again, please do sit down to your dinner," said Mrs. Potts, excusing the footmen so they could join the maids and other staff for their own dinner.

"This is a treat!" said Mrs. Potts, picking up her

glass and examining it. "This looks lovely, Lumiere, thank you."

"Yes, Lumiere, thank you," said Chef Bouche.

"Shall we make a toast? Will you mind if I do the honors, Mr. Cogsworth?" asked Mr. Potts, putting his arm around Grosvenor.

"As you wish." Mr. Cogsworth's expression made him look as if there were a foul smell in the air.

"What is wrong, Mr. Cogsworth? Does the aroma of dinner offend your senses somehow?" asked Chef Bouche, looking agitated. Everyone at the table looked surprised at his directness. "Have I somehow gone afoul with the execution of this evening's meal? Does it not meet with your exacting approval?"

Chef Bouche, who was known for his bad temper, was now out of his seat, red-faced and scowling from under his large blond mustache. There weren't many people Mr. Cogsworth found intimidating, but it was very well-known he always did his best to keep Chef Bouche in good spirits if he could help it, else the chef would explode into a fiery rage.

"Not at all, Chef Bouche. If anything, I am just eager to partake of your divine masterpiece before it becomes a midnight feast," said Mr. Cogsworth. This seemed to calm the chef, to everyone's relief, especially Mr. Cogsworth's.

"Mr. Potts . . . if you will," said Mr. Cogsworth, giving Mr. Potts the cue to make his toast.

"Tchin mon ami," said Mr. Potts, raising his glass to Grosvenor. "To our dear friend, returned to us at last. May this be the first of many more nights to come."

"Tchin tchin, Monsieur Grosvenor!" said Lumiere, raising his glass along with the others at the table, all of them looking at Gaston's father.

"And to Rose!" said Mrs. Potts. "Much loved and never forgotten."

"And to Gaston, my dear brother!" said a voice they did not expect. When everyone turned, they saw the prince standing in the doorway still in his finery he wore earlier that evening to dine with his parents. At once everyone at the table stood, taking their cue from

Mr. Cogsworth, who bolted up from his seat to stand at attention.

"Is there something we can do for you, Your Highness? Why didn't you ring?" Mr. Cogsworth looked even more uncomfortable than before. It was one thing having Gaston and his father to dinner, but now the prince? It was unheard of. Or at least, it should have been. Everyone knew this was the sort of thing Mr. Cogsworth would have no truck with. In his mind it was a slippery slope leading them all into chaos and a disintegration of order, tradition, and propriety. But there was little the man could do if the prince insisted, which seemed very likely.

"I hoped you'd let me join you for dinner," the prince said, smiling slyly at Gaston.

"Here!" said Gaston, pulling one of the chairs over so the prince could sit next to him. Everyone in the room seemed perfectly happy to have the prince join them except for Mr. Cogsworth. He was a man who liked order and rules, and letting the prince dine with them felt like a crumbling of everything he believed in, a shifting of the ground beneath him in a way that made him wonder how long it would be before everything just fell into mayhem.

"Of course you can join us for dinner, dear! Sit down, sit down. Chef Bouche has made more than enough," said Mrs. Potts, who was clearly ignoring Mr. Cogsworth's discomfort.

"This is highly irregular, Your Highness. Are you sure the king and queen will approve? Won't they wonder where you are?" Mr. Cogsworth twitched and fiddled with his waistcoat, a habit that betrayed when he was feeling nervous.

"They went to bed shortly after dinner," said the prince.

"And shouldn't you have done the same, young sir? I know Mr. Willowstick is expecting you in the schoolroom first thing tomorrow," said Mr. Cogsworth.

"You're mistaken, Mr. Cogsworth, he is away visiting his brother for another week yet." The prince smirked, knowing he was winning this match. Mr. Cogsworth's expression seemed to wind even tighter, and it looked as though the prince was enjoying it.

"I'm sorry, Your Highness, but it seems he's decided to cut his trip short. He arrived earlier this evening," Mr. Cogsworth said, tugging at his waistcoat again.

"So where is he, then?" The prince made a show of looking around the room. "Why isn't he joining the staff for dinner?"

"He made an early night of it since he had such a long journey back, Your Highness." Cogsworth appeared even twitchier than usual. Everyone held their breath, wondering how this would end. They all knew the prince wasn't the sort of aristocrat who hid behind a thick veil of convention. When he was angry, he let you know, and they had all been on the receiving end of such wrath.

"I am not doing lessons tomorrow! Do you hear me? This isn't fair. Why did no one tell me he was back before now?!" The prince did nothing to hide his anger. It was a relief Mr. Willowstick hadn't joined them for dinner, or the prince's wrath would have been directed at him. And if the raised voices that were often heard from the school room were any indication, poor Mr. Willowstick had been on the

49

receiving end of the prince's anger rather frequently.

"Come on, Kingsley, it's fine. I have lessons with my papa tomorrow anyway. I'll come find you when they're over," Gaston said, pulling out the chair for his friend to sit down, and added, "Think of all the stories you'll have for me tomorrow after your lessons. Want to make a bet now how many times you'll fall asleep while Mr. Willowstick prattles on?" This made the prince laugh and seemed to bring him out of his sour mood, to everyone's relief, including Gaston's. But that's all it would usually take, making him laugh, and Gaston was rather good at it.

"Kingsley? What's this, now? Why are you calling him that?" asked Mr. Cogsworth, looking at Gaston and then the prince with a befuddled expression on his face.

"It's nothing, Cogsworth. Never mind. Now, what are we having for dinner?" The prince sat down next to Gaston, giving him a cheeky smile that made Gaston laugh.

Aside from Mr. Cogsworth, no one seemed to mind the prince joining them for dinner. In fact, they seemed pleased Gaston had a friend his own age to visit with while the adults chatted. Mr. and Mrs. Potts's younger children were already off to their beds, and though Lumiere, Plumette, Mr. and Mrs. Potts, and even on occasion Chef Bouche enjoyed Gaston's company, it was a good opportunity for them to catch up with Grosvenor while the boys occupied themselves. It was a fun evening for everyone, and when it ended there were promises to do it again and many hugs were exchanged before Grosvenor and Gaston made their way into the night back to their cottage.

This time they talked as they walked, marveling at starlit sky sparkling above them. It was a perfect evening. At least, Gaston thought so.

"What was that name you called the prince? Kingsley, was it?" his father asked as they passed one of Gaston's favorite oaks on their way home.

"It's just a nickname," said Gaston, regretting he had used their secret name in front of everyone. He hadn't intended to make that little slip, but he could tell his friend didn't seem to mind. Nevertheless,

Gaston didn't feel like explaining it to his papa or anyone else. They wouldn't understand.

"I heard you two talking during dinner. Did I hear the prince say you beat him at archery the other day?" Gaston thought this would make his father proud, but it seemed to only cause him concern.

"I did beat him! Why? What's it matter? You should have seen it, Papa. I hit the bull's-eye every time! The prince didn't even hit the target half the time," said Gaston, laughing.

"You don't always have to be the best, Gaston," his father said, surprising him.

"But you're the best, Papa! You're the best at everything!"

"Not when I'm in the company of the king I'm not. Then *he* is the best," his father said, rather more serious than Gaston had ever seen him.

"You mean you let the king *think* he's the best." Gaston scoffed. "Kingsley would never fall for that."

"Indeed I do, and you should do the same with the prince."

"But the king has to know, Papa. He must know.

Doesn't that make him look foolish, pretending while everyone knows you're the best? Kingsley would be cross if I did that," said Gaston, stopping so he could look his father in the eye.

"He might be cross with you now if you always let him win, but I doubt that will be the case when he's older. Kings always want to be the best, and it's our job to make sure that they think they are." He put his hand on Gaston's shoulder and gave him another serious look.

"You sound like stuffy, old Mr. Cogsworth!" Gaston said with a laugh.

"Goodness forbid!" said Gaston's father, his tone softening into a laugh as well. His father seemed content to drop the subject as they continued walking.

The sky was an inky black, and there wasn't a cloud in sight. The moon and stars glowed brightly, winking at them as they walked through the forest on their way home.

"Does the prince often lose his temper like that?" his father asked casually, stopping in front of the little cemetery where Gaston's mother was laid to rest. Gaston could tell his father was concerned even though he was pretending not to be. That's how his father was, always calm, never wanting to make a big thing out of anything, even if Gaston could see his father was clearly vexed.

"Like what?" Gaston knew what his father meant, but he didn't want to let on that his friend lost his temper easily. He didn't want his father to worry, he was already troubled by Gaston's friendship with the prince, he didn't want to give him any more reason to fret. Or worse, tell him they shouldn't spend so much time together.

"He seemed very upset when Mr. Cogsworth told him Mr. Willowstick was back early from his trip." His father bent down to pick some wildflowers that grew along the stone wall surrounding the little cemetery. Gaston had always wondered where he picked the flowers he often brought home from his walks to put on his bedside table, but he should have guessed.

"Oh, don't worry about it, Papa. He was just upset because we had plans tomorrow, and it made him all, you know, *kingly*," said Gaston, laughing.

"Ah, that's why the nickname," said his father, bundling the flowers and standing back up. "And he doesn't mind your letting him know when he's acting that way?"

"No! He's made me promise not to let him become one of those horrid kings you hear about, chopping off heads and stuff like that."

"I believe you're thinking of the Queen of Hearts, but I understand what you mean," his father said, chuckling.

"Who is she? She doesn't live in the Many Kingdoms, does she?"

"No, she rules in another world called Wonderland, if the legends are to be believed. You might be able to find a tale or two about her in one of your books," said his father, looking like he was lost in his thoughts while gazing at the wildflowers he had gathered.

"What is it, Papa? You seem worried."

"I suppose I am, son. I'm just starting to wonder if it's a good idea for you and the prince to be such good friends."

"You sound like Mr. Cogsworth again."

"You'd better stop saying that or I will have to grow a long pointy mustache and start twitching at you!" said his father, laughing again.

"Papa, do you ever think you will tell me how Mama died?" asked Gaston, looking at his mother's tomb. It was the largest in the graveyard, and the prettiest. The queen had one of the most famous and talented sculptors in the land carve a statue of his mother Rose from light pink marble. It stood graceful and serene, as if beckoning Gaston to come inside. Gaston had always found it frightening, as if his dead mother was trying to take him to the other side to be with her. Now that he was older, he wondered if that wasn't the sculptor's purpose. Not to frighten Gaston, of course, but to look as if she was waiting for her family and friends to join her when they were ready to pass into the next realm. He wasn't sure if his theory was right, and he didn't have the courage to ask the queen, or his father, so it remained a mystery.

"Oh, son." His father looked tired suddenly. "It's not a story for young ears." He started down the path again, signaling that Gaston should do the same.

"Perhaps when I'm older, then?" asked Gaston, running to catch up with his father.

"Perhaps, my boy. We shall see."

Once Gaston and his father got back into their cottage and tucked snuggly in their beds, Gaston ran over the day and the evening's events in his mind. It was probably one of the best nights he'd had. And he hoped there would be many more nights like that to come.

CHAPTER III

The Ghosts in the Library

After Gaston and his father had been invited to dinner with the staff that first wonderful night five years ago, to Gaston's delight, dinner in the servants' hall soon became part of their routine. Life was perfect, as far as Gaston was concerned. He spent most of his time with his best friend the prince, and he had his evenings with his father and the other servants, who he looked at as his family.

Even though he and the prince were a bit older, they still filled their time with wild adventures and exploring. They sometimes found themselves feeling rather cooped up in the castle, especially on occasions when they were stuck indoors for any length of time. And this particular time it had been raining almost constantly for the greater part of a fortnight. Having already explored every inch of the castle and its foundations, they came up with a way to entertain themselves, and it was an impish plan. Because they knew the librarian, Monsieur Biblio, hated to have any of the books leave the library, Gaston and the prince thought it would be great fun not only to sneak out books they wanted to read but to rearrange Monsieur Biblio's meticulously organized system to distract him from noticing some of his treasured books were missing. And poor Monsieur Biblio's increasing frustration only inspired the boys to get up to more mischief.

Of course, Monsieur Biblio suspected Gaston. But he was a smart man, and he wouldn't come right out and accuse Gaston in front of everyone, at least not at first. He would make little remarks and steer the conversation in ways he hoped would slip Gaston up, revealing it was he who had been sneaking into the library and rearranging his precious books. This had become an almost nightly event, Monsieur Biblio bringing up mislaid books at dinnertime, or really anytime anyone would listen. The mystery of the books had become an all-consuming obsession, and the rest of the staff didn't have time or patience for his longwinded pontifications.

"I do believe I saw some of your books in the West Wing attic, Monsieur Biblio," said Plumette one night when Monsieur Biblio was on one of his rants. "It was when I was up there dusting. I wondered why they were there, but I supposed you had your reasons." It was obvious to everyone at the table except for Monsieur Biblio that Plumette was teasing the librarian.

"There would be no reason! No reason whatsoever, Mademoiselle! Every self-respecting bibliophile knows a damp and dusty attic is the worst possible place for any book, let alone the treasured tomes that are housed within the royal library!" Monsieur Biblio's face was screwed up in anger, making his eyes even smaller than usual, and his fists were clenched tightly.

"If it wasn't you, I wonder how they ended up in the attic, Monsieur?" she asked with a wink to the others at the table. This had become the staff's nightly entrainment.

"I have a culprit in mind," Monsieur Biblio said, eyeing Gaston. But Grosvenor had joined them that evening, and he dared not say anything in front of the boy's father.

Almost everyone in the household staff seemed happy Grosvenor and Gaston had been taking their meals with them more frequently ever since that happy evening five years prior. And Gaston was pleased his father didn't find spending time with his old friends to be as painful as he had imagined. Gaston understood that being in the castle might remind his father of the days when his mother was alive, and it might cause him pain, but now it seemed Grosvenor felt comfortable spending his evenings among friends, among others who loved and valued Rose almost as much as he did.

Mrs. Potts was especially delighted Grosvenor and Gaston frequently joined them. She loved hearing Gaston's stories about his and the prince's adventures, which were becoming bolder now that they were young teens. Even Mr. Cogsworth had gotten used to seeing them at dinnertime on most evenings. The only person who still grumbled about it and gave Gaston side glances was Monsieur Biblio, who had become singularly focused on solving the mystery of his wandering books.

The boys, of course, found all this rather amusing, watching Monsieur Biblio hunt around the castle looking for his books, sent on wild-goose chases by the other servants. Gaston and the prince began to leave clues that would lead the poor man to search in strange places like the castle graveyard, only to find nothing there. It was a stroke of luck for the boys that Monsieur Biblio had brought about his own misery by annoying everyone so much they were unwittingly part of what was turning into an elaborate prank. Gaston didn't understand why Monsieur Biblio was so ill at ease about books leaving the library, why it was he and the prince had to sneak them out in the cover of darkness. If Monsieur Biblio were a bit less regimented in his approach, then perhaps things wouldn't have gone so terribly wrong for the poor man.

"Ah, I think I agree with your theory, Monsieur Biblio. There can be only one culprit. I am sure it is obvious to all of us sitting at this table," said Lumiere, playfully smiling at Gaston.

"I knew it! At last, someone with some sense. Thank you, Lumiere! It's time we all stop pretending we don't know who is to blame and punish this thief!"

"But how do we punish a ghost, Monsieur?" asked Lumiere, nudging Plumette so she would stop giggling.

"Excuse me, sir? Did I hear you correctly? Did you say *ghost?*" Monsieur Biblio was aghast, but the others at the table nodded along as if they were convinced the castle was haunted. Gaston felt a swell of warmth, knowing they did it to protect him. But it was Lumiere's complicity in their little ruse that made him most happy. Gaston could always count on his creative flair in situations like this.

"Indeed you did, Monsieur Biblio. It is the only explanation," said Lumiere.

"Do you really think so? Has anyone noticed

anything else in the castle gone missing or put in strange locations?"

"I think this particular spirit has a fondness for books, Monsieur. And who can blame him? Perhaps it's the ghost of the previous librarian," Gaston said with a straight face.

"I doubt it's a previous bibliophile, young man. The attic is the last place they would hide books, trickster or not! Well, if it is a ghost, I know just how to deal with pesky specters. I was just reading a fascinating book . . ."

"Good. It seems you have it all in hand, Monsieur Biblio. I'm sure you will find your books in no time. Now, it's getting late. I think it's time we all say good night," said Mrs. Potts, who seemed to feel bad for the man. But then again, Mrs. Potts was a very kind and patient woman.

Yet Monsieur Biblio managed to test even Mrs. Potts's kindness and patience as the days wore on and would still not drop the matter of the missing books. It wasn't until he marched into her sitting room a few days later that she lost her temper. Mrs. Potts had been busy at her desk, with a stack of papers in front of her, writing up her lists for an upcoming house party when Monsieur Biblio came blustering in without bothering to knock.

"Books! Books! More missing books! I'm at my wit's end, Mrs. Potts!" Monsieur Biblio was standing in the doorway, waving his hands and yelling so loudly the other servants passing him in the hallway looked to see what was the matter. When they saw who it was, they just rolled their eyes and kept walking.

Mrs. Potts by this time had gotten used to Monsieur Biblio blustering in, disturbing her peace, and complaining about missing books. On this occasion, however, she had been less patient than usual because she was frantically trying to finish writing up the menus for the house party so Mr. Cogsworth could plan the wine list. They all had more work than usual, planning this party, and Mrs. Potts didn't have time for this nonsense.

"I demand someone do something about this at once!" Monsieur Biblio continued. "Books out of place, books missing altogether! This is complete chaos! And don't insult my intelligence by suggested we have a ghost!" It seemed after a few days of ghost hunting Monsieur Biblio had given up the idea of a supernatural trickster and was back to suspecting Gaston.

If Mrs. Potts had bothered to look up, she would have seen Monsieur Biblio clenching his fists and shaking them with anger. It was no matter; she didn't have to look up to know his expression. This scene had played out several times before over the past few months. And each time Monsieur Biblio had become more agitated and more demanding. And more determined to prove Gaston's guilt.

"I know Gaston is the booknapper!" he said, almost causing Mrs. Potts to look up from her work.

"*Booknapper?* Now really, this is getting silly, don't you think? Are you sure you've not mislaid them, Monsieur Biblio? Perhaps take a good look around the library and you'll find they were there all along," she said, still focused on her work, desperately trying to finish writing the menus before Mr. Cogsworth came in wondering why they were late.

"Are you suggesting I don't know how to do my

job, Mrs. Potts? I must insist Grosvenor's cottage be searched. I know Gaston has taken the books! And I know you have all been covering for him!"

Monsieur Biblio was testing Mrs. Potts beyond her limits. She looked up from her papers and glared at Monsieur Biblio, clearly agitated. Now, Mrs. Potts was by all accounts a very kind woman, the kindest woman any would ever be lucky to know, but the one thing no one did was threaten her family. That she would not stand for. And that's how she saw Grosvenor and Gaston, as part of her family, and she wasn't about to sit there and entertain the thought of Grosvenor's cottage being searched for any reason whatsoever.

"I am sure you're aware we have a big house party coming up. And you must have guessed we would all be busy making the arrangements, which is exactly what I should be doing this moment rather than discussing your missing books. Twenty lords and ladies will be here in a matter of days, Monsieur Biblio; we do not have time for this." Mrs. Potts was stone-faced and much more serious than usual, but the angry librarian didn't back down.

"I know, that's why I didn't bother Mr. Cogsworth with this."

"I see. Well, I assure you, we all have our work cut out for us. Are you looking for something to do, Monsieur Biblio, since you seem to have so much time on your hands fretting about missing books. Perhaps you'd like to write up the seating charts, plan the menus, place the orders, assign rooms to all our guests, and arrange the entertainment. I assume you saw the legion of maids scrubbing, dusting, and arranging the flowers. Or perhaps you noticed the footmen rolling up the carpets to make room for dancing, while the others are polishing the silver. Not to mention the new pavilion that's being built—or how about the tent that's being erected for the outdoor activities? Every single member of the staff, outdoor and in, is preparing for the king and queen's house party. All except for you. But since this is an emergency on the grandest of scales, I will ask everyone to stop what they're doing and look for your missing books at once!"

"If you won't help me, then I will be forced to take this up with Mr. Cogsworth!"

"Why don't we go speak with him together," she said, standing up. "He's in his pantry, grumbling and pacing. I'm sure it won't bother him at all to learn the menus are late because you're vexed about some missing books!"

"I won't bother him just now. But perhaps you can tell me where I might find Grosvenor? I think I will take this up with him directly."

"Feel free. He's in the courtyard." Mrs. Potts smiled mischievously as she watched him storm down the hall on his way to have words with Grosvenor. And just as he was about the round the corner she called out to him, stopping him in his tracks.

"Oh, and, Monsieur Biblio, could you please tell His Majesty the king that Mr. Cogsworth will be late coming down to go over the wine lists because we were unavoidably delayed by a book emergency?"

"What? Me, the librarian, taking a message to the king? That's unheard of! I don't even know where he is."

"He's in the courtyard with Grosvenor planning the hunt, of course. I'm sure once the king hears of your troubles he will insist we all drop what we're doing to discover the mystery of your missing books!" Mrs. Potts hoped this would finally put an end to his antics, at least until the house party was over.

"You haven't heard the last of this, Mrs. Potts, I assure you."

"I'm sure I haven't," she said, sighing and shaking her head.

"What was that all about?" asked Mr. Cogsworth, suddenly popping his head out of his pantry after Monsieur Biblio stalked away in a huff.

"Oh, nothing, Mr. Cogsworth. It seems the ghost in the library is up to his shenanigans again," she said, laughing.

"Do you have those menus written up?" he asked, hardly paying attention. Mrs. Potts could see Mr. Cogsworth was feeling the strain of their impending events, though only Mrs. Potts would have noticed. She had known Mr. Cogsworth for a long time and could recognize the little signs that gave him away. She saw the pressure of this house party bubbling under the surface of his smooth, stoic facade. It had been many years since the family entertained at this level. The king and queen were so often away in recent years they didn't have the opportunity. So it had been a surprise when the queen said they would be hosting a house full of guests for an extended period of time, which would include lavish dinner parties, nightly entertainments, hunting parties for the men, picnic and scenic outings for the women, and, for the big finish, an exquisite ball on the grandest scale since the king and queen's wedding. It was no surprise the staff was run off their feet; preparing for this event was a Herculean task. And it was no wonder the staff was annoyed with Monsieur Biblio for distracting them when they had so much to do and thus blew off a bit of steam by teasing him.

"I do have the menus," she said, handing them to Mr. Cogsworth. "I was making my final adjustments just as Monsieur Biblio interrupted my work."

"What do you mean, ghost in the library? Monsieur Biblio doesn't actually believe the castle is haunted, does he?" asked Mr. Cogsworth, as if her words had just registered.

"No. He blames Gaston and demanded Grosvenor's cottage be searched."

"That's ridiculous."

Mrs. Potts was surprised to hear him defending Gaston.

"What would Gaston want with books, anyway? Unless they had pictures. The ghost theory makes more sense. Think of it, Gaston reading." He laughed, and Mrs. Potts frowned.

"That's quite enough of that, Mr. Cogsworth! If you know what's good for you *and* would like to remain in my good graces I suggest you keep those comments to yourself. And if you haven't noticed, Gaston isn't a boy any longer, neither of them are. They're both thirteen now. Almost men."

Mr. Cogsworth was frequently stuffy and a notorious snob, and it wasn't a secret he didn't approve of Gaston having the run of the house, but he wasn't often a cruel man. And in this instance Mrs. Potts thought he was being cruel, and she couldn't have been more disappointed in him. And by the look on his face, it seemed he was disappointed in himself.

"That was a low blow, Mr. Cogsworth, even for you," she said, making it clear he had gone too far.

"I'm sorry, Mrs. Potts. That was over the line. This house party has me rattled, I won't even try to deny it. It's been so long since we've had a guest list of this magnitude. Please tell me you have everything under control."

"Of course I do, Mr. Cogsworth. Not to worry. We're all under pressure, but I am sure it will be a tremendous success," said Mrs. Potts.

At that moment, she spied Gaston round the corner into the kitchen and stop short when he saw Mr. Cogsworth standing there. He ducked behind the wall and waited.

"I don't like it when we are at odds, Mrs. Potts," Mr. Cogsworth said, looking a bit sheepish. And she knew he was telling the truth. Further, there was no time for one of their discussions, not with so much more to do for the party. And certainly not with Gaston in earshot.

"Off with you. You still have the wine to plan," she said, ushering him back to his pantry with a wink for

Gaston, who was peeking around the corner, waiting for the conversation to end. But Mr. Cogsworth would not budge.

"Oh, and, Mrs. Potts, I will treat Gaston like a young man the moment he starts acting like one."

"Does that apply to the prince as well?" she asked with a cheeky smile. Mr. Cogsworth didn't answer. He just shook his head and went into his pantry. She didn't mind. She knew he was eager to get the wine list written up for the king, and Gaston was waiting to pay her a visit. Though today she didn't have a moment to spare. It would be a wonder if she took a break at all that day before it was time to sit down for dinner.

"Mr. Cogsworth looked like he was in a state. What happened?" asked Gaston, laughing in her doorway.

"Get in here, young man," she said, quickly pulling him into her sitting room and shutting the door. "Haven't you heard? It seems the library ghost is up to his trickery once again," she added, giving him a knowing but indulgent look. "Luckily for you, Mr.

Cogsworth is too busy to take this book debacle seriously. But might I suggest you and the prince replace Monsieur Biblio's treasures before he takes this further? He's threatening to have your cottage searched, and you know what that would mean, they would discover your secret tree house, and no doubt find the books you hiding within it." Mrs. Potts walked over to her tea table and poured them both a cup.

"Hey, how did you know about our tree house? What makes you think we have the books?" asked Gaston, taking a small round cookie covered in powdered sugar from the plate on Mrs. Potts's tea table.

"There is very little that goes on around here I don't know about."

"I see," said Gaston, munching one of Mrs. Potts's delicious cookies with a guilty expression.

"Don't worry, my boy, your secrets are safe with me. Only your father and I know about the tree house. But it's no secret you and the prince have the books, but for the life of us we don't understand why it's such a problem. That's why we all tease the poor man. But I worry this might have gone a bit too far, and

I don't have time to deal with it with everything else going on."

"He's angry because we broke his rule. That's the problem," said Gaston, taking another cookie.

"But why have such a rule? Aren't books for reading?" Mrs. Potts threw up her hands in exasperation.

"Exactly how Gaston and I feel," said the prince, ducking into the room with an impish look on his face. "So what did I miss this time?"

Mrs. Potts wasn't sure she liked what she saw in the boy on occasion, but she didn't have time for one of her lectures.

"Monsieur Biblio is making a fuss again. Maybe you and Gaston can help him discover the mystery behind the missing books while I get back to planning your parents' house party," she said, motioning to the plate of cookies so he would take some.

"Perhaps we'll do just that, Mrs. Potts," said the prince with a sneaky grin. "I think I know just the thing."

Later that night, long after Monsieur Biblio had gone to sleep, exhausted from many hours of searching the castle for the missing books, he was roused by a strange noise in the men's corridor outside of his room. He could hear the floorboards creaking and could swear there was someone was lurking right outside his door. He peered into the darkness at the sliver of light shining from under the doorway of his pitch-dark room and saw a shadow move across it which made him start with a bolt. Someone *was* there.

"Who's there?" he asked in a weak voice as he pulled the coverlet up under his chin like a frightened child. But whoever it was didn't answer; they just stood there in terrifying silence.

"State your business or leave!" he called out rather more loudly, trying to sound brave as he mustered his courage to light the candle on his bedside table. The room exploded with light when he struck the match and ignited the candle's wick. He quickly slipped on his dressing jacket, adjusted his sleeping cap, and picked up the plate that held the candlestick with shaking hands. He made his way to the door slowly, very much afraid of what he might find on the other side. But when he opened the door, he saw something completely unexpected. Books.

"That damnable boy!" he said, looking at the stack of books on the floor. When he leaned over to collect them, he heard someone scurrying around the corner and down the hall.

"Gaston! I know it's you!" Monsieur Biblio rushed down the hall, hoping to catch Gaston in the act, but what he found was a trail of books scattered along the corridors. As Monsieur Biblio followed the trail, he felt a chill in the air that made him shiver, and he wondered if Gaston had taken the books after all. Perhaps there really was a ghost. He had read in one of his books on the nature of supernatural entities that almost every account of a spectral encounter was accompanied by a distinct chill in the air. And there was indeed a distinct chill that penetrated his very being. There was no denying it. But *could* there really be a ghost? It didn't seem possible.

"Don't be an old fool!" he said aloud to himself. "There are no ghosts in this castle." But he wasn't sure. He looked around for an open window, for some logical reason it was suddenly so cold, but he could not account for it. He knew old castles were, by nature, cold places, and he knew not only because he lived in one but because he had read so many books about others. Yet he also knew castles were notorious for being haunted places, and he wasn't sure if he was shivering from fear or because the gallery was particularly cold that evening. The conundrum made him quite dizzy as he followed the trail of books. He wasn't sure if he was feeling faint due to seeing his precious tomes littering the gallery in such a disgraceful manner or if he was truly fearful the castle was haunted. Whatever the reason he regretted not waking up at least one of the footmen to accompany him on his frightful mission.

He finally found himself standing in front of the library doors, where he could hear strange noises coming from within. Wailing and thumping sounds that sent terror into his heart as he stood there in his pajamas and sleeping cap, holding his candle and looking like an illustration from one of his books. He couldn't believe this was happening. If he didn't know better, he would think he was suffering some sort of walking dream sickness. How could his library really be haunted? The idea was preposterous.

When he opened the library doors, he was astonished to see ghosts, *actual ghosts*, dancing on the grand upper gallery. They were pulling books off the shelves and throwing them every which way. The ghosts were just as Monsieur Biblio had imagined they would look: white, billowy, and frightful, with large, round, expressionless black eyes. And they paid absolutely no attention to him whatsoever; they were taking delight in their mayhem, laughing and hurling Monsieur Biblio's treasured tomes with wild abandonment.

All trembling and fear left Monsieur Biblio in that moment, seeing his books treated in such an ill fashion, and it was replaced with indignation, giving him the courage to confront the mischievous spirits.

"Stop this at once, I say! Show some respect!" And to his surprise the ghosts stopped, looking as if they were frozen in time, standing there holding great stacks of books while peering down at him from the gallery.

"Spirits, please! I command you to put those books down carefully and leave this place at once, never to return!" he said, managing to muster an authoritative tone. He had read that spirits were more likely to do your bidding if you spoke to them in such a manner, and so far it seemed to be working. He was feeling rather proud of himself. After all, he was a librarian, and not a spiritualist or master of the magical arts. But one of the things Monsieur Biblio loved most about his work, what he loved most about books, was that there was almost nothing he couldn't do as long as he took the time to research it first.

"Now, off with you, trickster spirits. Go back to the dark places where you belong!" he said, feeling more like a powerful wizard than a librarian. But then something happened he did not expect: the ghosts started laughing! Actually laughing at him—he couldn't believe it. And they were throwing books right at him from the gallery above.

Monsieur Biblio screamed as he tried to dodge the books as they came raining down all around him, slamming onto the floor with a clatter that sounded like thunder. He shielded his head as the ghosts laughed and threw book after book at him, sending him running from the library. Monsieur Biblio was so afraid he didn't stop running until he reached Mr. Cogsworth's room in the men's corridor, where he found himself pounding the door furiously and with great fervor.

"Mr. Cogsworth, Mr. Cogsworth! Please wake up!" Monsieur Biblio was trembling in fear but was brought out of his stupor when Mr. Cogsworth opened his bedroom door abruptly with his mustache askew, his hair mussed, and his face full of wrath.

"What is the meaning of this, Biblio? What's the matter now?" asked Mr. Cogsworth. Monsieur Biblio had never seen him so angry. Never seen him looking anything other than perfectly composed.

"It's true, Mr. Cogsworth! There *are* ghosts in the library! Come quickly!" said Monsieur Biblio, adjusting his sleeping cap, which had slid down while he was running and now almost covered his eyes.

"Poppycock! You're having nightmares again, man.

Go back to bed." Mr. Cogsworth was about to slam the door in Monsieur Biblio's face, but Monsieur Biblio put his foot out to stop him.

"No, Mr. Cogsworth, I swear! They're in there now. I must insist you come with me." The poor man was out of breath from running and from his frightening ordeal. Surely Mr. Cogsworth could see he was telling the truth. Surely he wouldn't dismiss this as trivial nonsense. There were ghosts in the library, and something had to be done.

"Very well. Wake the footmen and tell them to meet us in the library. If we do indeed have ghosts, then we should face them prepared." Mr. Cogsworth took his dressing jacket off the hook on the wall next to his door and pulled it on. He tied the belt with an angry flourish and ushered Monsieur Biblio out of his way.

Monsieur Biblio woke the footmen as Mr. Cogsworth had asked and led the groggy and confused young men to the library, where Mr. Cogsworth was waiting for them. But before they walked into the room, Monsieur Biblio stopped them so he might prepare the footmen for the frightening spectacle they were about to witness.

"Now, gentlemen, you must harden your resolve. We must stand our ground no matter what may happen. Apparitions such as these feed on our fear. So whatever you do, don't appear frightened," said the librarian as they walked into the library. But once they were inside, his jaw dropped open. There were no ghosts, or even any books on the floor. Everything was neat and tidy and put away in its proper place. There was no sign anything had happened at all. It was confounding. He didn't understand.

"Yeah, it's a right old mess in here. It's full of ghosts," said Francis, one of the footmen, making the others laugh.

"I'm telling you, there were ghosts in here! I saw them with my own eyes." Monsieur Biblio spun in circles, looking around the room in confusion. "They were here, I swear!"

"You, Monsieur Biblio, have awoken the house for

nothing more than a trifling nightmare, and with all the work we have ahead of us before the house party," said Mr. Cogsworth, who seemed to have straightened his mustache and smoothed down his hair on their way downstairs.

"It wasn't a nightmare! I tell you, there *were* ghosts in here, and they were hurling books at me!" The librarian looked around wildly for any sign this hadn't all been a dream. Clearly the spirits had cleaned up after themselves. But was that likely? He hadn't read that spirits were particularly fastidious in that way. But nevertheless, it had happened. He didn't care what the library looked like now, just moments before it had been chaos.

"What's more likely, Monsieur Biblio, a haunted library, or an overwrought librarian suffering from nightmares? Now, if you don't mind, I think we will go back to bed. I suggest you do the same." Mr. Cogsworth motioned to the footmen to leave the room.

"But what of the ghosts? Something must be done! Wait . . . what's that? Did you hear that laughter?"

asked Monsieur Biblio. His eyes were wild as he darted to a bookcase behind which he could swear he heard laughing.

"First ghosts, and now someone laughing among the books? Monsieur Biblio, I do believe you need a rest. I wonder if we should have Monsieur D'Arque take a look at you?"

"Now look here! It's true, I say. I'll show you." Monsieur Biblio pressed a discreet button on the bookshelf, which slid open to reveal a stack of books tucked away in a secret compartment. The very books that had been thrown at him moments earlier. Suddenly, it all became clear, he knew what had happened, and his blood began to boil.

"Come out, Gaston, I know you're in there, you horrible, fiendish, wretched little . . . Oh!" Monsieur Biblio was shocked to see the prince come out from his hiding place, behind the stack of books. "I'm—I'm sorry, my prince. I didn't realize it was you."

"Clearly," said the prince. "What's this all about, Monsieur Biblio? Mr. Cogsworth? Why are you all here in your nightclothes?" The prince drew himself up and crossed his arms imperiously, as if it were perfectly normal to be hiding behind a bookcase in the middle of the night.

"I'm sorry, Your Highness. Monsieur Biblio must have had a nightmare. I do apologize," Mr. Cogsworth said, his face growing red.

"Of course I don't blame you, Cogsworth," said the prince, glaring at Monsieur Biblio.

"What are you all playing at? I know Gaston is in there with you! I know he's behind all this," Monsieur Biblio sputtered in rage. He had had enough of Gaston and the prince's tomfoolery, and he could only take his anger out on one of the boys. They had both been plaguing him for years, taking his books and not returning them. It wasn't as if he could lash out at the prince, call him out on his complicity, but he could make sure Gaston was punished for his wicked book-thieving ways. If there was one thing Monsieur Biblio could not abide, it was disrespecting books, and Gaston and the prince had shown disrespect of the lowest order. They had scattered them throughout the castle and thrown them onto the floor. And there was no way this would go unpunished if he could help it.

"Let's say Gaston is behind all this. So what if he is? What will you do about it?" asked the prince, more domineering than ever. It wasn't Monsieur Biblio's place to say, or even to have an opinion on such things, but as far as he was concerned the prince wasn't all he was cracked up to be, and he was getting more impertinent by the day. And Gaston was even worse. He didn't understand why almost the entire household worshipped them. It seemed it was only Mr. Cogsworth and he himself who saw Gaston for who he was. It made sense why old Mr. Cogsworth would make excuses for the prince and indulge him. But Monsieur Biblio was quite sure that in no time the prince was going to turn into a little monster if someone didn't take him in hand.

"Come now, Monsieur Biblio, you don't want to say anything you might regret. You forget yourself," said Mr. Cogsworth.

"I know this is all down to Gaston and the prince!

Stealing books, playing tricks! I have a mind to tell the king myself!" said Monsieur Biblio.

"And who do you think the king will believe? A bumbling old fool of a librarian who believes in ghosts, or his son? Now, go back to bed before you lose your position, Monsieur Biblio," said the prince with a mean-spirited expression.

"Yes, I suggest we all go back to bed," said Mr. Cogsworth, who seemed rather uncomfortable with the entire situation, fiddling with the belt of his dressing jacket.

Monsieur Biblio was defeated. There was nothing to be done. Not now, anyway. As he made his way out of the library with Mr. Cogsworth and the grumbling, groggy footmen behind them, he distinctly heard Gaston's voice along with the prince's coming from the library. He quickly shot a glance over at Cogsworth to see what his reaction would be. But there was nothing. The majordomo was stoic as ever, not a flinch, not even a look, as if they hadn't both heard the same thing.

"You're not really going to have Monsieur Biblio

dismissed are you, Kingsley?" Gaston had asked.

And the prince replied: "I haven't decided yet."

No, this wasn't the end for Monsieur Biblio. He and Mr. Cogsworth both knew the prince and Gaston had been behind the missing books from the beginning. Perhaps together they would find a way to punish the boys for breaking Monsieur Biblio's rules.

CHAPTER IV

THE BEAST OF GÉVAUDAN

When Gaston wasn't pulling pranks on poor old Monsieur Biblio with the prince, or up to their usual tomfoolery, he was at his father's side, helping prepare for the Great Hunt. Gaston's father had been preparing for it since the king came to him with the news he would be hosting a hunt on the grandest scale during the upcoming house party that had all the staff in a flurry of panic and work over the past several weeks. Gaston accompanied his father on his rounds, seeing to the beaters who drove the game out of cover for the shooters to make sure they were outfitted with everything they should need; supervising the arrival of the visiting lords' horses, which had been sent ahead of the lords and ladies; and scouting the best areas to host the various outdoor activities, all while consulting with the king and queen. Gaston couldn't believe how much responsibility his father had and found it inspiring to watch him work.

On this particular day, Gaston and his father walked out to a clearing where the builders were putting the finishing touches on the construction of an enormous outdoor pavilion. It had been an ongoing project for quite some months, long before the news of the house party, but when Gaston's father learned he was to arrange a royal hunt, he and the king decided to expedite the process so it would be ready for the shooters' lunch that would be hosted by the queen.

Luckily, much progress had already been made on the pavilion, so the builders felt they could have it ready in time. Gaston's father could, of course, have left this to the head builder, just as he could have left the care of the horses to the head groom, and so forth, but Grosvenor knew how important this event was to the king, and he wanted to make sure it was perfect.

Gaston had been in awe at his father's attention to detail, astonished by all the arrangements he had to make and things he needed to remember. Gaston felt the weight of his father's responsibilities pressing him as if they were his own, though there was no sign of any of it seeming to faze his father. He had never seen such a strong and capable man, always remaining so calm, even gentle, and never cross with anyone, no matter if he was given cause.

As they approached the pavilion, they could see from a distance the structure was indeed almost finished, and there were a number of staff members there bringing in the tables, chairs, and other things needed to host the queen's luncheon. There had even been a special chandelier—fashioned with little mirrors that would reflect the light—imported from a neighboring kingdom. The prince had told him about how the queen had been talking of almost nothing else because she was so excited, and she had been going on and on about how the chandelier was made of fragments from the collection of a renowned maker of mirrors who had passed away some years before. And Gaston's father had just said this morning he knew the queen had great plans for the pavilion beyond hosting the luncheon; the chandelier was the centerpiece for her plans, so he was happy he was there to supervise its arrival and make sure the builders treated it with care. As they got closer to the pavilion, Gaston noticed Mrs. Potts was also there and must have had the same idea.

"I see you're here to supervise the installation of the queen's new treasure as well, Grosvenor," said Mrs. Potts, looking very pleased to have run into Gaston and his father. She was such a jolly woman, always with a smile on her face—unless, of course, she was cross with someone. But it seemed the strain of the upcoming events, and even Monsieur Biblio's outbursts about the "library incident," as he called it, couldn't diminish Mrs. Potts's spirits.

"That I am, Mrs. Potts. I know you have a lot to look after in the house, so you can leave this to me, if you'd prefer," said Grosvenor.

"It's nice to get outside for a while, Grosvenor. I envy all the time you get to spend outdoors. And how are you, Gaston? Are you ready for the Great Hunt?

Will you be joining your father in his duties attending the king?" said Mrs. Potts, who was somehow able to have an entirely pleasant conversation while simultaneously watching the workers with a hawk eye as they removed the chandelier from the wooden crate.

"Gaston will be attending the prince, serving as his loader," said Grosvenor, smiling at his son and patting him on the back.

"His *loader*? I am a way better shot than Kingsley. Won't I be allowed to shoot as well?" asked Gaston, whipping his head around in shock.

"We're servants, Gaston. It isn't our place to shoot with the royal company. And you're not better than the prince, remember that." Grosvenor glanced at Mrs. Potts to see if she would chime in.

"But Kingsley *knows* I'm a better shot than him."

"Oh, I don't think anyone would mind if Gaston joined the hunt, Grosvenor," said Mrs. Potts. "I really don't. And he's right, you know, he is a better shot than the prince. He's the best at everything. He takes after you."

"If he took after me, then he would see the wisdom

in letting the prince believe *he* was the best," said Grosvenor.

"You sound like Mr. Cogsworth," said Mrs. Potts. "And I'm not sure how wise that is, especially if it's not the truth."

Their conversation was interrupted by the sound of a group of men yelling from the woods. They seemed to be some yards away from the pavilion, but Gaston could hear they sounded panicked as they called to the men working on the pavilion. One of men came running from the woods, his face filled with terror.

"Someone, please, get Monsieur Grosvenor!" he said, breathless, hardly able to speak. "Does anyone know where he is?"

"I'm here. What's the matter?" Grosvenor called out as he ran to the other side of the pavilion to see what was happening, leaving Gaston and Mrs. Potts behind.

"Oh, Monsieur! Come with me. It's terrible," said the young man. "This way." He led Grosvenor into the woods, where a group of men were huddled, looking down at something. At first Grosvenor thought an animal had been mauled by a wolf or some such creature. It was a bloody scene, gruesome and terrible, but he didn't understand why the men were panicking. When he got closer he realized it wasn't an animal at all, but one of the young men on the outdoor staff by the name of Andre, who Grosvenor liked very much. He couldn't bear to look at the poor fellow lying on the forest floor, caked in blood and dirt, like his life meant nothing at all.

"What's happened?" he asked, realizing he already knew the answer the moment he asked. He had seen an attack like this before, and it made his stomach drop and his heart race so fast he thought his knees might buckle. Grosvenor recovered his nerves and examined what was left of the poor young man's body with shaking hands.

"He's been lying here since last night!" He couldn't keep the tears from falling when he looked up at the grief-stricken faces of the other men. All of them friends with this poor young man who had lost his life. "Why didn't anyone tell me Andre was missing?"

Grosvenor asked, taking off his jacket and putting it over the poor man's face.

"Someone fetch Jean!" he continued. "I want to know why he didn't let me know Andre didn't come back with the other builders last night." His voice was cracking, his grief turning to anger and reproach.

"We thought he was off at the village tavern, Grosvenor. We couldn't have imagined—" Grosvenor didn't let him finish. He wasn't the sort of man who cut others off or barked orders, but Jean, the head builder, had arrived, and there was no time to lose.

"Never mind that. Jean, I want a full count of the outdoor staff immediately! And tell everyone the entire kingdom is under curfew until further notice. Do you understand? No one is to go out after dark. I want everyone inside no later than twilight," said Grosvenor as the others started making their way over from the pavilion to see what had happened.

"And what are we to say to the king and queen when they ask why we haven't followed their orders to work late? You know we can't stop working at twilight if we're going to be ready for the festivities!" Jean protested.

"The entire house party will have to be canceled, Jean. I'll talk to the king," said Grosvenor. The small group was now surrounded by the outdoor staff, as well as the maids who were there to help with the preparations of the pavilion, now talking among themselves and asking Grosvenor questions.

"We can't cancel the party now, surely. What will the king and queen say? Their guests have been traveling for weeks to get here," said one of the maids, who was there to polish the chandelier before it was installed.

"They will say the Beast of Gévaudan has returned, and we are under siege," said Grosvenor, making everyone gasp and then fall into an eerie silence just as Mrs. Potts and Gaston came onto the scene.

"What's this? Are you sure, Grosvenor?" asked Mrs. Potts.

"Stay back, Mrs. Potts. I won't have you see this. Gaston, take her back to the castle, now, and inform Mr. Cogsworth I will be there shortly to speak with him and the king," said Grosvenor.

"Can it really be the beast, Grosvenor? Truly? Are

you sure?" Mrs. Potts looked unsteady on her feet, wobbly, as if she might faint, causing Gaston to put out his arm for her to take it.

"Gaston, see to Mrs. Potts and get her back to the castle. We will speak of this later," said Grosvenor.

"Of course, Papa." Gaston put his arm around Mrs. Potts and tried to lead her back to the castle. "Come on, Mrs. Potts, my papa will take care of this," said Gaston. He wanted to stay there with his father. He couldn't see what had happened to make everyone so scared, but he could tell it was serious.

"But are you sure, Grosvenor?" Mrs. Potts was refusing to budge; she looked as though she was in a trance of fear.

"I am quite sure, Mrs. Potts. Now let Gaston get you inside."

"Come on, Mrs. Potts," Gaston said again, giving her a small kiss on the cheek like a loving son. "I think you could use a cup of tea."

Gaston had never seen Mrs. Potts so upset. He took her to her sitting room, sat her down, and wrapped her shawl around her shoulders. "Now sit here, Mrs. Potts, I will be right back with a pot of tea," he said as Plumette came into the room.

"What is this I hear? Is it true, Mrs. Potts? Is it really—"

Gaston interrupted Plumette before she could finish. He didn't want everyone plaguing her with questions.

"Mrs. Potts has had a shock, Miss Plumette. My father will be back as soon as he's done talking with the king, and he will explain. Could you please see if one of the kitchen maids could make Mrs. Potts a pot of tea?" he asked.

"At once!" she said, running off to the kitchen.

"Are you all right, Mrs. Potts?" Gaston adjusted her shawl and took her hand. He hated seeing her so afraid. She had a faraway look in her eyes that reminded him of the way his father looked sometimes when he sat alone looking at the stairs.

"Yes, dear. Don't you worry about me. You go see to the other servants, and I'll join you in a moment." But Gaston didn't want to leave her alone. He had never known Mrs. Potts to be afraid, not like this. Come to think of it, he had never seen his father afraid either.

Gaston knew this must be serious for Mrs. Potts and his father to be so unnerved. He had seen his father sullen, and thoughtful, and maybe even agitated at times, but never frightened, never overwhelmed, and it made Gaston feel afraid. His father's hands had been shaking as he talked to Mrs. Potts, and his face was so stricken with fear and grief, terror, and sadness. And now poor Mrs. Potts was in a state, so shaken, so unlike herself, he wondered if he should have left his father alone. Wondered if his father was safe. If Mrs. Potts didn't need him he would have gone back to make sure his father was okay.

Gaston knew only fragments of the stories surrounding the Beast of Gévaudan, even though the stories were well-known in their lands. The beast hadn't been heard of for many years, and they had all thought it was dead. It was said to have been a large gray wolf of massive proportions that terrorized the countryside for years. If the tales were to be believed, it hadn't been seen since shortly after Gaston was born, so to him they were just stories, made up to frighten children into minding their parents like the other fairy tales and legends he and the prince grew up on. The thought that this beast was real sent terror into Gaston's heart. Not because he was afraid of it, but because his father was. His father wasn't, as far as he knew, afraid of anything, until today.

Gaston could hear everyone in the hall talking loudly, panicking about the news that had clearly spread to the castle in the time it took Gaston and Mrs. Potts to make their way back.

"Where is Grosvenor?" Mr. Cogsworth stood in the doorway of Mrs. Potts's sitting room. "How do we know this is truly the Beast of Gévaudan and not simply a wolf attack?" Mr. Cogsworth had lost all composure. He was not himself.

"Calm down, Mr. Cogsworth, please. Mrs. Potts has had a shock, and my father will be back soon to talk to everyone. I'm sure he wouldn't want us to panic," said Gaston, trying to take control over the situation in the way he thought his father might.

"Now look here, young man. I won't have a servant's son telling me to calm down." But Gaston didn't care. He wasn't going to let anyone upset Mrs. Potts any more than she already was, but before he could say anything more Mrs. Potts made the situation more than clear to the majordomo

"Of all of us, Mr. Cogsworth, Grosvenor would know an attack by the Beast of Gévaudan. And there is no reason to bite Gaston's head off," said Mrs. Potts.

"Did you see . . . the poor lad?" Mr. Cogsworth could barely bring himself to say the words. As if talking about it would make it all real.

"No. But I trust Grosvenor. He is speaking to the king now, and they will decide what to do," said Mrs. Potts.

"I am the majordomo of this house! It is for me to help the king decide what to do." Mr. Cogsworth's mustache twitched so fast it looked like hands on a clock being wound quickly. The fact was, Mr.

Cogsworth was tightly wound, and who could blame him with everything going on.

"You know as well I, Mr. Cogsworth, this is Grosvenor's province. I am sure once he has spoken to the king, you, Grosvenor, and I will meet to discuss how the king wishes to proceed," said Mrs. Potts. She still looked rather pale, and Gaston wished Mr. Cogsworth would leave her alone, but he wasn't about to push him. He was in such a state as it was, Gaston was surprised Cogsworth hadn't thrown him out of the sitting room. Not that Mrs. Potts would stand for it.

Gaston hadn't truly appreciated his father's place in the royal staff until that moment, but he was proud to hear his father was every bit as important as Mr. Cogsworth and Mrs. Potts. Gaston couldn't help but smile when he saw Cogsworth's resignation at Mrs. Potts's words.

By the time Gaston's father made his way to the servants' hall where Gaston, Mrs. Potts, Mr. Cogsworth, and most of the senior staff had assembled, everyone in the castle had already heard the news. They were in a tizzy of panic, and full of questions.

"I was just with the king. He wishes me to inform you all of the curfew that is in immediate effect. No one is to go out of doors after dark for any reason what-soever. The king expects everyone to obey for their own safety. And that includes you and the prince," Grosvenor said, looking directly at Gaston.

He continued, "The king has suggested Gaston should take a room in the castle so neither of them is tempted to sneak out to see each other after dark, and knowing their history, I have to agree. Mrs. Potts, will it be a problem finding Gaston a room?"

"Of course not, Grosvenor. I will arrange a room for both of you," said Mrs. Potts.

"That won't be necessary, Mrs. Potts, but thank you," said Grosvenor.

"What is this? Of course you will be staying in the castle with us, Grosvenor!" said Lumiere.

"We do not have the room to house all of the outdoor staff within the castle, and I will not stay safely within its confines while my men are at risk." Grosvenor sounded stern and resolute. That's the sort of man Gaston's father was. He was good, and honest, and always tried to do the best for his men. Gaston was in awe of his father's bravery.

"Surely they will be safe in their quarters, as long as they don't go out after curfew," said Lumiere.

"And I will be safe in mine," said Grosvenor. Gaston was proud of his papa. Even if the idea of him staying in the cottage on his own frighted Gaston, he was impressed that his father wouldn't hide behind castle walls unless all of his men were with him.

"But, Grosvenor, we are all so frightened. Is it true, then, what they say? The Beast of Gévaudan has come back? How can this be? I thought you killed the beast long ago," said Lumiere.

"I hoped I had, Lumiere, but it seems I did not." Grosvenor looked at his son. Gaston didn't understand. His father never told him he once faced the Beast of Gévaudan. He never mentioned it at all. This seemed like the sort of thing someone would brag about, a story to share by the fire, but his father never even mentioned the Beast of Gévaudan, let alone that he had thought he killed it.

"Yes, Grosvenor, please stay here with us. The men

will be fine," said Mrs. Potts. "We need you here to protect us." She still looked so pale and frightened. Gaston could see his father was in an impossible position, but he wasn't going hide away inside a castle while his men fended for themselves in their cottages in the dangerous woods.

"My papa will not abandon his men, and I will not abandon my papa. I will stay in the cottage with him," said Gaston. He now realized where his father had gotten his scar: it must have been while fighting the Beast of Gévaudan. He knew his father was brave, he knew he was the best at everything, but this surpassed anything he had imagined. His father really was the most incredible man, and he hoped that one day he would be able to be as brave as him.

"The king has decreed you will stay in the castle, Gaston. Mrs. Potts will arrange a room for you. And please, everyone, stop plaguing Grosvenor with pleas to stay in the castle. If he feels it is his duty to be with his men, then we must respect his choice." Mr. Cogsworth spoke with conviction, his hands firmly placed on his hips, which put an end to the panicked chatter and endless questions. And all around the hall, eyebrows shot up at his support of Grosvenor.

"Thank you, Mr. Cogsworth. The king and queen would like to speak with the two of us and Mrs. Potts, but first I need to have a quick word with my son. I will only be a moment. Excuse me." With that, Grosvenor took Gaston by the arm and led him out of the servants' hall.

"You may use my sitting room, Grosvenor," Mrs. Potts called after them, a worried look on her face. Gaston and Grosvenor took Mrs. Potts up on her offer and used her sitting room so they could speak privately. The room was cold and dimly lit, with the fire having dwindled to embers and none of the candles burning. It felt strange being in there without Mrs. Potts.

"Listen to me, son. I know you're worried, but I need you here to help Mrs. Potts stay calm. I am counting on you to keep the prince out of trouble. I do not want either of you getting it into your heads to leave the castle after dark. The king is counting on you as well. It was his idea to have you stay in the castle. He knows you're the only person the prince truly listens to. This is a big responsibility, Gaston, but I know you can handle it. I'm trusting you to keep your little brother safe."

"You've never called him that before, Papa. Why now?" asked Gaston.

"Because I know you love him like a brother, and I want you to understand how important and serious this is. You would never forgive yourself if something happened to your friend, and I would never forgive myself if anything should happen to you. My heart has been broken once already; please do not break it again. Promise me, Gaston, you must keep yourself and the prince safe." Grosvenor wrapped his arms around his son almost desperately, as if it might be the last time.

"I promise, Papa," said Gaston returning his father's hug, sensing the weight of what was happening, even though he had a feeling his father wasn't sharing everything.

"Very well. I must go with Mr. Cogsworth and Mrs. Potts to speak with the king and queen. You be a good boy and do what Mrs. Potts says," Grosvenor said, giving him a kiss. "I'll see you in the morning for breakfast."

Gaston lingered in Mrs. Potts's sitting room for a moment after his father left, thinking about everything he had just heard. He couldn't remember seeing his father so scared before, so serious. And he couldn't help but feel there was more to this than what his father or Mrs. Potts was saying, but he also couldn't say why he felt that way. It was just something in the way they were acting, something they were not saying and the looks in their eyes.

"Gaston! There you are. Did you hear, you're staying in the castle! I insisted you be allowed to stay in the room that's connected to mine," said the prince, bounding into the room as if they weren't in the middle of a crisis.

"I assumed Mrs. Potts was going to arrange a room in the servants' wing," said Gaston in surprise.

"Don't be ridiculous. I just told Mrs. Potts to make the blue room ready. Don't worry, my mama and papa don't care. It was Papa's idea, anyway. Can you believe our luck? A chance to hunt the beast!" The prince seemed rather more jovial than he should have been. Acting as if someone hadn't just died.

"I'm not sure poor Andre would agree with you," said Gaston, remembering the body with the coat over it, the look of terror on his father's face. "Besides, we're not going after the beast, Kingsley. I promised my father we would stay inside and keep safe."

"Since when do we follow the rules? Come on! This is just the sort of adventure we have been waiting for. A *real* adventure. We're ready, Gaston." The prince was so cavalier about it, Gaston was almost ashamed of him. How could he be thinking of this as an adventure? Didn't he see how frightened everyone was? His friend was not taking this seriously. But then again, there was very little he did.

"We are not ready, Kingsley! Leave the beast to my father and his men!" said Gaston, feeling frustrated with his friend, but before he could say more Lumiere opened the door and peeked into the room.

"And what are you two up to?" asked Lumiere, narrowing his eyes at both of them. Gaston was happy he had come into the room; he didn't want to get in a fight with his best friend. He knew what was going through the prince's mind, and the last thing he would do is betray his word to his father.

"Oh, nothing, Lumiere. Just wondering what's for dinner," said the prince.

"I suppose that depends on whether you are dining upstairs or down, Your Highness. But somehow I doubt that is what you were talking about," said Lumiere, still looking at the boys as if he had caught them doing something they shouldn't.

"Perhaps you're right, Lumiere, but I think we will be eating dinner downstairs tonight."

CHAPTER V

THE BEAST IN THE WOODS

Downstairs dinner was rather subdued. The servants' hall was not filled with the happy voices of friends or ringing with laughter that evening. Everyone was shocked and saddened by the discovery of Andre's body in the woods, and they were frightened by the threat of the Beast of Gévaudan. It had been so long since the beast was last seen in their part of the countryside they had thought it was a distant memory. And now they were not only faced with the violent death of a friend, and an impending menace, but by the tragic events of the past they tried so hard to put behind them.

"I suppose the king and queen wanted to make an early night of it," said Plumette, her eyes still red from crying. Everyone at the table looked sad and frightened. But there seemed to be something more behind their eyes and the shared glances between those who had had been working in the castle longest. Those who were there when the beast attacked years before. And Gaston could tell there was something they were thinking, but not saying to each other aloud.

"Yes, they had dinner in their private quarters and retired to their rooms early. I daresay we will all want to make an early night of it," said Mr. Cogsworth, who had hardly touched his own dinner. No one at the table had much of an appetite, except for the prince, who had already had seconds and was looking to the sideboard to see what was for dessert.

As the others chatted, Gaston was distracted, thinking about his father alone in the cottage while the beast was out stalking the woods for its next victim. He wondered if his father had thought to bring the cat in before dark. Horrible images filled his mind, flashing like lightning, his body seized by fear with each invasive thought. No matter how hard he tried, he couldn't banish the images of the giant gray wolf ripping out his father's throat and tearing the limbs from his body. He imagined his poor father's body scattered on the forest floor, and their cat dead and mangled, her fur caked in blood. He closed his eyes against these horrible thoughts but couldn't will them away no matter how hard he tried.

"Gaston, are you all right? You look peaky," said Mrs. Potts. She didn't look well herself. She was exhausted by the day's events. It had taken her longer than usual to get all of her children to sleep that night. All of them afraid of the vicious beast lurking outside their castle walls. And no doubt she was also worried about Gaston's father.

"Gaston's is fine, Mrs. Potts. He's just worried about his papa being alone in the cottage," said the prince. "But we'll make sure he's okay, won't we, Gaston?" He patted his friend on the shoulder.

Gaston was happy the prince was having dinner with them, even if it seemed like everyone at the table looked uncomfortable in his company, for some reason.

It wasn't usually like this when the prince had dinner downstairs—and hadn't been for many years now. Even Mr. Cogsworth usually seemed less rattled by it, though everyone knew, strictly speaking, he didn't approve. No, this wasn't about the prince joining them, it was something else. Of course, everyone was upset over Andre, and they must have been worried about the beast. And now many of the king's and queen's plans for the house party had to be changed at the last moment, but this felt like something else. Something they all wanted to talk about but wouldn't.

"Monsieur Biblio, does the library have any books on the Beast of Gévaudan?" Gaston asked, taking Monsieur Biblio by surprise. He had noticed the librarian trying to avoid looking in his direction all through dinner and didn't understand why, until he remembered the prank he and the prince had played on him. He felt foolish right after he asked. The truth was he had almost forgotten about their silly stunt with everything else going on. But it was clear Monsieur Biblio had not forgotten and was still fuming.

"I'm surprised you have the audacity to ask me

about a book, young man, let alone speak to me at all. You're lucky I didn't have your father's cottage searched," said Monsieur Biblio, clearly not caring the prince was sitting there. He was far from the frightened man trembling in his night cap he had been the other night. He seemed like a man with a renewed sense of anger who didn't care what might happen.

"You're welcome to go search it now," said the prince, to audible gasps from Monsieur Biblio and a few others at the table. Shocked he would suggest such a thing under the circumstances.

"Go now? With the Beast of Gévaudan afoot? I daresay not, young sir, I daresay not!" Monsieur Biblio dropped his fork and knife, causing everyone at the table to jump at the clatter. "I think I hear the beast snarling at the back door. Why don't you go open it and take a look?" said the prince with a wicked smile.

"Never mind, Kingsley. That's enough. It's not worth it." Gaston put his hand on his friend's shoulder. He hated when the prince was like this. And he was starting to resent being the only person who could talk him down from these moods. He had enough to worry about tonight without the prince needling Monsieur Biblio. Never mind the fact they *were* the reason he was so vexed. They had dressed like ghosts and pummeled him with books. Anyone would be angry. But the prince didn't see it that way. He felt the man had brought it all on himself, and maybe he had, but the prince didn't have to take it this far. And Gaston knew from experience the prince was going to keep pushing the man until he exploded with anger. Gaston loved his friend, but he hated how relentless he could be when carrying a grudge.

"Did you really hear something, Your Highness? Is the beast really here?" asked Plumette, grabbing Lumiere's hand in fright.

"No, my darling, the prince is just teasing Monsieur Biblio. The beast would never come so close to the castle. At least, I hope not." He gave a fearful look out the window, which had a view of the servants' courtyard.

"But what if it did? How would we know? It could be out there right now!" said Plumette, taking a shaky sip from her glass.

"There are armed guards on the ramparts, Plumette. They will shoot it on sight and sound the bells. You have no reason to fear," said Mr. Cogsworth.

"I'm sorry, Miss Plumette. I didn't mean to frighten you. I was just teasing Monsieur Biblio," said the prince. "Please forgive me, Monsieur Biblio, I know you are in a fragile state of mind, and you should not be teased."

"Balderdash! My mind is perfectly sound, I assure you," said Monsieur Biblio. Gaston could see the man was on the precipice of explosive anger and decided to try his best to calm the man down. He wished he had never brought up the subject of books. This was his fault, and he felt he'd better try to fix it.

"Of course it is, Monsieur Biblio. You are just agitated by the events today. We all are, including the prince. Isn't that right, Kingsley?" said Gaston, kicking his friend under the table, but Kingsley just sat there, looking at the man with an arrogant, contemptuous expression on his face.

"And who wouldn't be agitated, as you say, after being hectored by you ruffians? And I'm sure I don't need defending by the likes of you!" Monsieur Biblio pointed a bony finger at Gaston, giving him a start.

"Did I hear you say *ruffians*, sir? You couldn't possibly be speaking of the prince." Mr. Cogsworth slid his chair back violently as he stood up. He looked as if he was about to instigate a round of fisticuffs.

Everything had fallen into chaos, with Mr. Cogsworth and Monsieur Biblio yelling at each other, and the prince seemed to be enjoying every moment of it. He leaned back in his chair with his hands behind his head, just smiling as the two men carried on.

"Calm down, the both of you!" said Mrs. Potts getting up as well. "I'm sure Monsieur Biblio didn't mean what he said."

"Indeed I did! That damned boy has been needling me all through dinner! No one cares a jot they attacked me! No one in this house has respect for books! Books missing, books put back in the wrong place, books mysteriously scattered all over the castle, books being thrown at me by ill-tempered, spoiled little brats. I still have the bruises from their attack! These boys are out of control, running roughshod over everyone without any consequences." The prince just smiled at Monsieur Biblio's outrage, and the sight of it made Gaston feel slightly sick. He knew his friend did this on purpose. And he couldn't believe Monsieur Biblio had taken the bait.

"That's enough, Monsieur Biblio. You will leave this house forthwith, without a reference," said Mr. Cogsworth, slamming his fists on the table so hard it made the china rattle. "You have taken things too far. You have stepped over the line!"

"I'm sure Monsieur Biblio didn't mean what he said," Mrs. Potts hurried to repeat. "He's just upset, like we all are. Maybe everyone will feel differently in the morning." The fact was, Gaston knew none of this would have happened if he and the prince hadn't pranked Monsieur Biblio. Things had gone too far, and Gaston felt as if everything was spinning out of control. Yes, Monsieur Biblio was annoying, and stuffy, and rather oddly obsessed with the books being kept in the library, but he didn't deserve being dismissed without a reference.

"I agree with Mrs. Potts," said Gaston.

"I don't need an illiterate little miscreant to defend me!" said Monsieur Biblio, locking eyes on Gaston. And in that moment any bit of pity or guilt Gaston had washed away. Monsieur Biblio had been sailing perilously close to the edge of things since he first spoke, and there was now nothing Gaston or anyone else could do to save him.

"That is enough! Now I know we are all wearied by this horrible day, but let's not say anything else we might regret. And we will not be sending Monsieur Biblio out into the night, no matter how impertinently he's treated the prince or Gaston. Not with the beast roaming the woods. I am sure not even they would wish death on poor Monsieur Biblio," said Mrs. Potts, waiting for the prince and Gaston to answer.

"Neither of us wishes that," said Gaston, nudging the prince. "Do we, Kingsley?" But the prince didn't reply. Instead, he directed his gaze to his tutor, Mr. Willowstick, who looked rather startled by the prince's attentions. He had been sitting silently, trying to stay out of the line of fire. He knew all too well what it was like to be on the wrong side of the prince.

"If I recall, Mr. Willowstick is very knowledgeable about the beast, aren't you, Mr. Willowstick?" asked the prince, acting as though the ordeal with Monsieur Biblio hadn't just happened.

"I am indeed, Your Highness, but we shouldn't bore the others with the history lessons concerning the Beast of Gévaudan." Mr. Willowstick looked rather uncomfortable as he exchanged looks with Mrs. Potts and a few of the others at the table. Gaston could see they were all disturbed but didn't quite know what to do about it.

"Please, Mr. Willowstick, I think everyone here would be enraptured by your knowledge of the beast. I know I would be," said the prince. Everyone at the table, including Mr. Willowstick, knew the prince found nothing Mr. Willowstick said to be enrapturing. It was obvious the prince was digging for information the adults at the table had no intention of sharing, but that wasn't going to stop him, and Gaston wasn't sure he minded. He wanted to know what happened with the beast all those years ago, and he wanted to know how his father was involved. But unlike the prince, he knew that tonight wasn't the best time to ask.

"I wouldn't find it boring. I would like to know—" said Plumette, but Mrs. Potts interrupted her.

"I think Mr. Willowstick is right. Perhaps we should change the subject," she said, giving Gaston and the prince the eye. Gaston could tell she knew what the prince was up to, and she wasn't having it.

"Why won't anyone talk about the beast and what happened with Grosvenor? Even my parents won't speak of it. I demand someone here tell us, at once!" The prince looked to everyone at the table in turn for answers. Answers they were clearly unwilling to give, but the prince was in one of his moods and wasn't about to relent. Gaston kicked him under the table to get him to stop, but the prince's expression told everyone he wasn't going to let this drop.

"Because, Your Highness, it is not our story to share. It is for Grosvenor and your parents to tell you both when they think you are ready," said Lumiere.

"What do you mean, Lumiere?" asked Gaston.

"We're not children. If you know something, then just tell us."

"That's enough," said Mrs. Potts. "I assume no one will be eating anything more. I suggest we all go to bed." She glared at the prince. "I daresay we have had enough talk about beasts for one night."

"Mrs. Potts is right. It's been a long day, and we still have much to do before the house party," said Mr. Cogsworth, looking as though he was ready to collapse under the weight of everything that had happened that day.

"We're still having the party, then? I thought Grosvenor said it was to be canceled," said Chef Bouche, who had until then been quietly observing the drama but now seemed to be in a panic.

"Some of our guests have been traveling for days, we can't very well turn them away at the gates. We will just have to make the best of things," said Mrs. Potts. "And we will all have our work cut out for us. So please, let's everyone turn in for the night."

"But what are we to do about the meals we planned for outdoors? Am I to transform the buffets into indoor banquets at the drop of a hat?" demanded Chef Bouche.

"We will go over all of that tomorrow after we have finalized the new schedule with the queen." Mrs. Potts rubbed her head with frustration, clearly wanting nothing more than to go to bed.

"The queen must be terribly disappointed she won't be able have her candlelight dinner under the stars. She was so looking forward to lighting her new pavilion," said Plumette.

Lumiere took her hand. "My dear, I am sure the queen is the last person who would wish to put her guests or staff at risk simply because she is excited to put on a spectacle, not after what happened to—" But Mrs. Potts cut Lumiere short.

"That's enough, Lumiere. You forget yourself. Now please, let's go to bed. We will discuss this later."

"*Later!* After we've gone to bed, you mean? We're not stupid, you know. We can tell you're keeping something from us. And we know you're afraid because Grosvenor refused to stay in the castle," said the prince. Gaston wanted to know, too. All this talk

was making him more afraid for his father. "I demand
you tell us what happened!"

"Will someone please tell me if this has this something to do with my father?" Gaston added. "Do you
think he's out there hunting the beast? If so, shouldn't
we to help him?" He jumped up to grab his coat and
head out the door.

"Of course he's hunting the beast, don't be more of
a fool than necessary," said the prince making Gaston
turn around and give him a seething look.

"That's enough out of you, young sir!" said Mrs.
Potts, who was probably the only person other than
Gaston under their roof who could get away with
speaking to the prince like that.

"Your father isn't foolish enough to go after the
beast alone at night, Gaston. You're not thinking
clearly. Mrs. Potts is right, it's time for both of you to
go to bed," said Mr. Cogsworth.

"Yes, come along, dears. I will show you to your
rooms." Mrs. Potts stood wearily.

"We know the way, Mrs. Potts," said the prince

giving her a look Gaston didn't like, but Mrs. Potts took it in stride.

"I know, dear. But I promised the king I would make sure you went directly to your rooms, and that is what I intend to do," said Mrs. Potts with a knowing look.

Gaston couldn't sleep. It was weird staying in one of the upstairs guest rooms. It wasn't like he had never spent time in this room, or many of the other rooms that were meant for the family and their guests, but he had never stayed overnight. It just wasn't done. Servants didn't stay in the guest rooms. But these were unusual circumstances, which didn't make it any easier to sleep. He tossed and turned, thinking about his father, wondering if he really was hunting the beast like Kingsley said. And he wondered what the older staff was keeping from him, and when he was going to find out what it was. And he felt guilty about

Monsieur Biblio. Even if he was a horrid man, Gaston
didn't like the idea of anyone losing their job without
the ability to find another. What would the poor man
do? This had been a terrible day, and all he wanted
to do was fall asleep so he could wake up and see his
father in the morning. He wanted to know his father
was safe, and he wanted to learn the truth.

"Gaston, are you still awake?" It was the prince's
voice. He was standing in the doorway that connected
the two rooms. Gaston almost didn't answer him.
But there was no way Kingsley would believe he was
asleep. His friend knew him too well.

"Yes. I can't sleep," he said, sitting up and lighting
the lantern on his bedside table.

"Gaston, I'm afraid your papa is hunting the beast
alone. You know how he is, not wanting to put any
of his men in danger. Shouldn't we help him?" The
prince was now sitting on the end of the bed. His face
looked so serious in the lamplight, but there was no
way for either of them to know that for sure.

"I promised we wouldn't leave the castle," said
Gaston, even though everything within him wanted to

go out and make sure his father was safe. He wished he hadn't made that promise.

"You made the promise before we knew he was putting himself into danger. We have to help him, Gaston. Don't be a coward."

"First I'm a fool, and now I'm a coward." Gaston stood glaring at his friend. He knew what Kingsley was doing, and he hated that it was actually working.

"You know I don't mean it," said the prince. "You know how I am."

"I know exactly how you are," said Gaston, but that didn't change the truth. He'd much rather be in the woods protecting his father than in the castle.

Gaston knew there was more to all this than any of them were saying. This wasn't just his father and the others trying to keep them out of trouble. There was something larger, something sinister and something secret he and the prince didn't know. And no matter how much Gaston wanted to rush out into the night and protect his father, he had to trust his father knew better. He had to keep his word no matter how afraid he was, no matter how much it frightened him that his father might be hunting the beast alone. A beast his father faced before, and nearly killed him.

"I'm not a coward, Kingsley, and I'm not a fool either. I know what you're doing, but I am a man of my word. My father made me promise to keep you safe, and that's exactly what I am going to do. I am going to keep my little brother safe, just like he asked."

"Then keep your promise, and be by my side while I hunt the beast! Because I am going to kill it and mount its head on my wall, with or without your help!"

"It's too dangerous. We're not doing it, Kingsley, we'll get killed."

"But just think of it! We would be famous if we killed the beast!"

"You're already famous. You're the heir to the throne." Gaston was getting angry. This wasn't about making sure his father was safe. This was about the prince's ego.

"We'd be heroes, Gaston. Just imagine it! They'd write songs about our bravery."

"I hate it when you're like this, Kingsley."

"Like what?"

"You'll say or do anything to get your way. You're relentless, Kingsley, and it doesn't matter who gets hurt. You pushed poor Monsieur Biblio to the breaking point, and now he's lost his job."

"Who cares about silly old Monsieur Biblio? Come on, Gaston. He insulted you, threatened to search your father's cottage, and insulted me and all. He deserved to lose his job."

"But you pushed him, Kingsley. I saw you doing it. I saw what you were doing at dinner. And now you're trying to make me break my word to my father so you can be the hero. You don't even care if my father is in danger. It's all about you!"

"That's not true. I *am* worried about him. Why can't it be both things, Gaston? Can't I be worried about your papa *and* want to be a hero? Of course I'm worried. Now, are you coming with me or not?"

"I won't let you go, Kingsley. I made a promise."

"And here I thought I was the one who gave the orders. Get dressed, Gaston. We're leaving as soon as I am ready. That's an order."

After they got changed, and the prince had outfitted himself with his blunderbuss and Gaston with his bow and a quiver full of arrows, Gaston and Kingsley made their way through the catacombs under the castle that led to the forest directly.

As they emerged from the catacombs, the prince rushed ahead down the main path, twigs and leaves crunching loudly under his feet. "What are you doing?" Gaston said as he yanked his friend off the path. "Do you want to get shot?" He pointed up at the men on the ramparts. "And you're making way too much noise!"

Gaston whispered as softly as he could, "This is a mistake." But Kingsley didn't hear him, and if he did, he ignored him. Gaston was afraid they had already made too much noise as it was. Kingsley wasn't thinking. He never did. And he had already made clear he wasn't in the mood for taking suggestions from Gaston.

"You're just afraid," said the prince, walking

ahead, making his way into the denser part of the forest, where they wouldn't be seen by the guards. The comment annoyed Gaston. But the fact was, he was afraid. They were acting like characters from one of the books Kingsley had read to him when they were younger. Headstrong, foolish characters flying in the face of danger, not heeding the warnings from everyone around them. Blundering into the woods to hunt a dangerous beast. It was reckless. It was irresponsible. Both of their lives were in danger, and he hated breaking his promise to his father. He wanted to turn back, but it was too late. He had to keep following Kingsley, to keep him safe.

He finally caught up to the prince. Tapping him on the shoulder, he whispered, "I have a bad feeling, Kingsley. I think we should get to my cottage as fast as we can."

Gaston was thankful his father had made him learn his way around every inch of the woods, else they would have been lost in this pitch-darkness. Trepidation and fear filled his heart, knowing they had made a terrible blunder by going into the woods alone. They needed to get to his cottage as quickly as they could. They were too young to be in the woods hunting this beast. And they hadn't even bothered to come up with a plan, or even think through what to do about hunters in the woods who might mistake Gaston and the prince for the beast. This was foolhardy. They needed to get inside that moment before something terrible happened.

The prince nodded as if to say he agreed with Gaston's plan, but Gaston was still filled with apprehension. The new moon did nothing to help them make their way through the dark forest. The trees looked sinister and twisted in the darkness, and all the outbuildings and cottages were dark. It seemed everyone who resided outside the castle walls was living in darkness, afraid to lure the beast to their dwellings. And here they were, in the woods alone with a wild beast, while the grown, more experienced men were safely in their homes.

After walking a little farther, they saw flickering firelight coming from what they thought must be the cemetery. When they got closer, they understood. The

entire cemetery was illuminated by torchlight. *"Be
careful,"* Gaston whispered, squinting his eyes trying to
see if there was anyone else there hiding in the shadows, waiting for the beast to come into the light. This
had to be a trap of some sort. It was brilliant, really,
shrouding the woods in darkness except for one spot.
This had to be his father's doing.

The torchlight reflected on the crypts and headstones, dancing upon the statue of his mother, Rose,
standing in front of her mausoleum. As ever, she
looked as though she was beckoning him to join her
on the other side. Beckoning him to come through the
mausoleum door. How strange it was to see her face lit
by the fire of the torches; it looked almost alive.

It made Gaston wonder at his father's choosing
this spot.

They crept as quietly as they could and didn't dare
speak to each other for fear the beast or its hunter
would hear them. If only his father trusted him
enough to tell him his plans, he would have never let
the prince bully him into going out.

But his father did trust him. He believed Gaston

when he made his promise. He had no reason to think Gaston and Kingsley were lurking in the woods. This was even more dangerous than Gaston had thought.

This is a terrible mistake.

As they got closer to the cemetery, they saw a large shadow appear on the side of Rose's mausoleum. It had to be the Beast of Gévaudan, it could be nothing else. Its great, monstrous shadow was larger than any wolf Gaston had ever seen. Larger than any animal or man, and it was terrifying. He had to keep reminding himself that shadows could sometimes make things appear larger. There was no way this beast could be so enormous.

Despite his fear, Gaston motioned to Kingsley to keep pressing on. They crept as slowly and as quietly as they could, being sure to keep out of sight until they reached the low stone wall that surrounded the little cemetery. They tried to make out Gaston's cottage in the distance, to see if perhaps there was some sign his father was there, yet they saw nothing but darkness beyond the torchlight. They inched their way into the cemetery, creeping over the low wall, and once inside, they saw it, the largest gray wolf they had ever beheld. But it was like no other wolf they'd seen. It was massive and strongly built. Its legs were stout and muscular, and its tail was so long it reached the ground. Its head was huge, with a powerful set of jaws filled with sharp and terrible teeth it was using to rip away at an elk tethered to a tree. Blood sprayed from the elk's throat as the beast tore into the poor creature's flesh with such a great force it made Gaston shudder.

When Gaston saw the tethered elk, he knew he was right. His father must be there, somewhere waiting for his moment to take aim at the beast. Gaston waited, wondering when it would come. And he wondered if his father was alone or had brought some of his most trusted men to help him. Gaston strained his eyes, searching the surrounding woods to see if there was anyone hiding in the trees or perhaps with them in the cemetery, behind the crypts. However, he saw nothing but the beast devouring its meal. Knowing his father, Grosvenor wouldn't want to put any of his men in danger. At least in that Kingsley was right. So

Gaston guessed his father must have been there alone, out of sight, waiting for his chance to kill the lurid creature.

The beast was grotesque, its face covered in blood, ripping away at its meal. Gaston wanted to wait for his father to take the first shot, making sure to be ready with his own bow if it wasn't a killing blow. He was suddenly thankful he was there so he could help his father, and less angry with Kingsley for forcing him out into the dangerous night. Gaston was going to help his father. Everything would be all right.

Gaston looked at Kingsley and put his finger to his lips silently, mouthing the word *wait*. He stealthily took an arrow from his quiver, placed it in his bow, and pulled it back, aiming it at the beast as he waited for his father to take the first shot. It had only been mere moments since they came upon it, but it felt like forever, and now Gaston started to wonder if his father was there at all. Surely he would have taken the shot already, while the beast was distracted by the elk. And just as Gaston was about to let his arrow fly, a loud explosion erupted in his ear, causing him to fall to the ground and writhe in pain. The next thing he knew the prince was standing in front of him, reloading his blunderbuss and aiming it right at the beast, who was now just a few feet away from them. The prince was yelling something at him, but Gaston couldn't hear, and he couldn't get back on his feet, he was so dizzy.

The beast was toying with them, inching closer and closer, snarling as the prince fumbled to reload his blunderbuss and cried out something to Gaston. But Gaston could still only hear distorted muffled sounds through the waves of pounding thunder in his ears. He looked around for his bow but couldn't find it, and in that moment he realized he and his friend were going to die. He loathed the idea of his father finding their dead bodies scattered near the grave of his mother. And he hated himself for breaking his promise and for not standing up to Kingsley.

He sat there, still unable to get back on his feet, horrified as the beast advanced on his friend, snarling and snapping its terrible teeth. Would he close his eyes as the beast ripped into his friend's flesh? Was this the moment they would both die?

Just as the creature lunged forward, it stopped in its tracks and turned its head as if it heard something, a noise—perhaps another blast, Gaston wasn't sure—but whatever it was also startled the prince. And then Gaston saw it: a blood-bursting shot had penetrated the beast's shoulder. The creature howled in pain so loudly even Gaston could hear it over the pounding in his ears, and the monster sprang in the direction the shot came from. Gaston willed himself to his feet, finding his bow and running after the beast. He found it tearing at something at the foot of his mother's statue. He aimed and shot the creature, puncturing its side. The beast stood on its hind legs to its full height and howled in pain before it ran off into the woods, leaving a trail of blood behind it.

But Gaston didn't follow the trail; he didn't track the beast to discover if it would live or die. Something else held his attention. Something so horrible nothing else existed. His father was lying at the feet of his mother's statue, his throat torn out, his blood pooling at her pink marble feet. Gaston fell to his knees, and he cried. His cries were like those of the beast itself, howling with pain and anguish. Between his sobs, he said he was sorry. Again and again until his voice was wrecked, and the prince took him in his arms and led him away from Grosvenor's body.

Gaston's world ended that day. He was now living in a world without his father. A cruel, unjust world. A world where his promises meant nothing. He had let himself and his father down, and there was nothing he could do to change it. He was heartbroken and alone.

And his friend was to blame.

Chapter VI

The Place in His Heart

It was an overcast day, and the sky was filled with gray storm clouds threatening to burst at any moment. Nevertheless, the prince insisted Gaston ride out with him that day. It had been three years since Gaston's father died, and though he no longer outwardly blamed the prince for what happened, his love for his friend had diminished, and when he allowed himself to admit it, resentment still lingered within his heart.

In the days that followed his father's death, there were terrible fights between them. Gaston demanded the prince explain why he fired off that first shot. He told him again and again if it weren't for him, his father would still be alive. The prince would simply listen quietly and then insist they go on as before, saying they were brothers, more than brothers, in fact, and nothing, not even this, would tear them apart. No matter how angry Gaston was with the prince, no matter how harsh his words, the prince remained his friend, never speaking against him, insisting they go on as they always had, insisting they were still the best of friends, until the resentment in Gaston's heart started to quell.

Before their outing on this day, Cogsworth had been attending the prince in his dressing room, getting him outfitted in his riding clothes, while Gaston sat in the prince's adjacent room. He didn't understand why the prince wanted to go out on such a gloomy day, but there was no saying no to the prince; the harder you fought him on something, the more he wanted to do it. His mood was foul as the weather, and when Kingsley's mood was dark like this, Gaston would always find himself wondering why he was still there. Both of his parents were gone, and while he hadn't exactly taken over his father's position, everyone treated him as though he belonged there. He supposed he was there because he had nowhere else to go, and this was the only home he knew. He spent his days with the prince hunting, riding, and practicing combat at arms. He did it because the prince asked. And he supposed the prince asked because he knew how much Gaston enjoyed it. In a way it made Gaston sad, doing the things his father had taught him, but also proud he had become even better at them. The best, in fact, just like his father. But his father had been wrong about one thing: the prince never got upset when Gaston bested him. At least, if he did, he didn't say anything about it.

As Gaston waited for the prince he could hear him talking to Mr. Cogsworth. He had become insufferable with almost everyone but Gaston. It was as if it took all of the prince's patience to withstand Gaston's silent condemnations, and there was nothing left but impatience for anyone else.

"I don't understand why I need to be dressed by you like I'm a doll, Cogsworth. I am perfectly capable of dressing myself." Gaston felt the prince was sounding more peevish by the day. He wasn't sure if it was because he was still angry with him, or if the prince was truly becoming exactly what he said he would never be: one of those horrible, selfish, entitled princes who would eventually become a miserable tyrant of a king.

"Of course you are, Your Highness. Will Gaston be serving you as huntsman and scout on this outing?" Mr. Cogsworth asked as he made his finishing touches to the prince's outfit.

"No, Cogsworth, Gaston will be joining me as my friend." Gaston rolled his eyes. There was no doubt the prince considered Gaston to be his friend. His best friend and brother. And while it was true he would defend Gaston to the death if need be, he didn't shy from giving Gaston orders that Gaston had no other choice than to obey. Like following him out the night his father was killed. He knew the prince still felt guilty even after all this time. He knew the prince must have felt he made a mistake with that first shot. And he knew the prince had tried to make up for it ever since, and was trying even now to make up for it by defending Gaston to Mr. Cogsworth. But to Gaston, there was nothing the prince could do to make up for that night, and he still wasn't sure if he could ever forgive him—not that the prince had even asked him to. Perhaps if he had, things would be different.

"Maybe it will be an opportunity for Gaston to serve you, as befitting the position we all know he should eventually take. It's time he learns how to conduct himself properly with his betters," said Mr. Cogsworth.

"Who says I am Gaston's better? Just because I am a prince? I won't have this kind of talk, Cogsworth, do you understand me?" This made Gaston laugh under his breath. Of course the prince thought he was Gaston's better. That's how one thinks when they are raised to rule. They might think they treat people fairly, or even like family, but ultimately they expect to be obeyed.

"The law of the land says you are his better, just as you are my better." Cogsworth's voice sounded sheepish, even though it was clear he was doing his best to sound resolute.

"Well then, if that's the case, I must insist you drop this matter at once. I won't have it, Cogsworth. Do you understand? Gaston has lost his mother and father. And isn't it up to me to decide if he takes his father's position? We're very old friends, you and I, but I'm afraid you are overstepping the mark," said the prince in a very serious tone. It surprised Gaston to hear the prince bring up his father. He hadn't brought that night up directly since it happened.

"As you wish, Your Highness." Cogsworth made the final adjustments to the prince's outfit. "If there will be nothing else," he said rather solemnly, taking his leave, and Gaston entered the room.

"I think you hurt Mr. Cogsworth's feelings," Gaston said.

"So what if I did!"

"He's only doing his job, Kingsley. He's just looking out for you." Gaston felt bad for Mr. Cogsworth. He had looked out for Kingsley like a father might. It made him sad and angry that his friend didn't seem to appreciate how many people truly cared for him despite his being so difficult to be around at times.

"I was defending you!" said the prince, his temper beginning to flare.

"I know, but I bet you cut him to the quick with that remark about overstepping. You know he takes that sort of thing very seriously. And since when do you talk like that anyway? *Overstepping the mark!* Come on, Kingsley, you'd better tell him you're sorry later, or he might jump off the bridge," said Gaston, trying to make him laugh.

"Princes do not apologize to servants, Gaston. Cogsworth would be the first person to tell you that." Gaston shook his head. Where was all this nonsense coming from? Not the prince's mother and father. They were never there. Maybe this was Cogsworth's influence, or perhaps royalty were just hardwired to turn into entitled jerks? Gaston didn't know.

"You've apologized to me," he said. "At least, you have before." It was a reminder to himself, and perhaps the prince that he still hadn't said he was sorry for what happened to his father, even after all this time.

"You're not a servant, you're my brother. Now let's go, it will be a long ride."

When they got to the courtyard, they found their horses waiting for them, ready to ride.

"Mrs. Potts packed us a lunch. It's in the saddle-bags. Now let's go," the prince said as they mounted their horses. The prince had given Gaston a magnificent horse on his last birthday. A majestic, massively built black Percheron. Gaston adored him, and it was really the only reason he agreed to go riding that day. A chance to ride Noire.

They rode out deep into the woods, not minding the threat of rain or the dark storm clouds overhead. They rode for miles, past a small neighboring kingdom, until they reached the tallest peak of the Cyclopean Mountains. From there, they had a breathtaking view of the Many Kingdoms. The most awe-inspiring landmark was the Lighthouse of the Gods in the distant Morningstar Kingdom, which was bathed in sunlight. Gaston had only seen drawings of the lighthouse before. It was the tallest structure in the Many Kingdoms, built by the great Cyclopeans in the time before men, well before the Morningstars built their castle in the same masonry style to look as if it too had always been there. Gaston never dreamed they would ever ride out far enough to see it up close. He and the prince often said they would, but they never dared, and his father had never agreed to take him so far from home. Now his father was no longer there to keep him from doing anything his heart desired . . . even though what he desired most was to have his father back.

As they looked across the beautiful lands, Gaston once again remembered the days and weeks following his father's death. He had been in shock. He felt like he was walking through water, letting the prince and Mrs. Potts lead him hither and thither. Eating when Mrs. Potts told him to, keeping the prince company when he asked. No one said a word about what happened that night except to say how sorry they were. No one scolded him or the prince for going out when they shouldn't have. Gaston was sure everyone would be angry with him, but there were no reproachful looks, only sadness, and pity.

Gaston didn't feel like he deserved their pity. He didn't feel like he deserved to live. If he had stood up to the prince maybe his father would still be alive. And perhaps that was one of the reasons Gaston stayed there, did the prince's bidding, and remained his friend: because he knew in his heart it was both of their faults. And what would Gaston do without the prince, without his best friend, even if there was a place in his heart that still blamed both the prince and himself for what happened? He could only hope that one day he would be able to forgive himself and his friend.

As Gaston came back to the present and looked at the beautiful landscape, he felt almost thankful to be in the prince's company and witnessing this beautiful view. They dismounted their horses and stood together on the cliff, taking in the splendor of Morningstar Kingdom. Standing in silence for a long time as the mists surrounded them, clinging to their cloaks, they looked at the sun-drenched kingdom in the distance.

"My father wants me to go on my grand tour. It will start in the Many Kingdoms, but I will also go abroad to the world outside our realms. I asked if you could come with me, but the only way we could manage it is if you agreed to serve as my valet."

"I have no idea how to be a valet, Kingsley," Gaston said, frustrated with Kingsley for ruining this beautiful moment with talks of grand tours and valets.

"You won't really have to be my valet. Just pretend," the prince replied, turning on his charm. Gaston knew what would happen next. What always happened when Kingsley wanted his way.

"And who is going to get you in and out of all the ridiculous costumes you will have to wear to all those balls and dinner parties you'll be expected to attend while you're traveling the world and expanding your education?" Gaston pressed.

"We'll figure it out. I don't want to go without you. Besides, you will have to help me pick my future bride. I can't do it without you. We need to make sure she is right for us," he said, surprising Gaston. What a thing to say.

"You mean right for *you*," said Gaston, laughing at his friend.

"For us, Gaston! I won't have some prissy princess

trying to keep us from having our fun just because I'm married. If I am going to marry anyone, she's going to have to understand you come first." Gaston looked at him, and saw that the prince was completely serious.

"I don't think that's how marriage works, Kingsley."

"It's how *my* marriage will work. I don't even want to get married. I'm only doing it because it's my duty. I'd be happy spending the rest of my life with you, hunting, and fishing, and going on adventures. And of course sneaking books out of the library," he added, now laughing.

"Neither of us has to sneak books out of the library now that Monsieur Biblio is gone. And you might feel differently about marriage when you're older. We both might."

"Maybe. But I'm not sure there's room enough for more than one love in my heart."

Gaston didn't say anything. He knew what his friend meant. Despite everything, he loved Kingsley with his entire heart. *That* was why he was still there. He did sometimes wonder what it would be like when they were older, wondered how it would work, wondered what it would be like when Kingsley had to get married, but it always felt so far off, and he would push it out of his mind. Now it seemed to be upon them without any warning at all. Without even realizing, and it made Gaston feel apprehensive.

"I do love you, Gaston. And I am sorry for what happened to your father. I truly am. I would do anything to take it back."

Gaston could see his friend was telling the truth, though he was shocked to hear his friend say the words. He had hoped that was how Kingsley felt, but it was different hearing him say it. And it meant everything to him he was saying it now.

"I know, my friend. I think it will just take more time to become less painful."

"Why not come with me, then? See the world, help me find someone who loves us both and won't mind we are the best of friends. Even more than friends," said Kingsley, wrapping his arm around Gaston's shoulder. "Think of how much fun we will have. It will be like old times." It was the first time Kingsley looked truly happy and excited for something since they were boys together, and it made Gaston want to agree to his plan. But he had to say no. For once, he wanted to do something for himself.

"Maybe some time apart will make things less painful," he said quietly.

"Then what will you do? Take over your father's position? You don't want that." The prince's laugh sounded sharp. And he was right. Gaston didn't want his father's life. It would be like living in a world of memories and pain. A constant reminder of how he failed him. But he didn't have a choice.

"It's the only thing I can do. I have taken advantage of your parents' generosity for too long." Gaston was surprised he hadn't been forced to take over his father's position before then, that they allowed him to live there without working for as long as they had.

"Don't be silly. I've talked to my father. You are to be given an estate, lands, and money of your own." Kingsley looked positively pleased with himself. "The estate is in this kingdom of course, close enough that you won't be too far away, but with enough distance that you will feel independent."

"What are you talking about? I have no idea how to run an estate."

"There will be a steward and a land agent to help you until you do. And to look after things when you're away. It's all arranged, Gaston. It's there for the taking when you decide you are ready. In the meantime, it will be well looked after. That way you can go with me if you change your mind." The prince looked so excited. So happy.

And the truth was, Gaston was happy at the offer. He knew this was Kingsley's way of trying to make everything up to him, and despite everything, Gaston loved him for it. And he wanted to go with him, but he didn't want to go as his servant. He wanted to go on his own journey, on his own terms.

"Do you think your dad can throw in a title as well? If he did, then I could just travel with you as your friend," said Gaston, laughing.

"Don't think I didn't ask. And title or no, Gaston, you will always be my friend."

Chapter VII

A Change of Heart

Life had been good for Gaston while the prince was away. Spending most of his time on his singular mission: hunting down and killing the Beast of Gévaudan. And if he could end his evenings with the fine men of the village, all the better. Gaston spent most evenings after a long day of hunting in Old Man Higgins's tavern in the village. Every night he'd be greeted by the same friendly faces, all of them eager to hear about his exploits and happy to buy him a beer. On this particular evening, Gaston kicked open the doors and strutted into the tavern, his boots covered in mud and his hunting clothes splattered with blood.

He had an enormous elk slung over his shoulder, and he slammed it down onto the floor with a loud thud. Everyone looked up from their beers and conversations and cheered to see him. "Gaston!"

"Another beast to stuff and mount on your wall, Higgins!" Gaston announced, flashing his perfect white teeth. "No need for applause, men. I'm only doing my job. I am the royal huntsman, after all." He let out a booming laugh. And it wasn't a lie. He spent most of his time hunting the woods, and would on occasion arrange a royal hunt when the king was in residence. But as far as the other duties his father performed when he was alive, Gaston left that to the other members of the outdoor staff. No one complained. Not even Cogsworth. And Gaston was happy. For the first time, he felt he had a purpose. His own purpose, not dictated by someone else.

"Gaston! You did it again!" said Mr. Higgins. "Another trophy. We're running out of room, Gaston. I might have to build a larger tavern." Everyone laughed. The tavern was filled with the usual suspects. Most men who lived and worked in the village stopped by Mr. Higgins's establishment for a drink and a chat before heading home for the evening. Gaston was happy he had made this his nightly ritual. The men treated him with respect and admiration. It really was the perfect place.

"Here, Gaston. On the house!" said Higgins, sliding a beer down the length of the bar. Higgins had a talent for this, sliding it just the right way so it would stop just in front of his intended target. Gaston took the stein in his hand and raised it toward the company of men. "To the fine men of this village. And to those who have to put up with them!" he said, laughing.

"So, Gaston, any luck tracking down the Beast of Gévaudan? Any signs of the wretched creature?" asked the baker, sitting at a nearby table.

"No sign yet, my good man. But I pity the beast if he slinks back into our kingdom," said Gaston, finishing his drink and slamming the tankard onto the bar.

"Oh, it will be back, no doubt about that. I heard it wiped out an entire village in one night in a kingdom not too far from our own. People around here are afraid to go out after dark again," said the milliner, who was sitting with the baker.

"An entire village, you say?" Gaston wondered if this could be true. He remembered stories the prince read to him about a coven of witches with an army of skeletons that attacked entire villages, killing everyone, including the children. That seemed a more likely cause than a lone beast, no matter how large it was.

"Did anyone see the beast? Are you sure it was the Beast of Gévaudan?" he asked.

"Some say the beast travels with a pack of wolves, dire wolves of unusual size that, like the Beast of Gévaudan, crave human blood now they've had a taste for it," said the gentleman who ran the bookshop.

"This sounds likes a story in one of the books you sell, old man!" said Gaston, trying to play it off, but the man's words did haunt him, bringing the images of his father's death to the front of his mind, flashing before him like it was happening all over again.

"Well, don't you fear, gentlemen. Be it one or twenty, I will hunt every last beast I find until the end of my days, if that's what it takes to keep us safe," said Gaston.

Just then, a squat older man with a large bushy mustache and wild gray hair walked into the tavern holding a log in his arms. He was relatively new to the village, so Gaston didn't know him as well as the other men who frequented the tavern.

"Have any of you seen the owls this evening?" said the man from the doorway, holding his log in his arms as if it were a baby.

"Can't say that we have, Maurice. Not many owls come in here," said Mr. Higgins, making everyone laugh. "Why do you ask?" Gaston didn't like the way Higgins was teasing this man. Smiling at him cheekily and treating him like a fool. A far as Gaston could tell, he was an interesting character. Perhaps a little eccentric, but some of his favorite people were.

"The owls have been acting strange. Haven't you noticed?" the man asked, blinking at the confused faces looking at him.

"And what do you have there, Maurice, that you

are holding with such care?" asked Gaston, walking over to the man and motioning to his log.

"This is my log! My first log! Can you believe it?" Maurice said, holding it out for him.

"It looks like a very fine log," said Gaston, patting the log like one might pat a puppy on the head and smiling at the man.

"No! I'm sorry. Let me explain. I've been working on a new apparatus that chops wood! And today it actually worked," said the man with pride. "At least it did work, until . . ."

"Until it exploded," said Higgins, interrupting him and causing everyone in the room to laugh.

"It just needs a bit more tinkering," said Maurice. "And I'd better get back to it. Belle will be furious with me if I am late to dinner again. Goodbye, gentlemen." He rushed out, holding his log.

"Say hello to the owls, if you see them," said Higgins, laughing as the doors closed behind him.

"Oh, leave him alone, Higgins. He's a harmless old man. So what if he loves his log and thinks the owls are up to something," said Gaston. Everyone laughed, which wasn't his intention, but he laughed, too, despite himself.

"He sure is an odd duck, that old man. And I don't think I've ever seen his daughter, Belle, without a book in her hand," said the baker.

"She's in my shop almost every day," said the bookseller.

"She's a very . . . peculiar young woman," said the milliner. "Not at all interested in hats."

"That is very peculiar, but also rather intriguing," said Gaston, looking at the clock. "Gentleman, it's time for me to go as well. Mrs. Potts will blow her top if I am late to dinner." He got up from his stool and headed over to the door, where he had his blunderbuss and bow propped up against the wall.

The fact was, he had completely forgotten, until that minute, that he promised Mrs. Potts he would join her and the other servants for dinner that night. So he said his goodbyes, slung his blunderbuss, knapsack, and bow over his shoulder, and made his way through the village on the main path that led to the stone bridge that took him to the castle directly.

Gaston didn't take the catacombs or hidden ways anymore. It didn't feel the same without the prince. And the memories of those places caused an ache in his heart for the days before his father died. Time had allowed him to forgive his friend for what happened that night, at least that is what he told himself, but the memory was still painful, and he wanted nothing more than to return to a time when this horrible thing wasn't between them. He still believed everything they had said to each other that day before Kingsley left for his tour, but he wondered how things would be between them after so much time. Two years had felt like a lifetime; so much had changed.

When he finally reached the castle, he went around the side to the back kitchen courtyard, where he would find the servants' entrance. He had fond memories of that courtyard, visiting with servants while they were on their breaks and sometimes playing with the prince's dog, Sultan. He remembered the first night he and his father had joined the other servants for dinner after so many years of taking their meals alone in their little cottage. He remembered feeling like his life had changed that night. Seeing his father happy again, laughing and having fun with his friends. They had been so isolated before that night, and he felt as if there was nothing but joy to look forward to in those days. And he wondered if he was doing the same thing his father had done so many years before, hunting the woods, checking in on his estate on the other side of the kingdom, and spending leisure time in the village. It wasn't as if he didn't visit his old friends at the castle, it just wasn't as frequent since he started occupying his time with hunting the beast.

He could hear laughter coming through the open windows of the servants' hall, and it made him smile. How he wished his papa were with him now. How proud he would be to know Gaston had become such a skilled hunter. There were so many things he wished they could have done together, so many things he wanted to say, and now none would come to pass. Gaston knew visiting the castle would bring up these memories and make him feel alone in the world, without his father there. They always did. But he wasn't alone, not truly, he had Mr. and Mrs. Potts, and even

Lumiere and some of the others who were family to now, and he hoped they were proud of the man he was becoming just as he hoped his father would. He loved them all, really, and it cost him nothing to admit it.

He looked down at his boots, remembering they were covered in mud from hunting that day, and kicked them off on the stoop before walking in. He quickly tucked his blunderbuss, bow, and quiver away in the corner of the entryway. He didn't want to chance Mrs. Potts's wrath for tracking mud inside like he was a little boy again, but when he went inside, it seemed she still had reason to be cross with him. She was standing there waiting for him. He supposed she had been keeping a lookout for him because he was running late. And there she was, with a cross expression on her face.

"And what do you call this? Coming in late, covered in mud and blood! Out hunting again? Well, I hope you brought a change of clothes," she said, shaking her head.

"I did. Here in my knapsack." He wished he could have just slipped in unnoticed and changed before dinner. But leave it to Mrs. Potts to be waiting for him.

"I won't be a moment," he said, ducking into the washroom. He did look a fright. He really should have gone to the cottage before heading over to the castle, but he was already late as it was. He didn't like spending time at the cottage but didn't feel like he could ask for other lodgings to stay in while he was visiting the castle, since he hadn't taken on all of his father's old duties aside from arranging the infrequent royal hunt for the king. He preferred to spend most of his time at his own estate, which was a fair bit of distance from the castle.

At least he had thought to bring something decent to change into. When he returned, and was all smartened up, Mrs. Potts gave him one of her indulgent smiles and a kiss on the cheek, so he assumed she approved of his new outfit.

"Now, that's much better. Handsome as ever," she said, holding her youngest, Chip, on her hip. He was almost getting too big to hold now. He was a chubby little fella, with big round cheeks and a happy grin.

Gaston had lost track of how many children she and Mr. Potts had now.

"Kiss your uncle Gaston good night, Chip. All your brothers and sisters are already in bed, and you should be, too," she said, putting him down.

Gaston leaned over and let the boy kiss him on the cheek, then watched him totter way, which made him laugh. To him, toddlers always seemed to walk like men who spent too much time in the tavern.

"I'm sorry I'm late, Mrs. Potts," said Gaston, now kissing her on the cheek. "I lost track of time."

"In the tavern, no doubt, after a day of hunting. It seems that is all you ever do these days. And look at you, getting so large. I don't think the prince will recognize you when he gets home," she said, taking him by the hand and leading him to the kitchen.

"Will he be back soon, then?" he asked, ashamed to admit all the news he received about the prince was from the letters Mrs. Potts had read to him.

"He will. Very soon, I think. He told me to let you know. We're going to have a big celebration to welcome him home and to announce his engagement." She said this with a weak smile. She knew he was hearing this news for the first time and was probably worried how he would take it.

This was one of those moments Gaston wished he had tried harder to learn to read, so that he and the prince could exchange their own letters. There had been nothing stopping him after his father passed, but by that time, Gaston felt it was too late. He just didn't have it in him. After his father died, he was too depressed to concentrate on anything, really, and he felt ashamed to ask someone to teach him. And no matter how hard he tried when he attempted to learn on his own, he just couldn't grasp it. He had thought about asking Mrs. Potts to help him. He knew she would be kind about it, but the idea of asking even her filled him with anxiety. Instead, he focused on the thing he did best. Hunting.

"Come in, Gaston. I will give you all the news. The prince is very eager that I should tell you everything," she said, leading him into the servants' hall, where everyone was already seated, and dinner was just being put on the table.

"Luckily for you, dinner is late tonight," she added as Gaston pulled out her chair for her.

"I'm sorry if I kept you all waiting," Gaston said, taking his seat.

"No, not at all," said Lumiere. "We all just sat down, and we are so pleased you are here with us."

The usual senior household staff, Mr. Cogsworth, Plumette, Chef Bouche, Francis the first footman, a handful of others, and Mrs. Potts and Lumiere, of course, were there. It seemed like a jolly party, and Gaston was happy to join them. The staff were in a buzz over the impending arrival of the prince and news of his engagement. They seemed to talk of nothing else. Even the kitchen maids were chatting about it as they finished laying out the dinner. Everyone at the table was to be in high spirits, twittering about the upcoming events, as well as everything that needed to be done to help the king and queen make their arrangements for a sea voyage to a distant land shortly after the prince returned home. Gaston thought it was interesting the king and queen had spent so much more time at the castle while the prince was away, and even more interesting that they should plan another long trip away now that he was coming home. He wondered if there was something more to it other than happenstance.

"So, Mrs. Potts, tell us about this beguiling young woman, Circe, whom the prince plans to marry. Is she a princess? By all accounts, she seems enchanting," gushed Lumiere as he poured himself and Plumette each a glass of wine.

"Yes, Mrs. Potts, do tell us all about her. I wonder if she is as beautiful as everyone says. How did she and the prince meet?" asked Plumette, giving Lumiere a kiss on the cheek as a thank-you for refilling her glass. Gaston loved watching the two of them. He always had. When he was young, he just found them amusing, and he still did, but now he loved the way they doted on each other. Lumiere treated Plumette like a queen, always telling her she was beautiful, giving her sly kisses, and making sure she wanted for nothing. It made him wonder how Kingsley and Circe would be with each other. Gaston hadn't even thought about courting anyone while the prince was away. He was too busy hunting the beast. It never even occurred to him. He couldn't imagine what life would be like with a wife and a house full of kids, no longer free to do as he liked. When he looked to the future, wondering at the possibilities, he always imagined his life with Kingsley.

The only other person who sparked the slightest bit of his interest was Belle, and that was because of the comment the bookseller made in the tavern earlier that night about her obsession with books. Gaston hadn't known anyone more obsessed with them than him and Kingsley—that is, aside from their old librarian, the poor, doomed fellow. But honestly, he had never paid her any mind until that moment. Well, if Kingsley had his future all planned out with this Circe, then maybe he should start thinking of finding someone, too, as unlikely as it seemed.

Yet Gaston knew no matter how his thoughts drifted, it was unlikely he would court anyone from the village, even if she loved books as much as he did. It just wasn't a future he could truly embrace.

"Circe is not a princess, as far as I know, but she

is a descendant of the Old King," said Mrs. Potts with excitement. Gaston was pretending not to be interested in hearing about this woman his friend planned to marry. But Mrs. Potts knew him well, and knew he'd be keenly interested to hear what type of person she was.

"So she's related to King White, Snow White's father?" Chef Bouche seemed impressed. "That is rather magnificent, don't you think? She is from one of the oldest families in the land."

Gaston knew a bit about Snow White's family. He and the prince had learned about them in a book they found in the library. It was a history of the Many Kingdoms called the Book of Fairy Tales. Chef Bouche was right, Circe was related to one of the oldest families in the Many Kingdoms, but the family's story was mired in witchcraft and curses. Then again, almost every family in the Many Kingdoms seemed to have some sordid tale or another involving witches, evil stepmothers, or the like. So he couldn't fault them for that. And it's not as if strange and horrible things didn't happen in their own kingdom. They were plagued by the Beast of Gévaudan, for instance. He wondered what Circe would think of that. Or was the land she came from even more dangerous? This Circe woman wasn't mentioned in Snow White's story, so he didn't know anything about her. But if he recalled correctly, it did mention cousins of the king who were of an ill-favored nature, and he wondered if Circe was really related to that side of the family.

"Indeed. They are cousins, I believe," Mrs. Potts said, spooning some potatoes with cream, cheese, and chives onto her plate and passing the dish to Gaston, who started piling his plate high with potatoes absent-mindedly as he recalled the story of Snow White and the Old Queen, Grimhilde.

"Oi! Leave some for us!" said Francis playfully. He was a newly promoted footman Gaston didn't know well. But Gaston had just been piling a mountain of potatoes on is plate, and he didn't blame the footman for calling him out for it while he was daydreaming about King White's rather strange cousins.

"Sorry!" said Gaston, passing the bowl to him with an apologetic smile, realizing there were now more potatoes on his plate than there were in the serving dish.

"It is no wonder you have such an appetite, you have grown so large, Gaston. Look at your enormous arms," said Plumette with a twittering and lilting laugh.

It was true; Gaston ate more than ever. He spent most of his time outdoors, hiking and stalking, chopping wood, and building camps for when he would spend days in the woods hunting, and by the time he finally stopped for the day, he was ravenous. And it seemed he was just getting larger by the day. His father had been like that. A large, powerfully built man. Gaston had always thought he would be slight like the prince, until one day he looked in the mirror and saw the spitting image of his father staring back at him.

"Come now, Plumette, we don't want Lumiere getting jealous, do we?" Chef Bouche said playfully, making Lumiere laugh. They were all in high spirits that night, except for Gaston, who was brooding over the prince's return.

"Not that Lumiere here has reason to be jealous.

He is one of the most handsome men I know," said Gaston, taking some roasted meat from the platter and putting it beside the mountain of potatoes.

"Doesn't this Circe have rather odd sisters, though? I heard they're very peculiar and have an ill-favored look about them. Do you think Circe is quite suitable? I mean, just because she is a distant cousin of the Old King, I wonder if that makes her a worthy choice? And who are her parents, exactly? That's what I would like to know," said Plumette. Gaston wanted to know as well. It was starting to seem very likely Circe was a sister to the rather odd sisters whom Gaston had read about in Snow White's story, and if it were true, he had to wonder if Kingsley had put it together.

"I heard Circe and her sisters won't reveal who their parents are. I'd say it's a mystery if I ever heard one. For all we know, she's a poor farm girl," said Francis.

"Weren't you a poor farm boy before you came to work in this house?" asked Lumiere.

"I'm not going to marry the prince, she is! What do we really know about her?" asked Francis, eyeing Gaston, and his pile of potatoes.

"That will be enough gossip, I should think," said Mr. Cogsworth, giving Francis the side-eye. This wasn't the sort of talk Mr. Cogsworth encouraged. In fact he usually made it clear he found it distasteful, and disrespectful. As far as he was concerned it wasn't their place to speculate on such things.

"Apparently, the king and queen approve, or they wouldn't be holding a ball to celebrate the engagement. And Mr. Cogsworth is right. That's enough of that talk. We have plenty to do before the prince arrives. We have a ball to arrange, and don't forget, the king and queen are making their departure shortly after," said Mrs. Potts.

"I am sure Gaston will be happy when the prince is finally home. Won't you, Gaston?" said Francis with a cheeky smile.

"I am looking forward to seeing him." But Gaston wondered if that was true. He did miss his friend, but he also liked the freedom he'd had while Kingsley had been away. And he wondered what it would be like now that his friend the prince was going to be married. He'd imagined he would have more time with

Kingsley before he got married. The idea of adjusting to having him back at the same time as getting to know Circe felt daunting. But he supposed if he and Circe didn't like each other, he could always keep going on as he had been the past couple years: hunting in the woods and spending time at his estate on the other side of the village. Then again the prince could insist Gaston spend more time at the castle, and he would feel obliged to, so he could only hope he liked this woman as much as his friend seemed to.

"I hear you are making a name for yourself in the village, Gaston. No one speaks of anything else. You're quite a celebrity, being the prince's best friend," said Chef Bouche.

"I think it's because he's become such a respected huntsman," said Mrs. Potts, shooting Chef Bouche a sharp look.

"Too right. I hear there isn't a trophy on Old Man Higgins's wall Gaston didn't bring in himself," said Mr. Cogsworth, surprising everyone at the table with his praise for Gaston. Though it had been years since Mr. Cogsworth shot him disapproving looks, he never outright praised Gaston, either. It seemed Mr. Cogsworth had stopped thinking of him as the little boy who tracked mud into the castle and was a bad influence on the prince.

"But it doesn't hurt to be the prince's best friend, does it?" said Chef Bouche, laughing heartily.

"If you have something to say, Chef Bouche, some sort of grievance you'd like to take up with me, then I suggest you come out with it! Perhaps you think I am taking advantage of my friendship with the prince and using it as a way to become popular with the villagers? If that is the case, then I'd appreciate it if you'd say so!" Gaston was looking the man straight in the eye with a face full of fury. He could see he had taken Chef Bouche aback.

"I have no grievance with you, Gaston, I assure you. I meant nothing by it. I am sure everyone in the village sees your qualities just as we do," said Chef Bouche, looking a bit startled by the exchange.

Gaston could tell the man was being honest and felt bad for trying to call him out. The fact was, Gaston *wasn't* sure if the people loved him for himself or because it was well-known he was friends with the prince. He had done his best to play his friendship with the prince down, but everyone knew Gaston grew up in the castle and had been given lands and an estate of his own. But he hoped the reason he was so well loved and respected was because he was committed to hunting down and killing the Beast of Gévaudan, and because he had sworn he would never let the village live in fear again; he would be mortified if they only loved him because the prince was his greatest friend.

When he started spending more time in the village after Kingsley left for his tour and got to know the people who lived and worked there, really listening to their stories, he realized the people of the village were terrified. They were horrified by the tales of the Beast of Gévaudan, what it had done in their own countryside, and how it was now ravaging other nearby kingdoms. They were fearful it would return to hunt their lands again, so Gaston promised them he would protect them and put an end to the beast, if it was the last thing he did.

And more importantly, he promised *himself* he

would do everything in his power to make them feel safe. He would track and hunt down the beast no matter how long it took, and it had been an exhausting effort.

The day after Gaston's father had been killed, all the outdoor staff had gone searching for the beast's body, hoping it had been mortally injured and just gone off somewhere in the woods to die. But they found nothing. And even though there hadn't been a sighting of the beast in their lands since his father died, Gaston knew in his heart the beast would return, and when it did, he would be ready. He promised himself he would avenge the death of his father, and he swore this was a promise he would not break.

"I'm sorry, Chef Bouche. Please forgive me. I fear I have something else pressing on my mind that clouded my judgment. I know you meant well," said Gaston.

"We have all been guilty of that on occasion, Gaston. Not to worry," said Chef Bouche, looking like he was more at ease.

Dinner went on much as it started, everyone in good spirits, laughing and sharing stories and wondering what the prince's intended would be like. Gaston did his best to join in the conversation, but he was distracted. He wondered if he even wanted to be there for Kingsley's return. Now that the prince had Circe, Gaston didn't see a place for himself at the castle. Not that he spent much time there anyway. But he had imagined, before he heard of Kingsley's engagement, he would be there more often. Maybe he would go back to his estate and stay there for a while. See how things were going. And give the two lovebirds time to settle in without Gaston being there to distract them.

Before he realized, it had gotten quite late, and everyone was saying good night and making their way upstairs to their bedrooms. Gaston decided there was no sense in trying to make his way back to his estate this time of night and resigned himself to sleeping in his old cottage that evening, and heading home the next morning.

"Gaston, would you join me in my sitting room before you go? I would like to talk with you," said Mrs. Potts gently, leading Gaston out of the servants' hall.

He knew she must have something important to discuss because she closed the door behind them, and she had a rather serious look on her face. It was his fault, really. He had looked sullen and vexed all through dinner. And he had snapped at poor Chef Bouche, so he knew he was about to get a lecture, and he knew he deserved it. He told himself that the poor fellow deserved another apology and was planning to do just that the moment Gaston could find a moment alone with him.

"Sit down, dear. I want to know why you haven't been spending more time at your estate? The prince gave you lands and a home of your own, but you seem content to leave it all to your agent and staff there."

"I don't have a staff. Are you kidding, Mrs. Potts? If anything, it's a glorified hunting lodge."

"By all accounts it would seem you are spending all your time in these woods hunting and camping, and I think I know why. Everyone does. But it has to stop, Gaston, it really does," she said, taking him by surprise. This wasn't the conversation he was expecting. He thought for sure she was going to tell him to stop sulking about the prince getting married. Some sort of speech about how all princes should marry one day. How it's their duty and so forth. He wasn't expecting this.

"I don't understand."

"Oh, I think you do, my boy. You're still hunting the Beast of Gévaudan. The creature hasn't been seen since your father died," she said putting her hand on his.

"That's not true. People in the village say it's been seen in other parts of the countryside, in other kingdoms. They're scared out of their wits."

"I'm sorry, Gaston, and I hate to say it, but sometimes people in the village can be a bit . . ."

"Ignorant. Is that what you were going say?" he asked, feeling a bit annoyed with her.

"No, I was going to say superstitious. And they're not what you would call open-minded, but that's another topic altogether. I'm just saying maybe stories of the Beast of Gévaudan terrifying villagers in other kingdoms far from here are a way to fill their evenings by the fire and nothing more. It has been years since it's come to our lands. Maybe you and your father did manage to kill it," she said.

"But isn't that exactly what you thought the first time? Didn't you all think my father killed it years before it came back again and took his life? Who is to say it won't come back again? And shouldn't I be ready when it does? The people of the village are counting on me, they look to me for protection. I won't let them down. I won't break my promise, not to them."

"I feel like I am talking to your father. You look so much like him, Gaston. Especially now that you're older. I saw your father obsess over the Beast of Gévaudan in the same way, after . . ."

"After what?"

"Gaston, your father never told you how your mother died?"

"I thought you knew that. Isn't that what you were keeping from me? What you all have been keeping from me."

"I was never sure how much you knew, Gaston. But it's time you knew everything. Your father hunted the beast for years after your mother died. After it

187

slaughtered her. It was his obsession, and in the end, it destroyed him, too. It was horrible when your mother was killed, my boy. It was too ghastly, too heartbreaking. Of course your papa didn't tell any of it. And now I feel like I am breaking his confidence."

"He's gone Mrs. Potts. I don't think he will mind. But why wait until now to tell me? Why after so many years?"

"They weren't my secrets to tell. They were your father's, and the queen's." She wiped the tears that were sliding down her cheeks with her delicately embroidered handkerchief and began wringing it in her hands. "I've spoken with the queen, and she agrees it's time you learned the entire story. But you have to promise me, Gaston, promise me you won't let this come between you and the prince."

"What does Kingsley have to do with this? He wasn't even born when mama died."

"Well, that's just it," Mrs. Potts began. "She died the night the prince was born. . . ."

CHAPTER VIII

THE ROSE IN THE WOODS

"I don't know where to begin, my boy," said Mrs. Potts as she took a sip of her black tea flavored with vanilla, almond, and just the slightest splash of brandy. She and Gaston were still in her sitting room in comfortable chairs facing the modest fireplace, its mantel covered with little framed portraits of all her children among her collection of pretty teacups. Between the chairs was a small round table with a pot of tea, two cups, and a plate with two chocolate and fruit tarts a kitchen maid had brought in for them. Gaston was eager for Mrs. Potts to tell him her story, and he was doing his best not to push her. He could see she was upset, and feeling apprehensive, but he felt he had been kept in the dark too long about his mother's death. In the days after his father died he wanted to ask her, but he couldn't bring himself to. He felt lost and alone in those days, even though he was surrounded by people who loved him. He had been a ghost drifting from one place to another, at the prince's whim. And by the time the prince left, it didn't seem to matter anymore now that Gaston's father died before he was able to share his secrets. All that mattered was that Gaston broke his promise to his father. But all those old feelings were starting to bubble up again, and he wanted to know the truth.

"Please, Mrs. Potts, just tell me about the night my mother died." Gaston wasn't trying to be rude. That's the last thing he would want. He loved this woman, but he was starting to feel angry and frightened because he knew there was something they had all been keeping from him, and now that he was finally about to learn the truth, he was afraid it would change his life. He wasn't sure if he was ready.

"But there is so much more to the story, my boy. So much more involved. It's not just about the night your mother died. It's not just how she was killed. It's also about the love the queen had for your mother and how much your mother loved her. They were absolutely devoted to each other, Gaston. Like siblings, they were, like you and the prince. When they discovered they were both expecting children around the same time, the queen insisted you be cared for in the castle nursery. She wanted you and the prince to grow up together, thinking of each other as brothers."

"And so we did. Even closer than most brothers. She got her wish," said Gaston.

"And why do you think the king and queen are never at home? Why do you think the queen built such a magnificent memorial to your mother when she died? She did it because she felt responsible for your mother's death." Mrs. Potts took another sip of her tea and continued.

"It wasn't the queen's fault, of course. At least, I didn't think so, but the queen blamed herself nevertheless, and I think there was a place in your father's heart that blamed her, too. You had only been born a few months before, but your mother was back to work attending the queen during her confinement. Stories of the Beast of Gévaudan were sweeping the kingdom, and everyone was afraid to go out at night lest they be attacked or eaten by the beast. There had been several deaths at this point, and your father, along with a group of other hunters, including the king, were doing their best to put an end to the beast's reign of terror, which dominated everyone's nightmares." Mrs. Potts paused, gaze drifting away, as if she was imagining those days, lost in her thoughts with the emotions welling up inside her as she told Gaston the story.

"The queen was in distress throughout her confinement, making your mother fearful for her, and for the baby. The queen was overwrought, worried about what might befall the king while hunting the Beast of Gévaudan, and your mother was always close at hand in the days leading up to the prince's birth so she might comfort and calm the queen.

"And the queen wasn't the only person who was terrified. We all were. Your mother was in anguish, worried for the queen and also in constant fear something horrible would happen to your father. But she didn't confide this to the queen. On the contrary, she was like stone, like marble, unbreakable and strong, at least while she was in the company of the queen. But afterward, after the queen fell asleep, she would come down to visit me, and in a great gush she would say all the things she had to keep bottled up inside, all the fear building within her to the point of bursting. Every night your father hunted the beast, she worried he wouldn't survive the night, and she dreaded the day he didn't come back to her.

"That must have been exhausting for her," said Gaston, trying to paint a picture in his mind of his mother, but all he could conjure was the statue that stood in front of her eternal resting spot. As if she were made of stone, just as Mrs. Potts described, strong and unbreakable.

"It was horrible. But your mother was a strong woman and did her best to support the queen, even though there were times when she wanted nothing more than to cry. And that is what she did, sometimes for hours, after the queen fell asleep. Your mother would collapse into in my arms and sob. I wanted to tell her everything would be okay, but of course none of us knew if it would. So I just held her and let her know she could count on me, whatever befell us.

"One morning your father hadn't come to the servants' hall for his breakfast, as was his custom while your mother was sleeping in the castle. We were all worried, none more so than your mother, who seemed unwell. Her nerves were frayed, and she looked as if she hadn't slept for days, never mind having just given birth to you not long before. The queen insisted Rose go to the cottage to check on your father and to rest. We both insisted, in fact. I said I would care for the queen while your mother rested, and we both told her she wasn't to return until the following morning, if even then, instructing her to rest until she was well again. She tried to argue, of course. She didn't want to abandon her friend. But she agreed if for nothing else to check in to see if your father was all right."

"Your father later told me when she got to the cottage, she collapsed into bed after a long embrace and slept the entire day. He called off the hunt that night, wanting to be with your mother, and so the king could be with the queen. He was happy to have her home. Happy to care for her while she rested.

"He said she slept as if she were under a sleeping spell, like a maiden from a fairy tale, sleeping and sleeping, and not stirring except for once in the early evening when he roused her to eat something and take some tea. But afterward she slipped back under her covers and fell into the land of dreams again. Exhausted from her constant care of the queen and constant worry.

"But then something happened that night your father did not expect. He only told me this story once, but the images his words conjured in my mind burn so brightly, it's as if he just shared them with me this evening, and not many years ago.

"Your father woke to screams coming from the woods, not far from the cottage. Horrible screams that sent terror through his entire body. When he shook off his grogginess and confusion, he realized it was your mother he heard screaming. Then he heard the bells ringing from the castle battlements, which meant the king and queen were in need of aid. He didn't know why; we can only assume your mother heard the bells and feared the queen was in distress during her labors and ran out into the night without thinking. And that is what he did, too. He grabbed his blunderbuss and rushed out into the wilderness, following the sound of your mother's screams."

Mrs. Potts stopped for a moment to take another sip of her tea, doing her best to keep her teacup steady, while trembling and attempting to hold back more tears.

"And what happened then?" asked Gaston. His face was pale and passive, but his hands, too, were shaking.

"I don't know if I can continue, my dear. I'm sure you can imagine the rest," she said, casting her eyes down.

"Nothing could be worse than my imaginings. You forget, I saw my father being attacked by that damnable wolf."

"It's worse than anything you could imagine, my

boy. It was so horrible your father could hardly speak of it. I will only say your mother was still screaming while the monster . . . devoured her. There was no way she would have survived, even if your father had been able to lure the beast away. It's too horrible to think of, my dear. Just too gruesome to imagine the terror and pain your poor mother suffered in her last moments, and to know your father saw it happen. He did the only thing he could and put an end to her suffering, after which he fell to his knees sobbing, saying again and again how sorry he was, without a care for his own life, or without even noticing the beast was advancing on him as he mourned your mother. Nothing but grief existed for him in that moment. It didn't matter to him if the monster lunged at him, clawing at his face. Your father felt it was right that he should die. He wanted to be with your mother. He felt he deserved a horrific death in payment for hers, for not protecting her."

"But it wasn't his fault. She ran out while he was asleep. He didn't know." Gaston's stomach and chest were clenched in grief and horror. He had no idea his father suffered this. His body felt weak and seized with pain. He wanted more than ever to kill the beast. He had to. It was his duty, not only to his mother and father but to the people of the village. He wouldn't let any of them suffer this same pain, this loss and grief, this horror, not ever.

"I know, my dearest one, but in moments of grief we sometimes blame ourselves. And in moments of panic, we do not think. Which is why I never blamed the queen for ordering the bells to be rung." He could tell she was worried *he* would blame the queen. And why shouldn't he? She was to blame. His anxiety and anger were becoming a violent torrent, attacking him from the inside. His hands were shaking and he was doing his best not to cry, but he felt if he held it inside any longer, he might explode.

"She knew the beast was out there! How could she put my mother in danger like that? She knew if my mother heard those bells she would come," he said, hardly able to breathe, the pain in his chest so tight.

"Perhaps. But just as your mother didn't think before she ran out into the dangerous night, the queen was not thinking of the monster lurking there. She was in danger of losing her child, Gaston, and she wanted her friend to be at her side. That is all she thought of in that moment of desperation and fear."

Gaston saw truth in this. He wished it had been different, but he understood. He, too, had made a choice that killed someone he loved. Who was he to blame the queen for calling out to her sister in the throes of pain and fear of losing her child? Perhaps the anger he had felt toward the queen was really anger and disappointment toward himself. He didn't know.

"How did my father escape the beast?" he asked, trying to banish the gruesome images of his mother. Trying to forget what his father believed would be his last moments. Why must his life be so tied to this creature?

"Some of the other outdoor staff heard your mother's screams and came out to help. When they saw the beast attacking your father, they shot at it, giving your father a chance to escape. The creature staggered back, giving your father a chance to grab his blunderbuss and shoot it square in the chest.

Everyone was sure it was a killing blow, but the beast escaped into the woods. It was a bloody business, my dear. A bloody business. The queen was devastated, and your father didn't know whom he blamed more, himself or the queen." Mrs. Potts squeezed Gaston's hand tenderly and looked at him with sad eyes. He truly loved this woman and was so thankful he had her. She was the only person in his life who was like a mother to him. He didn't know what he would do without her.

"Is that why my father preferred to spend his time in his cottage? But surely he didn't think you blamed him." Gaston hated the idea of his father blaming himself. To think, all those nights, when his father looked at the night sky in silent melancholy, he felt responsible for his own wife's death. It was heartbreaking.

"No, my dear. None of us blamed him. And we understood why he obsessively hunted the woods. And why the king and queen were rarely at home. The queen loves that you and the prince are like brothers, it's what she and your mother wished for most, but it hurts her too much to see you together. It makes her miss her friend even more, and she can't bear that she took your mother from you."

"She didn't take my mother from me, the beast did, and I will kill it, Mrs. Potts. I swear I will."

"My darling boy, please don't walk your father's path. Don't dedicate your life to vengeance. This sort of suffering is far too terrible for someone so young." She stood up and took his face in her hands. "Please, my boy, promise me. I so wish you would choose happiness."

"We cannot choose our fates, Mrs. Potts," he said, startled by her talk of happiness. Wondering if it was even possible.

"So it is your fate to drown in a maelstrom of grief and vengeance? Don't lose your life hunting this beast, My dear one. If you did, I don't think I could ever stop crying." She was on the verge of more tears.

"I don't intend to, Mrs. Potts. I am glad my papa didn't tell me his story. I can't bear the idea of him having to relive it, or seeing the pain in his face in the telling of it. Thank you for being honest with me, Mrs. Potts. And please don't fret. I promise I will be okay."

He took her in his arms. She felt so small to him now. So tiny. Someone to be protected. It was up to him to protect her now, to protect them all.

"It's time you stop trying to look out for me, Mrs. Potts, and let me look after you. After all of you," he said, stepping back and feeling thankful he had someone who loved him so much.

"I will always look out for you, Gaston. Always. You're my sweet boy," she said, crying again. "And you don't blame the prince?"

"For my father's death? I did for a long time. But we were both young and foolish, Mrs. Potts. I don't know if I blame anyone anymore." He was not entirely sure if that was true. There was a part of him that still faulted the prince, and himself, but he was now saving his rage and grief for the beast.

"I meant for your mother's," she said, taking a shaky sip of tea.

"Of course not. Why would I blame him for my mother's death? And I don't blame the queen, not really. My parents are dead because a vile beast attacked them."

"I am proud of the man you're becoming, Gaston. But don't you think I will ever stop seeing you as my darling boy. And you must promise me you will put an end to hunting this beast."

"I don't make promises I can't keep, Mrs. Potts. Not anymore."

CHAPTER IX

THE INVITATION

$\mathcal{B}$efore they knew it, the engagement ball was upon them. Gaston had been dreading the ball since Mrs. Potts told him about it. He didn't want to see Kingsley for the first time in so many years on the same night he was going to meet Kingsley's fiancé, Circe. Gaston had hoped he would have some time with him alone, a mere handful of hours would have sufficed, but it seemed the prince and his betrothed would be arriving at the castle together in a whirlwind of excessive fanfare and pomposity. Gaston had thought he would sneak off to his estate and just avoid the spectacle altogether, but Mrs. Potts advised him otherwise, so he decided to stay in his father's old cottage that night to be nearer the castle. He tried to avoid staying there as much as possible. It reminded him too much of his father. And somehow their cat seemed to know where he was, always showing up for her scrinches and bowl of milk. She was usually out on adventures, that cat. Gone for weeks at a time, but she always found her way home, whether he was staying at the cottage or in his house on his estate. And he was happy for her company.

None of the plans for Kingsley's return seemed like something his friend would have planned himself. Gaston heard Kingsley and Circe would be riding in an open carriage throughout the Many Kingdoms, making their way through all the neighboring king-doms as well as well as the village in his own king-dom so he might show off his new intended as he made his way to the castle. And if that wasn't lofty enough, once he made his grand appearance he was to be greeted by a multitude of kings and queens, lords and ladies, and gentry from the surrounding kingdoms all there to celebrate his engagement to

Circe. No one spoke of anything else. It was sickening, really. At least, Gaston thought so. It was nothing like the Kingsley he knew. From the sound of it, this would be the most lavish event in the history of the Many Kingdoms, and that was saying something if the Book of Fairy Tales was to be believed. It was a far cry from eating smashed sandwiches in the hollow of an old tree while waiting to see if they could spy fairies. But then, Gaston supposed they weren't boys anymore. And the queen seemed pleased to have a reason to throw a party.

She had even arranged for some of the spectacles she had originally planned for the thwarted celebration that was to have taken place many years ago now, before the beast returned and Gaston's father died. Something about it made Gaston's stomach lurch. He remembered the day he and his father went to check on the queen's pavilion to make sure it would be ready for her ill-fated grand event. He suddenly felt angry with the queen for dragging him back into those dark memories. Mrs. Potts had just warned him about not letting himself drown in the past, and that's exactly what he was doing. But it wasn't the queen's fault. She wasn't pulling him under, he was letting the weight of his grief drag him down. So Gaston cleared his mind, trying to make himself ready to see Kingsley and Circe even though he was dreading it with all of his being.

Gaston was invited to the engagement ball that evening as a guest, not as a servant. He was surprised by a knock on the cottage door and opened it to find a royal servant, all spiffed up in a white powdered wig, flouncy coat, short pants, stockings, and silk shoes with flashy buckles, standing on the porch. The servant had even brought the invitation on a little silver tray, which made Gaston laugh. It wasn't as if someone couldn't have given it to him when he was in the servants' hall. Why all this pomp and circumstance? The servant gesticulated dramatically as he announced the contents of the invitation, as if he were delivering the most important speech ever uttered in the history of the Many Kingdoms.

"You are hereby invited by the king and queen to attend a royal ball to celebrate the engagement of the prince and his beloved," said the footman, standing awkwardly as he held the little round silver tray with the invitation sitting upon it.

"Francis, is that you under that wig? What have you come as?" Gaston laughed even harder, realizing the awkward servant was Francis.

"Shut up. I'm trying to be official," said Francis, sweating under all of his finery and clearly embarrassed Gaston recognized him.

"I'm sorry, but is all this nonsense really necessary?" Gaston took the invitation from the tray. When he opened it, he saw there was a small piece of paper folded up with a note scrawled on it along with the official invitation. "It is nonsense and all! Completely unnecessary! Having me run around in silk shoes like some sort of toff; whoever heard of a footman wearing silk shoes? I'm afraid I'm going to get mud on them or something." Gaston could see Francis hadn't meant to let out that little outburst, and his demeanor quickly snapped back into that of formality rather than familiarity. He cleared his throat, apologized, and continued.

"The prince wants you to know he has made

arrangements for you to have rooms in the castle, and there you will find your clothing for the ball this evening," said Francis, eyeing Gaston.

"I see." Gaston looked at the note. He wondered if someone had told Francis he wasn't able to read. And suddenly he felt ashamed, and like some kind of impostor. He wondered why he was he being invited to this fancy ball, and he was sure everyone else there would be asking themselves the same thing.

"Simply ask Mr. Cogsworth to direct you to your room. The dressing gong is at six. An intimate party will be meeting in the drawing room at seven, to be followed by a light dinner at eight, after which the ball will be officially opened by the prince and his betrothed. Now, if you will excuse me, I have my other duties to attend to," Francis said before he quickly walked away. Gaston felt bad for making a joke about his outfit. He didn't mean to, not really, so he called after Francis.

"Oi! Francis! I'm sorry!"

Gaston couldn't be sure if he heard.

"This is madness," Gaston said to his cat, who was

looking up at him with sleepy eyes after being awoken from her slumber by his booming voice.

"This is not like Kingsley, not at all!" he said to the cat. She just blinked at him before snuggling back into her cushion near the fireplace.

"Well, you're no help! I guess I'd better go see Mrs. Potts and see what this is all about," he said, grabbing his knapsack and weapons and heading out the door.

He made his way through the forest and to the castle, going around back to the servants' entrance, and found Mrs. Potts in her sitting room going over her lists.

"Look at this!" He stood in her doorway, waving the note and invitation in a flurry. "Francis says I am to have rooms in the castle? Did you know about this? What does Mr. Cogsworth have to say?"

"It's not for Mr. Cogsworth to have an opinion about any of it," Mrs. Potts said without looking up. "It was a royal order." Mrs. Potts was checking her lists and ticking off the tasks that had been completed. "I don't understand why you are so upset. I would think you'd be happy to see your friend!"

"I am. Of course I am. I mean, I think I am. But what's this about an intimate dinner before the ball? What does that even mean?" asked Gaston, trying to bring her attention back around to him.

"It's just a light dinner for the family. There will be an *at home* for the duration of the ball, in which food will also be served, and of course a late supper, and breakfast in the morning," said Mrs. Potts. "Don't worry, there will be plenty for you to eat."

"So it's an all-night event?" Gaston was surprised; the king and queen had not thrown a party of this magnitude since the one they'd been preparing for when his father died. "I heard the queen is going to light the pavilion, and yesterday I saw the gardeners making animal topiaries in the hedge maze. And now they've got poor Francis running around, sweating in his fancy livery and powdered wig, handing out invitations on a silver tray. She's given everyone a lot of work with very little time to do it." Gaston shook his head. "I can't imagine Kingsley wanted any of this."

"The queen didn't order all this; it was decreed by the prince. He seems to have—how shall I say

it?—come into his position while he's been away."
Gaston knew that half smile. The one that said Mrs.
Potts did not approve.

"I see," said Gaston, feeling even more nervous
about seeing his friend again than he had already been.
He had to wonder if this was all Circe's influence. She
was from a very old royal family and was probably
demanding all this cockamamy fanfare. He hated the
idea of some snobbishly annoying, pretty little princess
changing everything and making their court boring
and pompous, just like Kingsley had promised he
would never be. And what was she going to think of
him, the prince's servant friend, his childhood companion who didn't know how to read and whom he
felt sorry for? Maybe that's why the prince was picking
out clothes for him, making him look presentable,
respectful, so he would fit in, as if he was just an old
friend and not the son of a servant. Gaston was starting to get angry. Since when did his friend care what
anyone thought or make poor footmen run around in
powdered wigs? This was beyond intolerable. And he

wasn't going to stand for it. He wasn't going to get dressed up in some silly outfit and try to win anyone's approval.

"And I suppose I'm to wear some snooty outfit that he's picked out? I'll probably look like a fool." Gaston felt as if his stomach was full of fluttering bats.

"I *suppose* the only way to find out is to go upstairs and try it on, and let me get back to my work." Mrs. Potts was still glued to her lists. Gaston sighed, feeling defeated, and turned to walk away. He stopped when he heard Mrs. Potts's voice calling to him.

"I'm sorry, dear. There's just so much to do, and with Mr. Potts away on top of everything else. You know how I worry when he's traveling," she said. Gaston understood. He loved this woman and would forgive her anything. She was the closest thing to a mother he had.

"I didn't know Mr. Potts was away; is everything okay?" he said, remembering her husband wasn't at dinner the previous night. Gaston hadn't even bothered to ask after him.

He had been so consumed by his own problems he didn't stop to think of Mr. and Mrs. Potts were having troubles of their own.

"His brother isn't well, you see, and there is no one else to care for him now that his wife has passed away. I fear Mr. Potts won't be back for some time." She was trying not to look worried. Gaston felt bad he hadn't been visiting Mrs. Potts as often as she would like and made a promise he would come to dinner and visit with her more often, especially with Mr. Potts away.

"I'm sorry to hear that. Please send Mr. Potts my best next time you write him." There he was prattling on when she had so many other things on her mind. "And don't worry, Mrs. Potts, I'm here."

"I know you are, dear. Thank you. And, Gaston, the very last thing you will look like at the ball this evening is a fool. I guarantee you will be the most handsome man there," she said. "Now bend over so I can give you a kiss!" she said with her sweet giggle.

"You mean I will be the second most handsome man there," Gaston said. "I remember my father telling me I should never let Kingsley know I am better than him at anything. Shooting, hunting, riding, everything. He said that's what he did with the king. He always let him think he was the best."

"That sounds like your papa. But, Gaston, that's not the relationship you have with the prince. Was he ever cross with you when you were better at something?"

"Never. I tried telling my father that every time he warned me, but he said one day it would change. I wonder if he was right. All this pomposity and fancy, frilly stuff isn't Kingsley. Do you think he's changed? Does it seem like it from his letters?"

"Perhaps. But I doubt he's changed toward you. And between us, dear, I think you truly are even more handsome than the prince. And there isn't a thing you can do to change that." She smiled and patted his hand. "Now I really must get back to work. I think you will find Mr. Cogsworth is in his pantry. He's been expecting you."

Even though Gaston was no longer a child, he couldn't help but feel like one in the presence of Mr. Cogsworth. Things had been easier with him in recent years. He wasn't sure why things had changed, if it was because the prince told him to leave Gaston alone or if Mr. Cogsworth had finally come around to accepting Gaston's unconventional place in the household. He wanted Mr. Cogsworth to like him. Growing up he had been like a father to the prince, and in a way that's how Gaston looked at him now, though there was no reason in it, except that he no longer had a father, and he had known Cogsworth since he was a boy. He knocked on the butler's pantry door and heard Mr. Cogsworth's voice from the other side.

"Come in."

"Good afternoon, Mr. Cogsworth. I was told to come to you, that you would tell me where to find my rooms?"

Mr. Cogsworth was sitting at his desk decanting a bottle of wine. He looked like an alchemist with the wine bottle in a strange contraption and his candlestick nearby to give him more light.

"Yes, sir," said Mr. Cogsworth, standing up. "You should have come to the front door. You are a guest in this house and will be treated as such," said Mr.

Cogsworth rather stiffly, and not at all in the friendly, more familiar way Gaston had grown accustomed to in recent years.

"I mean, I could go back out and enter through the front, if you'd like," said Gaston, laughing to make things light. But Mr. Cogsworth didn't laugh. He stood there stoic as ever. Gaston felt as if he had been transported to another world. Was this how Mr. Cogsworth was with the family and their guests? It seemed so odd and formal, and it made Gaston uncomfortable.

"It's funny, isn't it, Mr. Cogsworth, for years you were always scolding me for going through the front door, and now you're saying I shouldn't have used the servants' entrance." Gaston was being jovial, but old Cogsworth was like a pillar of stone standing there at attention. Gaston didn't understand what was going on.

"Indeed. Things change, sir. And while you are a guest in this house, please just call me Cogsworth."

"Oh, stop with all these formalities, Mr. Cogsworth. We're old friends, you and I. There's no reason for pretense," said Gaston earnestly. Was Mr. Cogsworth angry that Kingsley had given the order to treat Gaston like a guest? Did old Cogsworth not approve? Whatever was going on, Gaston didn't like it.

"There is every reason for these formalities, *sir*. You are a guest of the prince and therefore the family, and you deserve the same respect as anyone who is a guest in this house. I wouldn't want to *overstep the mark*."

This reminded Gaston of the conversation he had overheard between Mr. Cogsworth and the prince, the day the prince told Gaston he was going away on tour. Mr. Cogsworth had suggested Gaston should learn his place, and the prince got angry with him and said he was overstepping the mark. Was the prince still taking this line with poor Cogsworth? And again, Gaston was sorry he never learned to read or write. If he had, he would have mentioned to Kingsley how things had been between him and Cogsworth in recent years. He hated the idea of Kingsley still being cruel to the old fellow.

"I'm not sure what Kingsley said to you, Mr. Cogsworth, but I have been very happy with how things have been between us lately. Let's not ruin it now," said Gaston, wishing he knew what the prince said had said.

"As you say, sir. Young Francis will show you to your room and will be taking care of you this evening," he said in this stiff manner.

"Taking care of me? What do you mean?" Gaston couldn't hide the incredulous look on his face. He was dumbfounded.

"As the first footman, he serves as valet when we have guests who don't bring servants of their own." He looked Gaston up and down.

"Of course I don't have servants. What's going on? I just saw Francis; he didn't mention any of this. I don't need a valet, Mr. Cogsworth," he said, shaking his head.

"Nevertheless, Francis will be there to assist you." Mr. Cogsworth opened his door and called Francis to come to his pantry. Francis arrived, no longer wearing his previous outfit, now having donned a sober black uniform befitting a valet.

"Francis, could you please show Gaston to his room?" asked Cogsworth.

This was all too much for Gaston, and he didn't understand why Cogsworth was making such a fuss. Kingsley must have said something to him. It was strange having people he knew, people he was friendly with and even grew up with, wait on him. He could hardly think of what to say, or where to look as he and Francis walked to his room together. So he tried to break the tension.

"Just how many costume changes are you expected to make in the course of one day, eh, Francis?" Gaston asked with a chuckle, but Francis didn't even crack a smile.

"This way, sir," said Francis, opening the door to the room assigned to Gaston.

"Oh, come on, Francis! Not you too!" Gaston was losing his patience. He knew Francis was just doing his job, but he felt like he had been transported into another universe, or was part of some elaborate prank everyone was in on except for him. And when Francis let him into his room, he was shocked.

It was a large set of rooms with wood furnishings and wood-paneled walls decorated with mounted elk, deer, and wolf heads. There was a massive stone fireplace with two comfortable chairs sitting across from the crackling fire, which was flanked by two enormous elk statues. And on the mantel were several crystal decanters, with matching glasses in which to enjoy the various spirits.

The rooms were at the back of the house and had a set of glass-paned doors that led to a balcony with a breathtaking view of the night sky, and below of the vast woods. The balcony connected to the adjoining bedroom, which had a massive four-poster bed carved from wood. The posts were intricately crafted to look like acorns, leaves, and small forest creatures like squirrels, rabbits, and foxes. The headboard featured a wolf sleeping under a night sky with a full moon. The bed was surrounded by heavy velvet drapes that matched the drapes on the windows, and red tapestries hung on the stone walls. On the other side of the bedroom was a dressing table and a wardrobe, where clothing hung waiting for him to put it on for the evening festivities.

This room was not the queen's style. It almost felt as if it had been decorated especially for Gaston, though the thought was ludicrous, even if he didn't remember ever seeing a room such as this in all the years he'd spent there. He couldn't believe he would be given such large rooms with so many royal guests coming to visit.

"A sitting room and a bedroom. How fancy. Are you sure it's for me?" he said to Francis, who was standing at attention, awaiting Gaston's orders.

"And a room with a bath," said Francis, motioning to a door hanging ajar Gaston hadn't notice. "I have had one drawn for you. I will be back later to help you dress."

"This isn't necessary, Francis. I don't know what the prince is playing at, but I am sure you have better things to do than help a grown man get dressed," said Gaston.

"But it's my job, sir," said Francis, and suddenly Gaston felt ashamed. He hadn't intended to belittle the man's position.

"Of course it is. I'm sorry. Thank you, Francis." He watched Francis leave the room with a bit of relief, sighed, and plopped down on the bed. He didn't know what was going on, but he decided whatever it was, he'd soon find out. And the last thing he was going to do was make a fool of himself. If Kingsley wanted him to dress and act like a gentleman, then that was what he was going to do. Gaston had no idea if his fears about this Circe were based in reality, but he decided he wasn't going to give her a reason not to like him. He would be on his best behavior.

CHAPTER X

THE ENCHANTRESS IN THE ROSE GARDEN

Gaston was surprised he had time to spare after he dressed for the ball, and he was rather glad Francis had been there to help him after all. It was no wonder royals needed valets and lady's maids—their clothing was so overly complicated, with little buttons and hitches he wouldn't have been able to manage on his own, especially with his large hands. He laughed, imagining himself having to fumble with all that himself. Thank goodness for Francis.

He had some time before he was expected in the drawing room, so he decided to take a walk around the gardens. He felt quite stylish, and perhaps even a bit dandyish (at least for Gaston) in his new outfit, which he didn't hate. Another surprise. Who knew he would enjoy dressing up and feeling so handsome. Of course Kingsley would pick out something perfect. Or at least give the instructions to someone whose business it was to procure Gaston's natty new clothing. The colors, fit, and style were perfect for Gaston. Red was Gaston's color, and Kingsley knew it. He picked out a handsome, deep red fitted frock coat that made Gaston feel like a gentleman without all the fuss Gaston detested in royal fashion.

And if the numerous compliments Francis heaped upon him were any indication, Gaston looked quite dashing in his new fashionable ensemble. Of course, such was what you'd expect a valet to say, but something in the way Francis gushed once Gaston was fully outfitted made Gaston feel he looked rather smashing.

He was off to a good start.

He was thankful for this time alone to think and walk in the gardens before he was thrust into a social situation in which he quite frankly had no idea how to conduct himself. But the new set of clothing did help. At least he would look the part, if nothing else.

As he was walking, he heard ladies' voices coming from within the rose garden. It was beautiful, abloom with pink rose bushes and enclosed by tall hedges with a circular stone path that led to the center, where one could sit and enjoy the view. Whoever was in the garden seemed to be arguing, unaware that Gaston was on the other side of the hedge wall and could hear everything they were saying. He knew a gentleman wouldn't linger to listen, but then again, he wasn't a gentleman, even if he was dressed like one.

"Please, sisters, stop trying to break us apart. He's done nothing to deserve your contempt!"

"He's not worthy of you, Circe."

"We've seen it in—"

"The Book of Fairy Tales."

Gaston could swear he heard three, maybe four different voices chiming in on the conversation. And how odd some of them sounded. So shrill, with such an awkward cadence to the way they spoke, finishing each other's sentences. These were voices he hadn't heard before, so he was almost sure they must have been Circe and her odd sisters. Plumette had said

Circe's sisters were strange, and she was right. He wondered if the prince had met them before proposing to Circe. He must have, if they were her guardians. Though it sounded as if she agreed to marry the prince without their consent, which meant she had a mind and will of her own. Perhaps he would like her after all.

"He's a monster, Circe!" said one of her sisters in a screeching voice so loud Gaston was worried they would draw attention from others. He looked around to see if anyone else was in the garden, but found no one except for the members of staff rushing about preparing for the ball.

"He's not a monster, Lucinda! He loves me, and I will marry him no matter how forcefully you protest!" said Circe.

Gaston was surprised. This Circe seemed to know her own mind and was clearly very much in love with his friend. He was rather impressed, hearing her stand up to her sisters, and he realized he was starting to like her despite himself. Maybe she was just the sort of person to keep Kingsley in line.

"He loves you for your beauty and title, and nothing more," said one of the sisters.

"What title? I have no title, and he's still agreed to marry me. He could marry anyone he wishes, and he wants to marry me," said Circe.

"You come from one of the most ancient families in the Many Kingdoms, Circe," a third sister spoke.

"You deserve better than this boy who is playing at being a king. We see into his heart. We see nothing but cruelty and selfishness lingering there. Mark my words, my girl, he will break your heart. Do you think he would love you if you weren't so beautiful? Or, say, if you were the daughter of a pig farmer?"

"I do! That sort of thing doesn't matter to him. He loves me unconditionally," said Circe, and Gaston tried not to laugh, wondering if that were true.

"We shall see, my girl. We shall see," said all of her sisters at once, which Gaston found unsettling. What must life be like for this young girl, living with these awful sisters controlling her? It was no wonder she was eager to marry the prince, if only to get away from her strange family.

Gaston could hear Circe crying as three sets of footsteps clicked toward him on the stone path leading out of the rose garden. He quickly stepped aside to make it look as though he hadn't been standing there listening, but he couldn't help being startled by them as they emerged from behind the tall garden wall. They were frightful-looking women, each of them exactly the same as the others. To think there was one woman such as this in their kingdom, let alone three, it was unbelievable, with their jet-black hair, ghastly pale skin, and bulbous eyes that were lined so heavily in black they looked as if they had just crawled out their graves. He felt a chill come over him as they cast their gaze on him, eyeing him up and down as they walked past.

These women were truly unnerving. They looked at him as if they knew him. Like they knew his story and what was in his heart. And he sensed they knew he had been listening to their conversation. And for some unearthly reason, all this seemed to please them.

He watched as they walked away toward the large elaborately carved double doors that led into the castle, and couldn't help but wonder what the prince had gotten himself into. Even the way they walked was unsettling, all huddled together as if connected, whispering and clicking their little heels on the path, their black-and-aubergine dresses floating about them like corpse flowers. They were like witches from a fairy tale. It reminded him of that book he and the prince had read, the Book of Fairy Tales. Were these the women from those stories? And then he remembered, one of them had mentioned the very same book. They said they saw Kingsley's story in its pages. How was that possible? He and Kingsley read that book cover to cover and never saw a story about their kingdom. These women were delusional, or lying.

Whoever they were, from everything Gaston had just heard, these peculiar women did not want their sister to marry the prince. The prince didn't need to get caught up in this family quarrel. He wouldn't want Circe's sisters clicking their heels around the castle, frightening the staff with their ghastly faces. Gaston didn't know what to think. Circe had defended the prince to her bizarre sisters; she seemed to love and trust him. But even if she were the most beautiful woman in all the lands, would it be worth having those frightful women as sisters by marriage?

When his mind stopped racing, Gaston couldn't help but hear Circe still crying in the garden, so once her sisters were safely away, he took out the handkerchief Francis had so thoughtfully put into his breast pocket and entered the garden. She was sitting there on the bench, her golden hair shining brightly in the moonlight; it looked as if she were glowing from within. Her head was down; she was unaware he was standing there looking at her. When she lifted up her eyes, he understood. She *was* the most beautiful woman he had ever seen. Her beauty was almost too painful to behold. He held out the handkerchief and watched her take it to wipe away her tears. Her sad eyes looked at him with kindness.

"Thank you, Gaston," she said, smiling up at him. He wondered how she knew his name. Kingsley must have told her all about him, about his greatest companion, but how did she know he was this person? "I apologize for my sisters. I imagine you heard what they said." She looked small and sad. So sweet, and nothing at all like he had imagined. It was no wonder his friend wanted to marry her and was putting everyone to so much trouble in planning this grand affair.

"They're protective of their little sister," he said, not knowing what else to say.

"You're too kind." She stood and took his hand in hers, blinking away more tears. "I wish you didn't have to go away." She said it so causally, it almost didn't register.

"What do you mean? Where am I going?" he asked, taking his hand away in surprise.

"Dear, sweet Gaston. I see into your heart. I see the pain the prince caused you, how it festers deep within you, and I fear one day one of you will lose your life as a result. Please trust me, it's better that you should never see each other again."

"Trust you? I don't know you, Mademoiselle! You come here with your gruesome sisters, making proclamations, telling me I will lose my life because of my best friend, my brother? Or that I will somehow cause the end of his? Who do you think you are?"

"Sometimes we cannot avoid our fates, Gaston." Though this woman might not have looked like her sisters, she was a witch, too, albeit more cunning and beguiling. She knew what she was doing, using her beauty and gentle voice, trying to trick him into thinking he would hurt his friend. But really, he knew she just wanted him out of the way.

"Did Kingsley tell you about how my father died? Are you saying I'm going to take some sort of revenge on him? That's insanity!"

"Not revenge. At least, I don't think so. What I see isn't clear. All I know is that it involves a beast," she said, reaching out for his hand, as if it hurt her to say these words. She was a good actress, this witch. Cunning, cruel, and vicious, disguised by a sugary voice.

"I don't blame Kingsley for that anymore. I would never hurt him. Never!"

"Yet something has taken hold in you. A hatred for something or someone, so strong it will put the prince's life in jeopardy," she said.

"My hate is for the beast that killed my mother

and father, not for Kingsley!" He took a step back. "What kind of women are you and your sisters? What kind of witches? You have it all wrong, Circe. I am not going to kill Kingsley."

"I know. I am worried he might kill you," said Circe.

"Are you threatening me?"

"I am only offering a warning. I wish I could see the events clearly in the mind. They are muddled and confused, but I know if you two remain friends, it will result in one of you killing the other," she said. "And it breaks my heart to say so, because I know he loves no one more than he loves you. Not even me."

"That's what this is about, then, isn't it? You're jealous. You're trying to get rid of me."

"If I was just trying to get rid of you, I'd ask my sisters to spirit you down to Hades. Trust me or not, Gaston, it's up to you. Either way, we have a dinner and ball to attend, and I imagine everyone is waiting for us to join them in the drawing room. So why don't you make the most of this time you have with your brother before you go away. And please trust I will do everything I can to make him happy in your absence." She smiled at him as if she wasn't tearing his world apart. This was worse than Gaston had imagined.

"Did you already tell Kingsley about this?"

"No. I didn't want to ruin your reunion for him. I thought I'd let you tell him you're going away. I think it would be better coming from you. It's for the best, Gaston, please trust me. I'm only trying to protect you both." And he almost believed she thought she was telling the truth.

"I understand," lied Gaston, offering his arm to Circe so he could escort her to the drawing room. He couldn't do anything about this now. Not here. Any moment someone would come looking for them. He had to act the gentleman. He had to act as if everything was exactly as it should be. He would look like the brute Circe likely thought he was if he made a scene. But the fact was, he didn't understand. This was all madness. Mysterious predictions, and her horrible witchy sisters. Something wasn't right. As grotesque as her sisters were, Circe was the dangerous one. She wanted Kingsley for herself. She had all but said it.

The prince loved him more than anyone, including her. That's what this was about. He didn't care if she was a dangerous witch or not. He wasn't going to let her send him away.

When they got to the drawing room, everyone was there waiting to go in to dinner. It was just the royal family, Circe's sisters, and a small number of family friends. Gaston didn't know what to do when he saw Kingsley. What he wanted was to embrace his old friend, to tell him how much he missed him, that being without him was more than he could bear. Somehow Gaston hadn't realized he felt this way until the moment Circe threatened to send him away. When he saw Kingsley standing there smiling at him, he knew he never wanted to be without him again. He had been telling himself he was happy Kingsley was away, happy to be on his own, but really, he was miserable and lonely without him. He had been filling days with hunting the beast, trying to forget the pain of the loss of his father, but also the loss of his closest companion. The moment he told Kingsley the truth about how his mother had died, he knew the prince would join Gaston in the hunt for the beast, and together they would kill it, forever rewriting all the pain and anguish it had caused. But if Circe was determined to separate them, to send him away from his best friend, his brother, and the only home and family he had ever known, how would any of that be possible? In a way, he was thankful to Circe for making him fear losing his best friend forever.

He needed to do something about her. But first he just needed to get through the dinner and the ball. He saw the queen smile at him from across the room. It made his heart hurt to think it was difficult for her to see him, that it made her remember her friend Rose. How hurt she must still be over the loss of her friend. He couldn't imagine losing Kingsley forever. And just as he got his courage to walk across the room to embrace his friend, Lumiere swung open the doors to the dining room with a wild and grand gesture that got everyone's attention. "Dinner is served, Your Majesties!"

"Thank you, Lumiere," said the queen said with a smile. "Everyone, if you could please follow Lumiere into the dining room." Lumiere directed them through.

"Gaston, won't you escort my sisters into the dining room? I am sure they would be honored," said Circe as she walked over to stand near the prince so they could enter the dining room together.

"It would be my pleasure," Gaston replied, cringing as he offered his arm to the sister on the end. *And it will be my pleasure to see you leave this kingdom, never to return*, he thought as he awkwardly walked the three witches into the dining room.

But the strange thing was, just as he thought that, all three of them looked at him and grinned eerily. They heard him. He knew it. They read his thoughts. It was uncanny, and unmistakable, but undeniable They *were* witches. But it was the oddest thing; they looked as if they wanted to help him. Well, of course they did, when he thought about it. They didn't want their sister to marry the prince any more than he did. Together they would find a way to make sure this marriage never happened. Even if it meant befriending these odd sisters.

CHAPTER XI

A Tale as Old as Time

To Gaston's horror he was seated between Circe's ludicrous sisters. He came to learn their names were Lucinda, Ruby, and Martha, though which witch was which, he didn't know. The dinner went on for ages as Lumiere introduced course after course, enough food that even Gaston was near the point of bursting. Every so often he would see Lumiere glancing over at him, as if he felt bad for Gaston's unfortunate place at the table. Gaston couldn't wait to go downstairs and tell them the rumors about Circe's sisters were true.

"How strange this must be for you in the dining hall, among people you once served," said one of the ghastly-looking sisters. It was true. It was odd to be there with the king and queen, and even with Kingsley, in this setting. It was all so formal, with the large floral arrangements and candles everywhere. With Cogsworth and all of his footmen lined up, standing at attention and waiting to see if any of the guests needed the slightest thing.

"It's even more uncomfortable, I think, to be served by people I consider to be my friends," he said.

"Speaking of friends, how sad you must be. The prince hasn't said a word to you all evening. I don't think he's even looked in your direction during dinner," said the witch on his left. That was true. But Kingsley did smile at him when they were in the drawing room, and that was all Gaston needed. He knew in his heart his friend was happy to see him again.

"Yes, I wonder if Circe hasn't poisoned him against you," said the witch to his right, who clearly didn't mind breaking the rules of etiquette.

One of the things Francis had imparted to Gaston during his crash course in court etiquette while helping him dress was that it was improper to talk across the table during formal dinner parties. Guests were expected to take their cue from the queen. If she was talking to the person to her left, then so did everyone else at the table. And once she switched to speaking to the person on her right, everyone followed suit. Which meant, to Gaston's dismay he spent the entire meal only speaking to Circe's frightful sisters.

"Come now, I would think coming from a family such as yours, so old and so well respected, that you would know how dinners like this worked," said Gaston, happy with himself that he remembered Francis's lesson.

"Are you scolding us, Gaston? Are you such the gentleman now that you would comment on our lack of decorum?" said the witch to his right.

"Not at all, my lady. I was simply giving a reasonable explanation as to why the prince hasn't yet spoken to me this evening." He wondered when this wretched dinner would end and he would be released from this torment, for it was clear that is what these women were doing, tormenting him, and taking far too much delight in doing so.

When the witches weren't whispering to each other, they were chatting away at him. Needling, and prying, and laughing shrilly in his ears. But the witch was correct. Kingsley didn't look at him once throughout the entire meal. And he wondered if the skeletal-looking witches in wigs, with far too much makeup on their faces, were correct that the accursed Circe had been filling Kingsley's head with lies about him, too. Maybe she had already told Kingsley he needed to send him away. One of the things he remembered from the stories of his childhood was that witches rarely, if ever, told the truth. So in all likelihood Circe was probably lying. But what did that mean for her sisters? Were they lying, too, or was this one of those rare occasions where they told the truth. He wasn't sure what to think except that believing Circe's sisters made it easier to plot against her.

As he sat there through endless courses and bewildering conversation, he wondered how these could be Circe's actual sisters. He thought they were frightful when he first saw them in the garden, but now, in the dining room with the candles blazing, he was faced with their true horror. Their faces were painted white, caked so thickly they looked as though they never washed them and just reapplied the makeup, layer over layer, creating a cracked effect. They looked like weathered glaze on a neglected doll's face. And it was alarming how thin they were, like skeletons: all bones, skin, eyes, and elaborate hairdos, with feathers that kept swishing across his face when they turned their heads. Lumiere kept giggling to himself when he saw Gaston batting the feathers out of his face or dodging a pointy elbow while trying to eat his soup. Gaston would laugh about it, too, if only he weren't so miserable. Perhaps he would laugh when he told the tale to his friends downstairs.

"I imagine your friends Lumiere and Francis, and perhaps even Mr. Cogsworth, will have already told them the story before you see them next," said one of the witches.

Gaston was abashed, forgetting the witches could hear his thoughts. It had been clear since the moment he met them. It wasn't as if he had been in the company of many witches, that he knew of at any rate, but he knew enough about them from the Book of Fairy Tales, and he was becoming increasingly convinced these might very well be the witches from those tales. Indeed, they seemed to resemble the witches from Snow White's story. The very witches who led her stepmother Grimhilde down the path of darkness and ruin. Nevertheless, he was embarrassed. It was one thing thinking something rude even if it was true. It was another having your secret thoughts shared without intention. He didn't know quite what to say except to make his apology. "I beg your pardon."

"We know people make fun of us, Gaston. We make fun of all of you, too," said the witch to his left.

"I suppose we're all even, then," he said, looking over at Kingsley and Circe. It was the first time he let his gaze linger upon them, and he wished he hadn't. His friend seemed very much in love with her, giving her kisses and feeding her little sweets off his own plate.

"We're not sure that's true," said one of the witches, taking his attention away from the happy couple. At first he thought she was remarking on how he said they were even, but then he realized she was reading his thoughts again.

"You don't think he loves her? Can't she read minds like you do?" he asked under his breath, so no one else would hear.

"Not when it's important," one of them hissed.

"Not when she needs it most," said another.

"Not when she's being stubborn!" they said together, much more loudly than he expected.

"I see," he said, looking around to see if everyone was looking at them. They had only gotten the attention of Mr. Cogsworth, which surprised him, and it was likely because the majordomo was always on constant alert. That was one of his jobs, to see things others did not. But everyone else at the table seemed to be too engrossed in their own conversations to notice. Without realizing it, one of the sisters started talking again.

"He loves aspects of her. He loves her beauty and that she comes from a great family, and he loves that she will pass these things along to their children, should they ever have any," said the witch on the end.

"But he doesn't truly love her. He doesn't know

her. He doesn't see her greatness, her intelligence, her talent," said the witch to his left, her eyes bulging from her blackened eye sockets fearfully.

"She doesn't see him clearly. She only sees there is love, which is displaced. She doesn't see that he loves how her virtues will reflect upon him," said the witch farthest away from him.

"I could say the same about you, ladies. I don't think you see the prince clearly," he said as the footmen started gathering the last of the dessert plates. Gaston hoped this was the final course and he would soon be released from his torture. He had read about the different circles of the Underworld, each of them being worse than the other, and decided being stuck with the Odd Sisters would be the most unendurable fate imaginable.

"Perhaps. But would it really work in your favor if we approved of him? Shouldn't you be focusing your efforts on talking your friend out of this marriage?" said the witch to his left, and before he could answer the infernal woman's question, they just started chattering away at him again.

"Your wish has come true at last, Gaston. It looks as though you will be released from our company. Behold." The witch on the left gestured to Lumiere, who stood at the front of the room preparing to make his announcement.

"Ladies are welcome to join the queen in the drawing room while the gentlemen partake of port and cigars here," he said with a flourish of his hands.

Gaston and all the gentlemen stood up with the ladies, waiting until they were all out of the room before taking their seats again. Gaston noticed the men clustering near the king and prince rather than going back to their original seats, so Gaston decided he would do the same. But by the time he got there, the prince stood up again. "Excuse me, fine gentlemen, but I fear I must leave you to your port and cigars. I cannot be away from my dearest Circe. I trust the company of the king will be more than satisfactory." He looked at Gaston for the first time since they first saw each other before dinner. Gaston had always been able to read Kingsley, but he couldn't make out the look on his face in that moment. Was it sadness? He wasn't sure. He went to stand so he could follow his friend, wondering if maybe he wasn't trying to signal for him to take his leave so they could finally talk, but the king stopped him.

"No, my boy, stay here with us. I daresay you have been too much in the company of chattering women. Stay, and have a drink with us," said the king, laughing.

"Perhaps you're right, Your Majesty" said Gaston, joining in the laughter.

The last thing Gaston wanted was being cornered by Circe's odd sisters in the drawing room. If he was going to plot with those fiendish witches, he didn't need Circe catching on. There was nothing he could do about having to talk with them at dinner, but if he were seen speaking with them in the drawing room as well, Circe would be sure to know they were up to something. He could only hope they wouldn't pursue him in the ballroom.

After drinks in the dining room, the men joined the ladies in the drawing room briefly before Lumiere swung open the french doors that led to the garden and beckoned dramatically for the party to gather on the terrace. Below, they saw a multitude of open carriages crossing the stone bridge. It was time for their intimate gathering to be turned into a gala affair, with lords, ladies, kings, and queens from various lands, some far and some near, all there to celebrate the prince's engagement, and to see the woman he was to marry. Circe and the prince stood closest to the terrace railing, waving to all their guests as fireworks exploded in the sky overhead.

"Come, let's welcome our guests," said the queen, taking the king's arm and motioning for Circe and the prince to follow them. Lumiere led all of them to the ballroom. It was glowing with candles sparkling from the chandelier and wall sconces. Gaston had never truly looked at this room before. He ran through it many times as a child, but he never lingered, never really saw it. It was a vast marble room lined with marble pillars that were accented with gold and draped with red silk bunting that matched the prince's frock coat. The ceiling was magnificent, painted to look like a celestial dreamscape, the chandelier hanging in its center. To the left was an orchestra near the piano, and to the right was a dais with thrones for the royal family to sit upon. And around the perimeter of the room were small round tables, with chairs for guests to take their repose upon between dances. But what Gaston loved most was the wall of windows and french doors that looked out across the entire kingdom, with a breathtaking view of the night sky, still sparking with fireworks.

The royal family took their seats on their thrones to await the arrival of their guests while the fireworks created bursts of colors in the ballroom. Gaston and the others who had joined the family for dinner took seats at tables closest to the royal family while Mr. Cogsworth stood at the entrance announcing the guests as they arrived, all of them paying their respects to the royal family and congratulating the prince and Circe on their engagement.

Once everyone was assembled, Cogsworth gave a cue to Lumiere, who rang a small brass bell he produced from his pocket. A legion of footmen entered, rolling a cart with an enormous cake. It was constructed to look like the castle itself, with little marzipan figures of the royal family. It was intricately decorated down to every detail, including the gardens, which even had little woodland creatures. Everyone gasped as the cake rolled into the room. It was a thing of art. Moments later, more footmen marched into the room with large trays of champagne they handed to all the guests. Once everyone had a glass in their hand, Lumiere made another announcement.

"And now the king would like to make a toast to the happy couple."

The king and queen stood from their thrones and smiled at their guests. The queen looked stunning in her red velvet gown embroidered with delicate lace and fine beadwork that cascaded from her bodice down the length of her voluminous skirt. The king was also wearing red, a red velvet frock coat with black epaulettes and gold buttons with black trousers. They were an impressive pair, imperious and majestic, and so happy to be celebrating their son's engagement.

"It is my and Her Majesty's honor to welcome you all here, and to lay our blessings on the heads of our son and his betrothed and wish them great joy in their forthcoming marriage. Let us raise our glasses to the future king and queen."

"To their happiness!" said the queen, and everyone following suit. "And with that, I declare the ball officially open!"

Cogsworth and the footmen whisked the cake to a corner of the room near trestle tables laden with refreshments as the prince and Circe stood and made their way to the center of the ballroom. The orchestra started to play. None of this felt real to Gaston, and just for a moment he was swept up in the pageantry, dizzied by the glamour and beauty of the evening.

The prince wore a red fitted frock coat, not unlike Gaston's, but trimmed in gold. His long auburn hair hung to his shoulders, and his blue eyes flashed with joy when he reached his hand out to Circe. Circe wore a silver dress with a tight bodice and full skirt, embroidered with small sparkling beads that glistened in the candlelight. The couple looked enraptured with each other as the prince put one hand around her waist and took her hand in his other, and they glided to the music that swelled around them. Everyone in the room clapped as they couple danced, spinning in circles and laughing, and soon other couples joined in circling around them.

Gaston sat at a small table alone, watching his friend dance. It felt like he was in some sort of dream as the other dancers floated around them. The ladies' dresses looked like blossoming flowers, reminding him of the conversation he had with Circe in the rose garden. His heart ached to see them dancing together so happily. Was he ready to ruin his friend's chance for true happiness?

"Circe is ready to ruin yours," said a voice that made his skin crawl. When Gaston looked up, he saw Circe's strange sisters looming over him. He quickly stood and smiled weakly, hoping they weren't looking for a dance partner.

"May we have this dance?" said the sister in the

middle, and Gaston's stomach dropped. Was there no end to his humiliation this evening? First at dinner, and now in the ballroom; was he never to be free of these women? It was too much. Not a word from Kingsley all evening, and now this? Dancing!

"How could I possibly pick which ravishing enchantress to dance with first?" he asked, rolling his eyes. He looked pleadingly at Francis, who was standing at the trestle tables handing out cake and champagne to the guests.

"You may have the honor of dancing with Lucinda first. She is the oldest. She should have the first dance," said two of the sisters, urging Gaston and Lucinda toward the other dancers. To his relief, Gaston saw Francis running in their direction with a slice of cake wobbling on a plate as he rushed over to them.

"Gaston, here is that cake you wanted," Francis said with a wink.

"Cake? You're serving the cake?" asked the two pushy sisters in unison, grabbing Lucinda by the arm. "I'm sorry, Gaston, I know you're heartbroken, but we can't dance now! It's time for cake." With that, they dragged Lucinda off, skittering their way toward the cake table.

"Thank you, Francis, you saved me. Who knew witches liked cake so much," said Gaston, watching the witches push the other guests out of their way who were standing at the cake table.

"Witches, sir?" asked Francis, looking on in horror as two of the sisters grabbed fistfuls of cake and shoved them into their mouths, while Lucinda was biting the head off a marzipan prince.

"Figure of speech. But they are odious women. Just look at them." Gaston rubbed his head in frustration.

"It's not my place to have an opinion," said Francis, looking as though he dreaded going back to his duties.

"Not while you're upstairs, anyway," said Gaston, making Francis laugh.

"I'm sorry you're having such a miserable time, Gaston. But if it's any consolation, you really are the most handsome man here," said Francis, making Gaston smile. Just then, Cogsworth appeared.

"Francis, the refreshment table is being woefully neglected. Please return to your post," he said with his hands on his hips. Francis stood there for a few moments, as if to muster enough strength to return to his post. He sighed deeply before turning to leave as the witches popped marzipan animals into each other's mouths and cackling.

"It's my fault, Mr. Cogsworth, I kept him talking," Gaston said, shooting Francis an apologetic smile. "You can hardly blame him, look at the mess Circe's sisters are making."

"Is there anything else you need, *sir?*" asked Mr. Cogsworth, stiff as ever.

"No, Mr. Cogsworth, you've been very kind," he said rather sarcastically.

To Gaston's relief, Circe's sisters were distracted for most of the evening by the cake. It was an unlikely distraction, but then again, they were exceedingly odd. It was strange how no one seemed to notice their antics, munching handfuls of cake, shooting daggers at the prince, whispering behind their fans, and laughing uncontrollably. At one point they seemed to be having a contest to see who could eat the most cake. No one paid them the slightest bit of attention. It was as if there was an unspoken understanding to ignore them. So that is what Gaston decided to do as well.

What he couldn't ignore was how happy Kingsley seemed as he danced with his duplicitous witch of a fiancée. At first Gaston wondered if it was right to ruin the life his friend might have with this woman he seemed to love so well, but as the evening wore on, Gaston became angry and bitter. Circe was trying to send him away, away from his best friend, the only family and home he knew, all because of some vision that she didn't even fully understand. He felt sick watching her dance with the prince, hiding behind her smile. It was all fakery, all smoke and mirrors. She was a pretender, plotting to rid herself of her competition. She had said so herself: the prince loved no one more than he loved Gaston.

As he sat there brooding, wondering if he was right, wondering if this was all a charade, he caught sight of Kingsley the prince standing alone near the tall paned windows, looking out at the view. It was the first time all night Circe hadn't been at his side. She was talking with the king and queen, likely charming them just as she beguiled everyone that evening with her seeming sweetness and grace. This was his chance. He got up from his table and slowly made his way across the ballroom. He had no idea what he was going to say. That didn't matter. He was going to be reunited with his friend at last. He rounded the room, taking care to avoid Circe and the royal family for fear Circe would intervene.

Just as he was about to approach, Kingsley turned around, as if he knew Gaston was behind him, and smiled to see his friend standing there. But Kingsley's expression quickly turned to horror. Gaston didn't understand. Why was he looking at him like this? Had Circe been weaving her web of lies all evening, whispering in his ear? Was his friend ensnared in her trap already? Was it too late for Gaston and Kingsley to have the life they dreamed of? Gaston felt his heart breaking, not understanding why his friend was looking at him like this, and even more confused when his horror turned to laughter. Gaston stood there silent and hurt, wondering why Kingsley the prince was laughing at him. Did he look like a fool after all? Were his thoughts so easily read upon is face? But then he understood. The prince wasn't looking at him. He was looking behind him, at the Odd Sisters running toward Gaston, their hands, faces, and dresses covered with frosting.

"Gaston! Gaston!" they screeched as they skittered closer, their faces full of expectation. "Oh, Gaston, it is time for our dance!" Gaston faced many beasts over the years, but the fear he felt as the Odd Sisters scrambled in his direction filled him with loathing. "You promised us a dance!" they said, cackling like the witches they were.

"I did no such thing," Gaston protested. "Perhaps you would like to go to your rooms and freshen up." He couldn't understand why no one there seemed to notice what a spectacle they were making of themselves.

"That is Circe's doing. She's enchanted us. We could scream the castle down and no one would notice or remember. No one of any consequence, anyway," said the witch he was sure was Lucinda.

"I see . . ." But before Gaston could finish his thought, he saw the prince being swept through the doors onto the terrace by Circe and his family.

"What's going on?" He looked around to see everyone following the royal family.

"The candlestick made an announcement," said one of the witches.

"Candlestick?" he asked, confused. What was she was talking about?

"Candelabra, not candlestick, you fool! And he's not one yet!" said one of the other witches.

"What are you going on about now? This is just too perfect. I'm in league with addlebrained witches who think the candlesticks make announcements. Next thing you'll see is dancing dishes."

"Perhaps we will, one day. But it's not you who will see it." The witches screeched with laughter.

"Shhh, Ruby, don't give away all our secrets."

"Can you please behave normally and stop talking your gibberish just for one moment?" He'd had enough. He wasn't going to suffer their insanity for one more moment. It was bad enough when they were needling and teasing him, but now they were just spouting pure nonsense. He followed the other guests onto the terrace, leaving the cake-stained witches behind to fight about dancing cutlery.

When he got onto the terrace, he saw why everyone was there. The queen's pavilion was sparkling like a jewel in the distance, casting dancing lights upon the castle and its grounds. His heart hurt seeing how much Kingsley loved Circe. He felt defeated and alone, not sure what to do. Should he give up and let Circe drive him away, or fight to live his life as he wanted? He wouldn't decide just now. He would sleep, and try to think about it more clearly in the morning. He would slip out while everyone was watching the lights. It was too painful seeing the pavilion lit up, too vivid were the memories of the days when everything began to crumble, changing his life forever.

The lights looked like dancing ghosts, flickering and moving with the breeze. Gaston was overcome by his own ghosts, the mother he never knew, the father he missed with all of his heart, and most of all the life he and Kingsley imagined for themselves when they were young.

Chapter XII

The Magic Mirror

The next day Gaston woke in his chamber to a knock on the door. It was Francis, holding a package wrapped in brown paper and tied with twine. Gaston was still exhausted from the night before, barely opening his eyes when Francis came into the room.

Gaston did his best to shake off his grogginess and say a tired hello.

"What's this, Francis? Who is this from?" he asked, turning it over to see if there was a note.

"It doesn't say, sir. It was dropped off this morning, and the messenger said it was to be given to you." Francis looked like he was bursting to talk about how ludicrously Circe's sisters had been acting the night before, but they were the last people Gaston wanted to talk about then.

"How strange. I bet it's from the prince," said Gaston. "Thank you, Francis." He reached to throw off his coverlet, almost forgetting he wasn't dressed.

"Would you like breakfast in your room this morning, or will you be joining the others in the dining room? I understand you are rather fond of eggs. Shall I bring some to go along with your coffee, sir?" asked Francis.

"I thought I'd have breakfast with the staff downstairs before I headed back to my estate." Gaston had had his fill of fancy dining rooms, pretending he was a gentleman, and, most of all, Circe and her sisters.

"The prince thought that might be your plan and said if it were so, to let you know he would be happy to join you for breakfast downstairs before your ride after breakfast," Francis said.

"Ride? What ride? Never mind. Thank you, Francis."

"Shall I draw you a bath before I go, sir?"

"Good gravy, Francis, no. I can draw my own bath, thank you." He wasn't trying to be rude to Francis. He just wasn't used to being waited upon by people he considered his friends. Gaston wasn't used to be waited upon by anyone, for that matter. And he was surprised Kingsley wanted to see him. What was this ride they were going on later this afternoon? He wasn't aware they had plans to go riding. Gaston felt ignored by Kingsley the night before, and it had been a nightmare being stuck with Circe's sisters, having to endure not only them but Circe's duplicity. Maybe Kingsley was just as disappointed they'd had no time together the previous evening and was making up for it. Gaston supposed he would find out. But that was no reason to take it out on poor Francis, who had been nothing but kind and supportive throughout this entire charade.

"I'm sorry, Francis. I'm not myself yet. I never am before my coffee, and last night was a doozy. I fear haven't quite recovered. Can you ever forgive me?"

"There's nothing to forgive. Your coffee is on the desk, sir."

"You're my hero, Francis. Thank you."

"If there's nothing else, I will go to the kitchen and tell Chef Bouche to make plenty of eggs for your breakfast. Five dozen, is it?"

"Yes, Francis. Thank you," he said, longing for his coffee, which he went straight for the moment Francis left the room.

Gaston was happy Kingsley was going to join him downstairs for breakfast. Hopefully he wasn't planning to bring Circe. The last thing Gaston wanted was to sit down to another meal with Circe and the prince, seeing her fawn all over him, pretending like she wasn't trying to end their friendship. But then again, it was probably beneath her to have breakfast downstairs. Well, at least Kingsley's new lofty ways weren't keeping him from having a meal with his old friends.

There hadn't been one moment the previous night when he was able to speak with the prince alone, so he was looking forward to this ride later and hoping he would be able to talk Kingsley into going out for a drink at the tavern afterward. He had to think carefully about how he was going to handle things with the prince. It was a delicate matter, telling someone they've picked the wrong person to marry, and he wasn't quite sure what to say. He could just be honest and tell him what Circe had said in the rose garden, but what if Kingsley believed her vision nonsense? The Kingsley he knew didn't believe in ghosts, magic spells, or curses, but Gaston had no idea what Kingsley believed in now. For all Gaston knew, Circe had him believing in all sorts of things. No, he had to calculate exactly what to say.

As he drank his coffee trying to figure out the best way to handle things, he remembered the package. It was sitting on the table near the double doors leading out to the terrace. He opened it, surprised to find it was a hand mirror.

"What a strange gift. What was Kingsley thinking?" he said, looking at his reflection. It was hard to look at himself; he looked so much like his father now that he was older. These days, he did his best to avoid mirrors altogether.

"The gift is from us, Gaston," said a voice from the mirror. Gaston dropped the mirror in shock, causing

it to crack. He could see one of Circe's sisters in the mirror looking at him with an insipid smile.

"Others have tried to break our mirrors, Gaston. They've even tried burying them in dark forests, or giving them away, but they always return good as new," said the witch from the mirror, who he was sure was Lucinda.

"What witchery is this? What devilry? What do you want?" Gaston flung the mirror on the bed as the woman laughed at him.

"We want you to bring your friend to our house in three days' time," she said with an evil grin. *"There he will find Circe in rags, caring for the pigs."*

"I see. And how are you going to get Circe to do this? I presume you're not a pig-farming family. Why would she agree to this farce?" he asked, then recoiled in shock as he picked up the mirror again and saw it was no longer cracked. He knew these women were witches, but he hadn't really taken them very seriously with all of their cake munching and making fools of themselves at the ball. He wasn't sure what to make of this. How powerful were these witches?

"*More powerful than you will ever know, Gaston. And you would do well not to cross us. So please, let us help you, and in doing so you will help us.*" Lucinda looked more serious than Gaston had seen her yet. She wasn't the fool he thought she was.

"*We will tell Circe if the prince truly loves her, then it won't matter if he finds her mucking it with the pigs, and since she wants nothing more than to prove us wrong she will agree,*" said the wicked woman as another one of Circe's strange sisters appeared in the mirror to chime in.

"*We think if you do this for us we will all get our wish, and your friend won't want to marry our sister.*"

"I have a feeling you intended for me to hear you in the rose garden," said Gaston, smiling at the three witches.

"*You're smarter than we thought, Gaston,*" said one of the women.

"*Yes, very interesting,*" said the other.

"*Not sure if that will do,*" said the third, right before the mirror went back to his own reflection.

"Vile women!" he said, turning the mirror over. He hated having to deal with these witches, and he was sure he couldn't trust them. But what choice would he have if Kingsley didn't see sense?

After changing, Gaston went around the back to the courtyard that led to the servants' hall entrance. And just as he hoped, the prince was standing there waiting for him. This was the first time he'd seen the prince alone, without being surrounded by a room full of people. It was a bright, sunny morning, and the sky was blue with fat white clouds that looked like someone had painted in the sky just for them. When Gaston saw his friend standing there, his heart began to race. He didn't expect to feel so nervous to be with him alone. Even though that's exactly what he had been hoping for since he first saw him the night before.

"My friend! My dear friend. I am so happy to see you," said Gaston, wrapping his arms around the prince. Kingsley looked even more handsome than he had the night before. Although maybe a little worse for wear, having been up all night and not shaving yet that morning.

"Gaston! Look at you. I barely recognized you last night. You are much changed. Mrs. Potts warned me, but I couldn't picture it, not until I saw you. You look so much like your father. It's no wonder Francis and almost everyone else in the kingdom has a crush on you." He returned Gaston's hug.

"I see you're already dressed for riding. Perfect. I've told them we will be out all day. Just you and I. We have so much to catch up on." This was the Kingsley Gaston was hoping to see. His heart felt lighter.

"Indeed we do. There is so much I want to talk with you about," he said, stopping himself for now. He decided it was better to talk once they were away from the castle.

"Circe tells me there is something important you wanted to tell me. I hope it's nothing too serious," said the prince with a smile. "I hope you like her, Gaston. I know she likes you."

"Does she? That's interesting." Gaston was unable to hide his surprise and disdain.

"What is it? Don't be jealous, Gaston, please. If you had come along with me like I wanted you could have helped me choose the perfect girl, but you decided to stay home. Now we both have to live with my choice. But she is beautiful, isn't she? The most beautiful woman I have ever seen."

"What else do you like about her?" asked Gaston, sincerely wanting to know.

"What else is there? She will look good on the throne and give me beautiful heirs."

Gaston winced. He had felt guilty, plotting to ruin his friend's chance at a happy life, but it seemed this was no love match after all. "So this is my punishment? You're going to marry the daughter of a pig farmer just to spite me?" Gaston didn't mean to blurt it out just like that. What was he thinking?

"What are you talking about? She's related to the Old King." The prince wasn't taking him seriously. Gaston knew his friend. He saw it on his face. There was no way he would ever believe the woman he loved could be a keeper of pigs. Convincing him of this was going to be hard. He should have waited until he could take Kingsley to see Circe with the pigs for himself.

"I wonder. I heard she and her vile sisters won't say who their parents are. Are you sure she's related to the Old King? Circe and her sisters don't live far from here, I'm told. I bet if we paid them a surprise visit, we would find her tending the pigs."

"That's poppycock and you know it! Come on, Gaston, you're just jealous I am marrying the most beautiful woman in the land. You want her for yourself!" While it was true he was jealous, he didn't want Circe for himself. He wanted her and her wicked sisters as far from their kingdom as possible. What would life be like for his friend under the rule of such witches?

"That's not true, Kingsley! I still feel the same way I did the day before you left for your tour. Remember what we said to each other? Remember our wish?"

"You know that dream is impossible, Gaston. You know I have to get married." The prince looked deeply disappointed. It didn't even occur to Gaston that he might be as disappointed as he was. Or maybe he was simply upset Gaston wasn't just falling into line and putting on a good face.

"I know you have to get married, Kingsley, but it doesn't have to be *her*. She's a liar! She and her sisters are witches. I promise you, she is not what she seems." Gaston stood there for a moment after he said those words, waiting for his friend to reply, but the prince just looked at him in silence. Gaston wasn't sure if he was taking it all in or if he was going the throw fisticuffs.

"You're honestly telling me Circe and her sisters are pig-farming witches?"

"I am! Who knows, maybe Circe takes after her namesake and the pigs are ex-lovers, or enemies. I haven't the slightest idea how the minds of witches work."

"Well, we shall see." Kingsley began walking away.

"Where are you going?" Gaston called out.

"To confront Circe!"

Later that day Francis gave Gaston a message from Kingsley saying he still expected to see Gaston that afternoon, and he was to meet him at the tavern in the village before they went riding. He had no idea how the talk had gone with Circe. It was typical Kingsley, cryptic and bewildering. What Gaston was sure of was that no matter how it went, Kingsley would want to go on as though nothing happened. That was his way.

When Gaston arrived at the tavern, he was greeted with great cheers by Old Mr. Higgins and the usual regulars. Kingsley wasn't there yet, so he ordered a drink for himself and had a chat with Mr. Higgins. It had been some nights since he ducked in to say hello to the old crew, and he was happy to be back.

"What's this I hear, Gaston? Too good for us now, attending fancy balls at the castle?" said Mr. Higgins.

"It was my best friend's engagement party. I could hardly duck out of that, no matter how much I wanted to," said Gaston, laughing heartily.

"And here we thought you had forsaken us now that the prince has returned," said Mr. Higgins. But Gaston did wonder if there were others in the village who thought he had given up on his friendships with all of them now that Kingsley the prince had returned, or worse yet, given up on his promise to hunt the beast.

"Of course I haven't forsaken you, you old fool! A promise is a promise! Besides, who else in all the land can kill the Beast of Gévaudan?"

"Good man!" said the baker, raising his beer with such enthusiasm it splashed all over the floorboards.

"We knew you wouldn't let that fancy lot go to your head," said Mr. Higgins.

"To Gaston! The hero of our village. The only man in this kingdom brave enough to hunt down the beast and mount its ugly head on my wall!" said Higgins.

Everyone in the tavern cheered. "To Gaston!" Gaston threw his head back and laughed as the other patrons all gathered around him offering to buy him another drink, but he wouldn't hear of it. Tonight, he was going to treat them. He owed it to them. It was they, after all, who kept his spirits up when Kingsley was away. And it was they who showed him his true quality. These fine men truly admired and respected him, and saw his worth. And he was happy to be in their company again.

"Drinks are on me, Higgins! In celebration of the prince's engagement!" Gaston felt happy, and like himself again.

"To the prince!" he said, raising his glass. But no one joined him.

"Sod the prince!" Higgins filled glass after glass, sliding them down the bar to everyone gathered around Gaston.

"To Gaston, our hero returned!" Higgins said as everyone raised their tankards and slammed them together so hard they spilled ale all over the floor. Gaston was in his element. It was such a change from the night before. He was in a place where he felt like he belonged. He wasn't putting on airs, or wondering what to say or how to act, or having to dodge Circe's sisters. The only triplets he cared to see ever again were the blond beauties Claudette, Laurette, and Paulette, the barmaids who helped Mr. Higgins out when the tavern was busy.

"Where are your lovely barmaids this evening?" He was surprised not to see them, with the tavern so packed at this early hour.

"They haven't been in the past few days. I thought perhaps you had eloped with Claudette, and the other two were home crying. Those women adore you, Gaston! When are you going to settle down like your friend and get married? There isn't a woman alive who wouldn't want to marry you," said Higgins, laughing.

"That Claudette and her sisters are the most beautiful girls in the village, besides Belle," the baker chimed in.

"You could easily have your pick, Gaston. There isn't a man alive more deserving than you! You're the strongest, most handsome, bravest man in the village. Just like your father was before you! You are the best, and you deserve the best! You only need to say the word, and you'd have the prettiest girl anyone has ever seen," said Higgins.

"Not prettier than my Circe," said the prince, having walked into the tavern without notice. Gaston knew that look on Kingley's face. He wasn't happy. And it seemed he was still going to marry that damnable witch. Gaston slammed a bunch of coins on the bar, demanding another round of drinks.

"Drinks are on me, gentleman! To the prince, and his beautiful bride-to-be!" he said, raising his glass and giving everyone in the tavern a look to say they'd better follow suit, or else.

"Thank you, gentlemen! Thank you." Kingsley

barely cracked a smile. Gaston knew he was in for it.

"She is the most beautiful woman in the village. I'd be jealous if we weren't the very best of friends," said Gaston. He was putting on a show for the other men, hoping to soften Kingsley's edges.

"You're lucky to have such a loyal friend in Gaston!" said one of the men, downing his drink and wiping his face with the back of his hand.

"Gaston is the best hunter in the land! There's not one trophy on this wall that wasn't brought in by Gaston!" said Higgins.

"Well, I've been away for quite some time. Perhaps that will soon change." The prince gave Gaston a look Gaston didn't like. Perhaps Gaston was wrong in his impression when he saw him in the courtyard, this wasn't the Kingsley he remembered after all.

"Right you are, Your Highness! We'll have to make some room!" said Higgins, laughing good-naturedly. But Gaston could tell Old Man Higgins doubted the prince would be bringing in any hunting trophies, let alone enough to rival Gaston. It was well-known Gaston had been besting the prince since they were boys. But it seemed that no longer would do for the prince. Something had changed.

"If you don't mind, gentlemen, I'm going to steal away my friend here. You can fawn over him later. Come on, *friend*," he said curtly, leading Gaston to a table near the fireplace where they could sit alone. They took two chairs that faced each other, and the prince scooted his closer to Gaston so they could talk without being heard.

"I've talked to Circe. She denies your accusations. We are, of course, going on with our plans to get married, Gaston, and you *will* stand by my side. You will be my best man!" Kingsley was talking through gritted teeth and keeping his voice low while eyeing the men at the bar who were looking in their direction.

"And how's that going to work, exactly? Do you think Circe will allow that, with how she feels about me?"

"Allow it? Who is the future king here, Gaston? Besides, I didn't tell her what you said. She needn't know. One day, we will laugh about this. I want to laugh about it now. It's all silly nonsense." It was just like Kingsley to make up his own version of reality, pretending everything normal when it's not. Exactly what he did after Gaston's father was killed. This was all too familiar, and too painful.

"It's not nonsense!"

"Oh, stop it, Gaston. Do you realize I actually believed you? You should have seen her crumbling into tears when I told her we had to call off the wedding, that I couldn't possibly marry someone so low. But honestly, Gaston, just look at her, how could she possibly be the daughter of a pig farmer, let alone a witch? It's laughable."

"I'm the son of a groundskeeper, and I'm pretty handsome," he said boastfully, and rather more loudly than he intended, making everyone in the tavern laugh but annoying Kingsley even more.

"Speaking of which, from this point forward we will say the kills on these walls are mine. Do you understand? Mine! I can't have you being the hero of this village, Gaston. It won't do." Gaston shouldn't have been surprised the prince was acting this way. His father had warned him this might happen, in fact, told him it *would* happen, but he hadn't believed it. All their lives, Kingsley didn't mind if Gaston was better at almost everything. It never mattered. But now, for some reason, it did. All of a sudden, now that he was getting married and closer to becoming the king, he magically had to be the best at everything?

"Isn't it enough you're the prince, Kingsley?"

"Why? Are you jealous of that, too?"

"Kingsley, come on! Every man here knows all these kills are mine."

"If you say something enough times, people will start to believe you. I do it all the time."

"What do you mean, you do it all the time? I have never known you to do that, Kingsley."

"Haven't you? How many times did I say you're my brother and my equal, until finally everyone treated you like my brother and equal?"

"I don't feel like we're equal now."

"I don't blame you for being jealous of all my achievements, Gaston. Just look at these walls!" The prince laughed as he motioned to the walls covered in trophies.

"What's wrong with you? Are you delusional? Everyone knows these are my kills, and I am the best hunter."

"Not anymore! Look, I know you're jealous. And why shouldn't you be? I am marrying Circe. You were overtaken by her beauty and it got the best of you, my friend. You wanted her for yourself, and that's why you made up that silly pig story. But who would want the marry the king of Buttchinland, *the king of nothing*, when she could marry me?" Kingsley's words knocked the wind out of him. It was a low blow, even for him. But Gaston didn't let it show.

"I suppose you're right. Didn't you say we were riding today? Come on, let's ride." Gaston stood up and walked toward the door. He was angry and hurt, but he wasn't going to give Kingsley the satisfaction of letting him know. He was going to show him who was best, even if it meant knocking some sense into him. Maybe then he'd have his old Kingsley back.

"All right, fellas! The prince and I are about to see who is the better rider. Any bets he beats me?"

"I wouldn't take that bet! Not in a million years,

Gaston!" said Higgins. Everyone in the tavern laughed as Gaston swung the doors open with a Lumiere-like flourish, letting the prince walk out of the tavern first.

"Did you hear that, *Your Highness*? Not in a million years!" Gaston was laughing, but both he and the prince were seething as they stood outside the tavern.

"Don't ever treat me like a fool in front of those men, or anyone else again, do you understand me? Never! You may be my best friend, but that's where it ends. I am the best at everything else."

"No matter how many times you say it, that won't make it true," said Gaston as he mounted Noir and took up his reins.

"Let's see who is best!" the prince said as he mounted his horse, and they both took off like a flash.

Gaston rode fast through the woods, looking back to see if his friend was following. He was, a few yards behind him. Kingsley's face was filled with anger as they both rode hard, Gaston easily jumping hedges and splashing through creeks as Kingsley the prince struggled behind him. Gaston had always been a better rider than Kingsley, and he knew it. Gaston steered his horse, weaving through the trees and laughing the entire way. He was better than the prince at everything, he always had been, and at the moment he was enjoying it much more than he should.

Then something happened he did not expect. The sky was darkening. At first Gaston thought a storm was coming, and he looked up, expecting to see large storm clouds looming, but it was something else. An eclipse. It was an eerie sensation, suddenly being enveloped in darkness. Gaston pulled on Noir's reins, coming to a quick stop, realizing where they were. They were right at the cemetery gates where his father was killed. He hadn't been there since his father was put to rest there with his mother.

Gaston stood there at the gate, looking at the statue of his mother beckoning him. Guilt washed over him as he looked at her marble visage, longing to know her, to talk with his father again. Wanting to tell his father he was right about the prince. Wondering how it was he knew. He had so many things he wanted to say to his father, so many questions he would never be able to ask. And he wondered how it was he found himself there, looking at his friend's angry and bewildered face once he finally caught up to him.

"What's going on? Why are we here? Did you plan this?" the prince demanded, dismounting his horse and getting in Gaston's face.

"How could I? I'm not a conjurer." Gaston wondered if there was some sort of magic at work, remembering he had packed the hand mirror in his bag. He wasn't sure why, but now he wondered if it was a mistake.

"I'm not talking about the eclipse, you fool. I'm talking about this place! Why did you bring me here?" Kingsley looked around, peering into the darkness. "What are you playing at, Gaston? Why are we here?"

"I didn't bring you here, Kingsley. And if you call me a fool one more time, we will both see who is better at brawling."

"Is that a threat? Are you threatening your prince?"

"Oh, shut up, Kingsley. What's wrong with you?"

"Circe told me you hold your father's death against me. She said one day one of us will die as result. After everything I have done for you, Gaston, you still won't forgive me? I still can't trust you?"

"It's not true, Kingsley. I don't blame you, I haven't for a long time. She's lying." So this was what this was all about it. She'd told him, and now he was hurt. No wonder he was acting this way.

"Why would she lie, Gaston? Why would she make up something like that? And how would she know about the beast and your father if she didn't have some kind of ability to see . . . things?"

"I thought you didn't believe in witches, Kingsley!"

"I don't know what to believe, except she knows things, Gaston. I don't think that makes her a witch."

"Everyone knows my father was killed by the beast. It is a very well-known story in these lands. They know we were there when it happened. And I didn't make it a secret I was upset with you back then, did I? We were kids, Kingsley, we were both foolish. It wasn't either of our faults."

"Is that how you really feel, Gaston? Then what is this about? Is it jealousy? I promise you, nothing has to change between us."

"Things have already changed. *You've changed*. You come home insisting you're the best at everything, calling me a fool at every opportunity, and you're marrying a woman who is trying to send me away. You can't marry her, Kingsley; she and her sisters are dangerous. You've seen her sisters; how long will it be until Circe starts showing her true nature? Do you want to live your life in a den of witches? She's making things up, telling lies about me. You've never let anyone break up our friendship, no matter how hard they tried. Don't let Circe do this to us."

"Why would she make this up? Why would she do it?"

"She told me why. She knows you love me more than you love her."

"She said that?" Gaston could see Kingsley was surprised.

"She did. She's trying to get rid of me, Kingsley. She knows I know the truth about her family." He felt guilty, but the fact was, her family was dangerous. The truth was more insidious than a story about her being some kind of pig farmer's daughter. This was lunacy, that his friend would be more affronted by her caring for pigs than being in a coven of witches.

"She really said that? That I love you more than I love her? Then she *can* see into our hearts," said the prince, looking off. "And that means I can't trust either of you." But before Gaston could defend himself, he heard something in the darkness. A crunching noise, twigs being broken under feet. The sound was coming closer and closer, and then he saw them, four pairs of eyes glowing in the darkness.

"What's that? Is it the beast?" The prince was panicking, spinning every which way trying to see where the danger was coming from.

"Shhh! No. I think it's wolves." Gaston slowly took his blunderbuss from his saddlebag.

"Stand behind me, between the horses. Go! Now!" Gaston said through gritted teeth, pointing the weapon at the advancing wolves. They were in a semicircle, moving closer and closer. Gaston took a handful of lead balls from his inside pocket and loaded them into his gun. He aimed his blunderbuss and took his shot, hitting all four of the wolves in the spray. As he turned to tell the prince they were safe, he saw another wolf coming out of the mist. It was sinister and large, snarling at him.

Without even thinking, Gaston dropped the blunderbuss and grabbed his hatchet from his belt as the wolf jumped at him, knocking him to the ground with a tremendous force. The wolf snapped its jaws at him over and over, trying to bite his face as Gaston held it off by holding the wooden handle of the ax on each end and pressing it against the wolf's throat. It took all his strength to keep the wolf from biting him, and there were moments when Gaston worried he wouldn't be able to hold it off for much longer. Its snarling teeth bared and snapped over and over, its face so close to his he could smell its foul breath.

He pushed the creature with all his might, trying to get out from under it, hoping to get some advantage so he could use the ax to kill it, but the wolf was too strong and too large. When he was finally able to see the creature clearly and look it in the eyes, he knew what it was. This was no ordinary wolf. It was the Beast of Gévaudan. He struggled beneath its tremendous weight, flailing, using everything within him to overtake the beast, but without warning he heard his blunderbuss go off, and he and the creature were pelted with rocks. Blood exploded as the rocks punctured them.

The beast looked up from Gaston, who was lying in the dirt, covered in blood from the numerous shots, and without warning pounced on the prince. The two went tumbling into one of the horses. Gaston struggled to get back on his feet as he watched the horse rear up and smash its hooves into the creature, nearly missing the prince. Kingsley rolled out of the way and tried to find anything he could reload into the blunderbuss while the beast was stunned. He scrambled backward as fast as he could until he reached the trunk of a tree, where he sat in terror watching the horrid creature take heavy steps toward him.

The blood poured into Kingsley's eyes as he closed them tightly against the encroaching beast. He couldn't see Gaston standing there, now with his loaded bow pointed right at the beast's head. Without even realizing he had actually taken the shot, Gaston saw the beast slump over the prince. At last, it was dead. Gaston pulled his friend out from under the creature, slapping his face and shaking him.

"Kingsley, Kingsley! Wake up! Please, please don't be dead."

"Don't be such a ninny. Of course I'm not dead." They both laughed as they embraced tightly, until Kingsley stepped back and took Gaston by the shoulders. "You saved my life, Gaston. I know now I can trust you. I'm sorry I faltered."

"We saved each other, Kingsley. We avenged my parents, together, as I knew we would." The beast was dead. The weight of avenging his parents was no longer suffocating him. No longer consuming his every thought. This was what he had wished for, to destroy the beast together with his friend, putting everything that happened when they were boys behind them. Gaston had his friend back. They had a chance to start over. To have the life they always wanted.

If only Circe wasn't standing in his way.

"Both of your parents? What do you mean?"

"I'll tell you later, my brother, I promise. But let's

agree we can trust each other, and we owe each other our lives. No matter what happens we will always be brothers, and you won't let Circe send me away," said Gaston.

Three days later, Gaston took the prince to see Circe at the house she shared with her odd sisters, with its witch's-cap roof and round windows. Gaston wasn't sure if Kingsley finally believed his darling Circe could truly be a pig farmer's daughter, or if he just wanted to prove to Gaston the rumors were untrue. Whatever his reasons, Gaston was happy he agreed to make the trip.

It was a strange sort of place, odd and foreboding with its stained-glass windows depicting fairy-tale images of beasts, a dragon breathing green fire, a sinister-looking apple, and other strange images that seemed to hold special meaning to the witches. There was even a cat who looked eerily like his own cat sitting in the garden near a lone apple tree, a tree that didn't look like it belonged there. Gaston wouldn't have been able to explain why it didn't look like it should be there if he could, but it just looked wrong, somehow out of place.

In the front of the house was a garden, and off to the side was a pen for the pigs. That was where they saw Circe. Just as the Odd Sisters had said she would be. The bottom of her simple white dress was caked with mud. Her hair looked dull, and her cheeks were flushed with hard work. She must have sensed them looking at her while she fed the pigs. Gaston could see how saddened she was by the look of disgust on the prince's face. She looked stricken with horror and shame. Gaston stayed with the horses and let the prince approach her; he couldn't bring himself to stand at his friend's side while he defamed and debased her and accused her of lying. Gaston saw Circe's heart break in that moment; the love of her life was ending their relationship because he thought she was lowly, that she was beneath him. And now her beauty was somehow tarnished in his eyes. All because Gaston and Circe's sisters tricked the prince into believing she was the daughter of a pig farmer.

Gaston's heart began to race, and he felt the heat rise in his face, realizing in that moment his friend Kingsley was truly horrible and that he himself was no better. They were bound to each other now, even more than before. Gaston had lied and let Kingsley shame and break Circe's heart. This was who he was now. Who his friend was. And he hated that this was who Kingsley had been for longer than Gaston would like to admit. Their lives would never be the same; he felt it in his core as Circe's sisters looked at him through the windows of their strange house, smiling at him, their grins wide and wicked while they danced and sang with joy because they had gotten their wish.

It made Gaston sick to see Circe fall to her knees and cry while the prince walked away as if she were a trifling piece of trash. Gaston had seen his friend treat people horribly in the past, but nothing quite like this. It was disturbing, and hard to watch, but even more disturbing was the part he had played in all of this, and the smiles on Circe's odd sisters' faces as they peered at them through the windows. Smiles he feared that would haunt his waking and dreaming mind for years to come. And he wondered if this would be the last time he would see these witches. He had a feeling it was not.

CHAPTER XIII

FROM THE BOOK OF FAIRY TALES

The Curse

The Odd Sisters here. Recall that bit at start of this tale when we said the Book of Fairy Tales is fluid and will reflect the events that took place before and after Gaston's story? Well, this is one of those moments, dears.

As you know, every story you've read or will read in this saga is from the Book of Fairy Tales, and we are its authors. And while that is true, our daughter Circe, who is the Queen of the Dead Woods along with fellow witches Primrose and Hazel, seems to be taking up our mantle now that we are living our best afterlives with Hades in the Underworld. The three queens are contributing to the Book of Fairy Tales, and have the inklings of their powers to change fate.

From our current vantage in the Underworld, we understand why some of you may feel we are the villains of these stories. You may even wonder how we could smile as the prince broke Circe's heart that day. How could Circe's overly protective and odd sisters take delight in her sorrow? Please, don't be more of a fool than necessary. Everything we did was for love of Circe. Yes, we danced and sang songs of joy, but who wouldn't? We saved her from a selfish, brutish twit of a prince, and believe us, we hated seeing Circe so wretched, but we did it for her own good, to protect her. We looked into the prince's heart, saw something foul and moldering there, and watched it growing by the day. We saw who he truly was, and we knew what was written in the Book of Fairy Tales. At least, what was written at that time.

If only we had seen what was growing inside of ourselves back then. If only we had listened to those who tried to warn us . . . Then again, if we had, perhaps we wouldn't be laughing and eating cake every night with Hades in the Underworld. So from our point of view, things worked out just fine. For us and for Hades, anyway.

And for those who have been paying attention, yes, we managed to find a way to get cake in the Underworld. We have all manner of goodies now, all of Hades's favorites. There's a lot that can be achieved when powerful witches and a god come together, even if it's just their own happiness.

But we digress; this is Gaston's story, and to understand it, you must know what happened to his best friend, because what happened next changed both of their lives forever, driving Gaston toward a disastrous fate.

Since the day the prince broke Circe's heart, many more stories have been added to this Book of Fairy Tales, some of which we did not expect. But we knew from the beginning that Circe was fated to be a powerful sorceress, a queen of an ancient kingdom, the only kingdom worthy of her unique and potent talents. And though we did not see her future clearly at the time, we knew she was going to exact change within all the realms. We worried marrying the beast prince would stifle her magical potential and keep her from becoming the most powerful witch of our age. We had to make sure she stayed on her path. We needed to keep her safe from a life of misery with a brat prince, no matter how much she thought she loved him.

If you've read the beast prince's story, you know what happened after he broke Circe's heart. It was a series of ruinous events that changed many lives, including Gaston's. And we have them immortalized in stained glass in one of our many halls in the Underworld, along with the rest of our histories.

The first in this series of unfortunate tableaus is Circe appearing to the prince at his castle. She will be forever immortalized in stained glass, dressed as a woman in rags. She pleads with the prince to take from her a single rose. A symbol of her heart, and the love she had for him.

When Circe showed up on the prince's threshold, she was heartbroken and sad, her eyes swollen from crying. To the prince she looked like a haggard old woman. Disgusted, he refused the rose, and therefore refused her love. But to the prince's astonishment, the old woman transformed into her true self, a beautiful enchantress. The prince was so overcome by Circe's beauty, and by learning she had indeed come from a long line of royalty, that he fell to his knees and begged her forgiveness. He asked her to marry him again. He had known, of course, from the start that Circe was from a great family, but he allowed himself to be tricked by Gaston, and by us. And it was all too easy. He had looked at her differently when he saw her keeping company with the pigs. She was lowly, he felt, and beneath him, and no longer worthy of becoming his wife, and eventual queen.

The astonishment on his face when he saw her transformed, realizing he had been mistaken, that Circe was everything she said she was, the image of him falling to his knees and begging Circe to marry him, was delicious.

But it was too late for the prince. Circe saw who he really was: a monster in the guise of a handsome young man. So Circe did what all great witches do in these situations.

The Curse

She cursed him, and everyone in his castle, with a little help from her older sisters.

But our sweet Circe still wanted to believe there was good within the prince, and in her generosity, she gave him another chance. She said if he learned to love, and became worthy of having that love returned, then the curse would be broken. She gave him the rose, the one he'd tried to refuse, and told him he had until the last petal fell, on his twenty-first birthday, to reform. If he did not, after that day he would forever stay a beast.

Circe's curse was an example of brilliant spellcraft. It was a degenerative curse that would slowly erode his appearance to match his selfish and cruel heart. Every time the prince committed a horrible act, his despicable deeds would show on his face, until slowly, over time, he would no longer recognize himself. And as he succumbed to the vilest aspects of his nature, his servants, his cherished childhood friends, would also transform one by one, in ways he could never imagine.

Circe's warning was clear, but the prince did not believe her. Instead, he became crueler and more vile than any of us thought possible.

CHAPTER XIV

GASTON'S GRAND IDEA

Kingsley had been in denial about the curse, insisting it wasn't real, but Gaston knew the true natures of Circe and the Odd Sisters, and he was worried for his friend's health. The prince was becoming more irrational by the day, and Gaston had made the mistake of remarking upon a portrait of the prince, asking when it had been painted, thinking it had been done maybe five or more years before. But to his and the prince's horror, it had been painted only a few months before. That was how quickly the prince's looks were diminishing. Gaston tried to play it off, teasing the prince, making light of the situation, but it was alarming how much Kingsley had changed in that time, and it was clear to both of them the curse was real.

Kingsley could no longer deny what was happening to him, and what would happen to everyone in the castle if he didn't find a way to break the curse. But accepting his fate only sent him spiraling out of control, leaving Gaston to try to bring his friend out of this deep pit of misery. Without warning, the prince's mental and physical well-being were in peril. He suffered terrorizing fever dreams, causing him to rant about the Odd Sisters and how the curse was real. Gaston was sure this had been brought on by an encounter with the Odd Sisters, but he couldn't be sure what the prince had imagined and what was real. Gaston and Cogsworth were by Kingsley's side around the clock, caring for him until he was well again. And after the prince recovered, Gaston came up with a plan to help his friend.

Desperate to help Kingsley break the curse, Gaston arranged for a ball, inviting every eligible young woman in the surrounding kingdoms. If Gaston understood the prince's fevered ramblings correctly, to break the curse they needed to find someone to fall in love with the prince before the last petal fell from the rose Circe had given him. If he didn't find someone to fall in love with him, he would fully become a beast. It seemed too easy. There had to be more to it, but the prince refused to say anything further than that. Gaston could see the subtle changes in his friend, the aging around the eyes, the bitterness in his face, the lines he didn't have before the curse. It seemed to Gaston that Circe's curse was causing Kingsley's features to match his increasingly foul nature—so as far as Gaston was concerned, they were up against a ticking clock, and he needed to find someone to fall in love with Kingsley before this wretched curse took complete hold of him and everyone else in the castle. And as a member of the castle staff, Gaston had a foreboding feeling this curse would change him into something terrible as well.

With the king and queen still away, it was up to Gaston to help his friend get out of this mess. They had left shortly after the engagement ball and likely knew nothing about what had transpired since. Gaston knew the king and queen had always wanted to join their house with Morningstar Kingdom, and that a marriage between the prince and Princess Tulip Morningstar would bring their great lands together in harmony. Gaston remembered one of the letters Kingsley had sent to Mrs. Potts from his grand tour, recounting his time with the Morningstars. He said the princess was a quiet, shy young woman who giggled easily and was rather agreeable but a bit dull and silly. By all accounts, she was besotted with the prince, but this had been early in his tour, and Gaston wagered the prince had hedged his bets that he would find someone more interesting. Who knew that what he would find was a nest of witches. Gaston wondered if perhaps Tulip wouldn't be a better match for him now. He remembered the prince going on about how lovely he thought she was, but he just hadn't been convinced they had enough in common to endure her for a lifetime. Gaston hoped another encounter with her might change his mind. So he went to Mrs. Potts for help.

"It hasn't been a month since the prince recovered

from his illness! Are you sure he's up to it?" Mrs. Potts wasn't convinced this was a good plan. Everyone in the household had been desperately worried about the prince, although only a few knew about the curse. And Mrs. Potts, of course, was also worried about Gaston and Mr. Cogsworth, refusing to leave his side during his illness. That was who she was. It wasn't enough that she had a brood of children of her own; she mothered everyone else, too, and Gaston was happy for it.

"It's exactly what he needs, Mrs. Potts. We need to get his mind off this curse, and we need to find him someone to marry. I think Princess Tulip Morningstar will be perfect!"

"Why throw an elaborate ball, then? Why not just advise the prince he should court Princess Tulip?" Mrs. Potts looked a little harried that day, likely because Mr. Potts was still away taking care of his sick brother. Gaston didn't know how she did it, running the castle and caring for all her children.

"Have you ever tried telling the prince to do something, Mrs. Potts? No, he has to think she is *his choice*." Gaston could see she agreed. Everyone in the house seemed confused about the prince's recent behavior, which was more erratic than ever. He was losing his temper and falling into deep melancholic moods. They were concerned, but no one knew what to do about it.

"Well, of course I am happy to help, but, Gaston, you have to tell me what this is really about. It's not like you to play Cupid." Mrs. Potts knew Gaston too well. She knew there was something he was keeping from her.

"Mrs. Potts, you would be shocked and revolted if I told you the truth. You would despise me, and that is something I just couldn't bear." He already despised himself. If Mrs. Potts was disappointed in him, too, he wouldn't know what to do.

"Despise you? Well, I think you *have* to tell me now," she said, motioning for him to sit down. Like for many of their talks over the years, they were in Mrs. Potts's sitting room. She was seated at her desk and Gaston in a chair nearby, across from the fireplace. The only thing missing was a pot of tea and cookies.

"All right, dear, out with it," she said, smiling at him.

"Circe claimed she somehow knew I secretly blamed Kingsley for my father's death and would one day kill him for it, or he would kill me. I don't know, it's all muddled now, but the point is, she said I had to leave the kingdom."

"Stuff and nonsense! You boys love each other, there is no way either of you is capable of that. What was she playing at?"

"I don't know. But I knew I didn't want to be driven away from my home and family."

"Of course you didn't. Who would, by heavens? So what happened?" she asked, but she answered her own question before Gaston could.

"Gaston, you didn't! You made it all up about her being the daughter of a pig farmer? But I don't understand—the prince saw the proof for himself."

"Her sisters were in on it. They helped me, and it broke Circe's heart. You should have seen her, Mrs. Potts. I hate to say it, but Kingsley was horrible to her." Gaston still felt guilty remembering how shamefully his friend treated Circe that day. Yes, she was trying to get rid of him, but there was lingering pain and doubt. He wondered if Circe truly believed her vision and was actually trying to protect him and Kingsley as she said.

"I see. But this isn't your fault, Gaston. The prince chose to break the girl's heart, not you. You were protecting yourself, my boy. I know it's not my place to say, but I do not like what I see in the prince. He's always had a mean streak and a sharp tongue, but it's gotten far worse since he's been back. You might have lied, my boy, but the prince chose to believe your lie. He was the one who decided the daughter of a pig farmer was beneath him, and he has been defaming her to anyone in the kingdom who will listen. It is he I am disappointed with, Gaston, not you."

"I knew what Circe and her sisters were like, Mrs. Potts, but I didn't think—I had no idea they would curse him, and it's all my fault. If I hadn't pushed him to break things off with Circe, he wouldn't be cursed now."

"It sounds to me like you were tricked, my boy, by those wicked sisters of hers. But you have to stop blaming yourself, Gaston. I saw you blame yourself when your father died, and now you're blaming your-self for this supposed curse. If you ask me, the prince is the author of his own misery, and it's time you stopped worrying about his happiness and worried about your own."

"But it's not just Kingsley, it's all of us; we're all cursed! Circe says if Kingsley doesn't change his ways, everyone within the castle will be transformed. Don't you see, this is all my fault."

"And you're sure the curse is real?"

"I am, and I intend to help Kingsley break it."

"All right, then, tell me what you want me to do," she said with a determined smile.

Mrs. Potts gathered the troops, and together with Gaston and the rest of the staff they planned a magnif-icent ball. Before he knew it, Gaston heard Mrs. Potts saying things like "This is a dream!" all through the house as she amended menus, made suggestions for little cakes to be served in the great hall, and told the gardeners which flowers to decorate with in each of the various rooms. Even Cogsworth had an extra bounce in his step. He was too austere to let it be known, but it was clear he was pleased to have a bustling house again to take control over, like a general at war. And that's what this was: a war. They were going to save the prince from himself and from this curse.

The prince, however, needed some persuading. "I hate these events, Gaston. I see no need to stuff the house with frilly ladies prancing around like decorated birds!" This made Gaston laugh because it seemed that was exactly the sort of thing the prince liked most these days. But maybe he'd had his fill of balls after the Circe debacle.

"If we invite every fair maiden in the Many Kingdoms, I daresay every girl will attend!" The prince seemed more than a little trepidatious.

Gaston didn't understand why Kingsley found this so daunting, why he was protesting. This was the point entirely: no woman would pass up the opportunity to shine in the prince's eyes. After his long illness, and everything that happened with Circe and the Odd Sisters, he deserved a diversion. And if Princess Tulip wasn't to his taste, then surely there would be many more lovely ladies to choose from. Gaston didn't see the problem.

"But that is what I fear!" the prince exclaimed when Gaston told him so. "Surely there will be far more ghastly-looking girls than beautiful! How will I stand it?"

Gaston put his hand on his friend's shoulder and replied, "No doubt you will have to wade through some ugly ducklings before you find your princess, but won't it be worth it? What of your friend who had such a ball? Wasn't it a great success after the matter of the glass slipper was sorted?"

"Indeed, but you won't catch me marring a house-maid like my dear friend, no matter how beautiful she is! Not after the disaster with the pig keeper!"

Talk like this went on for many days before Kingsley finally agreed. Little did he know Gaston and Mrs. Potts had already set everything into motion. The ball was going to happen with or without his approval. Luckily for everyone involved, Kingsley had come around.

Arranging a ball was the last thing Gaston ever expected or longed to do, but if he could convince Kingsley Princess Tulip was his best chance at breaking the curse, perhaps then Gaston could drag his friend out of the deep pit of depression in which he had been languishing. And then they might go back to living their lives as they always had. As they had always wished.

Every young woman in almost every neighboring kingdom was invited to the ball. It was a gala affair, bursting with palpable expectation and excitement. The ballroom was decorated this time with silver bunting along the tops of the marble pillars to match the prince's frock coat, which was, in Gaston's opinion, decidedly fussier than was necessary. But the prince had in recent months become vainer and more ostentatious in his style and manner. The silver frock coat was adorned with diamond buttons and accompanied by a white shirt with a lace trim collar and cuffs, short silver breeches, white stockings, and silver shoes encrusted with diamonds. Gaston had never seen anything like it. Kingsley looked silly to Gaston, sitting on his throne in the ballroom and sparkling like his mother's pavilion, but the women who attended the ball didn't seem to share Gaston's opinion. He couldn't help but laugh as he watched them promenade past his friend, giggling behind their fans. With giant feathers in their hair and enormous ball gowns, they resembled floats in a parade.

Every woman there wanted to marry the prince, all except for one. Someone Gaston knew from the village: the inventor's daughter, Belle. She was sitting alone on the sidelines, reading. She didn't seem to notice anything going on around her, so engrossed in her book it was as if she were in another world. It was as if she didn't want to be there at all, and Gaston had to wonder if her father had made her accept the invitation. She was completely unimpressed by the castle, the glittering spectacle swirling around her, and the prince. And the prince was hard to miss.

Something about watching Belle sit there reading in the midst of a royal ball swirling around her made Gaston want to whisk her off to the library to show her all the delights waiting for her on the shelves.

She was the only person he knew who liked books as much and he and Kingsley, and perhaps that was why Kingsley was drawn to her. The prince demanded to be introduced.

Instead, Gaston steered Kingsley in Princess Tulip's direction. The prince needed a wife who wasn't headstrong, someone from a royal family who knew the ways of court and wouldn't mind that her husband made all the decisions. And most of all, she should not mind that he spent all of his time with Gaston. Belle was none of those things, at least as far as Gaston could tell from the few interactions they'd had, and besides, he knew Kingsley wouldn't be content with an inventor's daughter, no matter how beautiful she was.

Nevertheless, Kingsley insisted Gaston introduce them.

Gaston wrinkled his nose in distaste, hoping Belle wasn't looking at them and catching on that they were talking about her. But it seemed Belle was used to people talking about her. It's all everyone in the village seemed to do, talk about her and her father. He didn't understand why the people in the village found it strange that she loved to read, or that she doted on her father. Gaston found it endearing.

"You wouldn't be interested in her, trust me," said Gaston.

The prince raised an eyebrow.

"Wouldn't I? And why is that, my good friend?" Gaston could see Kingsley knew he was up to something. Perhaps he thought he wanted Belle for himself. Gaston didn't have time to want anything for himself, let alone time to court a young woman from the village. Even if she seemed perfect in every way.

Gaston lowered his voice so those nearby wouldn't hear. "She's the daughter of a cuckoo! Oh, she's lovely, yes, but her father is the laughingstock of the village. He's harmless enough, but he fancies himself a great inventor. He's always building contraptions that clank, rattle, and explode. She isn't the sort you'd like to get mixed up with, good friend." Gaston glanced around to see if she was looking in their direction.

"Perhaps you're right, but nevertheless, I would like to meet her."

"I daresay you would find her very tedious with her endless talk of literature, fairy tales, and poetry," he said. Suddenly, he worried he had made a mistake mentioning her love of books, though it seemed Kingsley's love for such things was a thing of the past. He was concerned he had only succeeded in sparking an interest. He wondered if he was trying to protect Belle by flinging Tulip in his friend's path, and would he now have to protect Tulip as well as Kingsley and everyone else?

"You seem to know a lot about her, Gaston."

"I fear I do! In the few moments I talked to her just now, she prattled on of nothing else but books. No, dear friend, we need to find you a proper lady. A princess. Someone like Princess Morningstar over there. Now she's a delight. No talk of books from her. I bet she's never read a book or had a thought of her own."

Gaston could see Kingsley thought that was a very good quality.

"Yes! I can do the thinking for both of us! Bring over the Princess Morningstar. I'd very much like to meet her again."

Princess Tulip Morningstar had long golden locks, with a milk-and-honey complexion and light sky-blue eyes. She looked like a doll draped in diamonds and pink silks. She was a perfect match for Kingsley. At least, a perfect match for this new, strange version of Kingsley who Gaston was still trying to get used to. Gaston had felt so guilty about the prince being cursed, he hadn't had time to process everything that had happened since his return. He realized he hadn't been calling Kingsley out when he acted horribly. He wasn't reminding his friend not to turn into a beastly tyrant prince like he promised he would when they were younger. And he wasn't sure what Kingsley would do if he did. He even let Kingsley think he was the best at everything, and acted as if that had always been so, just because it made his friend happy. This was indeed a different Kingsley. It was easier for Gaston to go along with his friend, and after a while it bothered him less, because Gaston's nature was also changing, sometimes without him even realizing it.

There were moments when Gaston would step back and really look at himself and wonder who he was. It wasn't like Gaston to run someone down for having never read a book or to assume they never had thoughts of their own. And even if that were so, would it be her fault? As far as he could tell, aristocracy only made it their business to educate their male heirs. And who was he to talk, anyway? The greatest regret of his life was that he had never learned to read, and he feared now it was too late.

It became clear to Gaston and everyone at the ball that Kingsley had decided he was going to marry Princess Tulip, and it almost brought the evening to a sulky end, with all the other ladies so sorely disappointed (save for Belle, who barely seemed to notice). Gaston did his best to look pleased with himself, to be happy his friend had made not only a love match but had chosen the very lady Gaston had pushed him toward. But part of him couldn't help wondering if he was pushing Princess Tulip toward a ruinous fate. He felt as if he were throwing her into a den of wolves to fend for herself, and that his complicity in bringing them together only further besmirched his darkening heart.

CHAPTER XV

FROM THE BOOK OF FAIRY TALES

Princess Tulip Morningstar

The Odd Sisters here again. This is where things could get complicated, so try to keep up, and please do forgive us if we've said this before, but it is worth repeating: All time moves concurrently. That means all time is happening at once. Imagine if your past, present, and future were all happening at the same time. That is how time works for powerful witches, and for gods. Some of us decide to tether ourselves in one timeline, giving ourselves the illusion we are experiencing the events of our lives the way nonmagical people perceive the passing of time. For witches, it's easier that way, and far less maddening. This is nothing to the gods; they're built differently and can withstand knowing everything at once. So it goes without saying the Book of Fairy Tales struggles to tell stories in a straight line, and that is why we go back and share more layers of the stories than were in the previous volumes.

But things are even more complicated now. We are no longer mortal witches; we live among gods and goddesses now that we reside in the Underworld with Hades, ruling beside him as queens. So forgive us if we step out of Gaston's timeline and talk about things that were, and will come to pass, because for us, it is all the same.

If you've read the volumes of the Book of Fairy Tales in the order of our choosing, then you will perhaps remember that Princess Tulip Morningstar started her journey out very differently than how she continued. And if you only know her from the pages of this volume, the one you hold in your hands now, not only have you gone against our wishes, but you are going to be pleasantly surprised to see where her journey takes her. Princess Tulip is the only princess in the Many Kingdoms we have taken an active interest in—that is, an active interest that wasn't plotting her demise. We've had an eye on her since our old friend Nanny came to be her caretaker. This was during a time when Nanny didn't remember who she was—when she thought she was just the nanny to a young girl who needed protection and guidance, and not the most powerful fairy in the Many Kingdoms. We knew who she was in those times even if she did not, and we waited in hopes she would wake up and destroy the beast prince for his ill-treatment of her dear sweet Tulip. To our bewilderment, someone else stepped in and saved Tulip, someone we did not expect.

Gaston.

After the ball, Princess Tulip went back to her father's kingdom and awaited the various ceremonies, parties, and other trappings that would take place during her engagement with the prince. By custom she would live at home, visiting the prince frequently with her mother or Nanny as chaperone. There were many such occasions, and all of them went disastrously, each one moving poor Tulip closer to the edge of possible oblivion.

These are the occasions that burn brightly in our minds, and we know they burn brightly for Tulip, too, even now after it has been so many years since she was so ill-treated by the prince. We wonder sometimes what Tulip has been up to, spending so much of her time with the Tree Lords and Cyclopean Giants. We hear of her escapades, and we wonder if someday she won't bring her army to the prince's castle gates. Of course, all we would have to do is look in the Book of Fairy Tales and know the answer, but sometimes it's better not to spoil all of the afterlife's surprises.

The engagement between Tulip and the prince was doomed from the start. She was out of her depth, and nervous, but who could blame her? She had only just left the schoolroom, if that's what you could call it, and was now thrust into an engagement she wasn't ready for, and which the prince himself didn't truly want. She was a means to an end, and she paid the price when things did not turn out as the prince thought they would. During this time, it was rare for young women belonging to royal families to receive the same sort of education as their brothers. They were taught how to play piano, how to sew, how to plan parties, how to direct the conversation at dinner, and how to support their husbands. They were not encouraged to have opinions of their own, and if they did happen to stumble on an opinion, they were discouraged from sharing it. And Tulip felt the weight of all that when in the company of the prince.

She felt dimwitted and foolish when a renowned painter called the Maestro came to stay at the castle during one of her visits to paint their engagement portrait. He was a widely celebrated painter and in great demand, an eccentric and dandified gentleman who fancied himself to be the wittiest and most intriguing man in the Many Kingdoms. Tulip didn't know how to act when the natty painter showed up in his velvet-and-lace outfit in various shades of lilacs and blackberry, with his large sad eyes set into his slightly swollen oval face. And she especially didn't know how to act, or what to say, when he would make flowery pronouncements such as:

"It seems every portrait that is painted with any real feeling is a portrait of the artist, and not of the sitter. I daresay you will both be magnificent!"

Poor Tulip blinked more than a few times, trying to grasp his meaning. "Will you be in the portrait with us, Maestro?" The poor dear didn't know if he and the prince laughed at her because what she said was clever or dull-witted, but she decided to act as though it had been the cleverest thing she could have possibly said, even though upon reflection she was sure it was not. That visit was a nightmare: the prince was brooding over the curse, and the Maestro's temperament grew increasingly bad because of the prince's foul mood, and Tulip found herself constantly melting into tears. The prince and Gaston escaped to the tavern every evening, leaving Tulip to entertain the Maestro alone. She consoled herself by playing with Gaston's old cat.

It had not been a very happy visit for the princess, but it somehow managed to get worse once the engagement painting was revealed. Quite the party was assembled on the day of the unveiling. Tulip's mother, Queen Morningstar, was there, along with some of her attending ladies. Also present was Gaston, as well as a few close friends of the prince's whom he had met on his tour. Mrs. Potts had arranged an outstanding dinner, and after their feast, all went into the great hall, which had already been filled with paintings of the prince and his family. Among them was the eagerly anticipated engagement portrait.

"Ah, I see you have hung the Maestro's painting here in the great hall, where it belongs. Good choice, old man," said Gaston, looking at the faces he had grown up with.

"Yes, I thought it was best suited in here," said the prince as the Maestro cleared his throat loudly. It seemed the painter felt the occasion required more ceremony, and this idle chat was debasing the situation at hand.

"Yes, without further delay, I would like to share the latest of my greatest treasures."

And at that, Lumiere pulled a cord, which dropped

the black silk cloth that had been concealing the painting. The room erupted into a clatter of sighs and applause, and the Maestro soaked it all in like an actor on the stage, bowing at the waist and placing his hand on his heart to indicate he was very touched.

Gaston could see Kingsley was shocked by how he looked in the painting. Though it shouldn't have been a surprise, since the Maestro was renowned for doing highly realistic portraits. He couldn't count how many times Gaston had heard the Maestro say he was "capturing a single moment in time to be forever preserved," or some other such nonsense. But maybe the prince hadn't realized until that moment how much he had truly changed, even more so since the ball. It was unnerving, looking at the painting, seeing Gaston's friend look so harsh, with his cruel eyes piercing, almost wolf-like, as if he were seeking his prey. Even his mouth looked thinner, more sinister than it looked before. Kingsley just stood there staring at the painting until Gaston jabbed him with his elbow.

"Say something, man! They're expecting a speech!"

he whispered in his friend's ear, bringing the prince out of his stupor.

"I couldn't have asked for a more beautiful portrait of my bride-to-be!" he said finally, still horrified by the painting, while Tulip blushed deeply, trying to find the right words.

"Thank you, my love. And I, too, couldn't have asked for a more handsome and dignified visage of my prospective husband," she said, feeling very proud of herself that this time she didn't allow her nervousness to make her mind and words a jumble.

You might wonder why we felt pity for Tulip. We are notorious for despising princesses. They do, after all, typically have more than their fair share of magical protectors. But Tulip's fairy, Nanny, didn't even know she was a fairy, didn't know she had magic, couldn't even recall who she was. And the prince saw to it Nanny was distracted by Mrs. Potts and the other staff so she didn't see what Tulip was going through. So we watched from a distance as the prince treated Tulip cruelly. When he wasn't ignoring her, he was belittling her and making her feel small. We watched her walk the gardens on the castle grounds, wandering through the hedge maze, wishing she knew more of the world, wishing she had the same education as her brother, wishing she was stronger. She needed a protector. She needed a fairy or a witch to keep her safe from harm. We saw the future. We knew eventually Tulip would write her own story. But while she was with the prince, she withered. She loved him with all her heart, even though he treated her with nothing but cruelty and mockery. And we feel, even now, one day, the prince will pay for what he did to her.

The prince sent Tulip and her family away the day of the unveiling, angry that she had called him *dignified*. Angry because he felt that was what men were called when they looked older. And he did look older. He had changed. The curse had him in its clutches. And after Tulip and the rest of the guests left, the prince made a sinister request of Gaston.

"I need a little favor. Sometime back, you mentioned a particularly unscrupulous fellow who could be called upon for certain deeds."

Gaston raised his eyebrows. "Surely there are ways

to get out of marrying the princess other than having her killed." Gaston was glad his comment made the prince laugh. It had been a while since he had seen him smile, let alone laugh.

"No, man! I mean the Maestro! I would like you to make the arrangements for me. The incident cannot be traced back to me, you understand?"

"Absolutely." Gaston looked at his friend with new eyes. This man standing before him, this wasn't his old friend Kingsley. And Gaston wasn't himself, either, because he agreed to make the arrangements for someone's death simply because he painted an unflattering portrait of his friend. Even if the image was accurate.

Chapter XVI

From the Book of Fairy Tales

The Winter Solstice

We kept a close eye on Gaston, taking delight in the terror we were causing. We saw him watch in horror as Kingsley became more bitter and cruel, witnessing the evidence on his dear friend's face as it became just as monstrous as his blackened heart. Gaston, too, felt monstrous, for encouraging this romance between Kingsley and Princess Tulip, seeing how terribly Kingsley treated her every time she came to visit.

We smiled when he tried to lift Kingsley's spirits by arranging a splendid solstice celebration, remembering how much they both loved the solstice as children, thinking maybe the magic of all the trappings would help lift his friend out of his gloom and perhaps bring the prince and princess closer together after their previous disastrous visit. Gaston would see to it they had a romantic solstice, and again he solicited the help of the staff to see to it that everything was perfect for the princess's stay.

As Princess Tulip Morningstar's carriage rolled up the path leading to the prince's castle, she couldn't help but feel there wasn't anything more breathtaking than the castle in wintertime. Morningstar was by far one of the most beautiful kingdoms in the land, but nothing quite compared to the prince's kingdom covered in pure white snow and decorated for the winter solstice. The entire castle was infused with light and glowing brightly in the dark winter night. Tulip had high hopes for this visit, and longed for nothing more than for the prince to treat her with kindness and love, as he once had. Like Gaston, she hoped the winter holiday would cheer his sour mood and bring him back around to the man she had fallen in love with at the ball. Little did she know she was moving closer to the edge of peril.

Lumiere opened the carriage door and greeted the princess at the castle entrance.

"Bonjour, Princess! Aren't you looking as beautiful, as always. It is so lovely to see you again." No matter how much Gaston had pleaded, he could not persuade Kingsley to meet his future bride when she arrived. At least Lumiere was on hand to make the princess feel welcomed and adored.

"Kingsley, you have to meet Tulip when she arrives! What will she think if you're not there to greet her?" said Gaston.

"I don't care what she thinks. You're the one who insisted she come here, and the castle be decorated for the solstice. It looks like a winter nightmare in here, trees everywhere, endless piles of gifts. I suppose it cost a fortune, all these gifts you bought for her. And where are all the servants? How was all this achieved?"

Gaston didn't want to tell Kingsley the curse had started affecting the servants as well. Every day there were fewer than the day before, every day there were new statues in strange places. Gaston had the creeping feeling the statues were watching him, moving when his back was turned. The castle was changing, too, within and without, gargoyles and dragons replacing cherubs, the castle becoming darker, foreboding, and frightening. He did his best to shield Kingsley from as much of it as he could, but he couldn't hide that the staff had dwindled down to Mrs. Potts, Mr. Cogsworth, Lumiere, and a handful of others.

"The servants are being turned into statues! Open your eyes, man, and look around. Tulip is our only hope of breaking the curse, so pull yourself together, put on your happiest face, and greet her when she arrives."

"Statues? Are you sure?" The prince looked horrified.

"Tulip loves you, Kingsley. And if you don't stop treating her so horribly we will lose everyone we love, all of our friends and family here. And we will lose each other. Please, just be kind to her. She's on her way now; won't you try to give her a nice holiday? If not for her, then for all of us?"

"I suppose. But I can't stand to be out of doors, Gaston. It feels too big. I can't explain it. My heart races, and I feel like I am going to pass out. I don't feel safe unless I'm in the castle."

"Fine, then meet her in the great hall. Lumiere will bring her in, and you will surprise her with all her gifts. Leave everything to us, my old friend. I promise, I know what's best."

The prince's absence upon Tulip's arrival, however, did not go unnoticed, and Nanny grumbled about it as she popped out of the carriage right after the princess. But Lumiere had it all in hand, saying their things would be taken to their rooms, even though there wasn't a footman in sight. Lumiere ushered the ladies past many vast and beautiful rooms until finally they arrived at a large door wrapped to look like an extravagant gift with a gold bow. The ladies were confused. Customarily they would be shown to their rooms so they could refresh themselves after their long journey, but Tulip was excited to find this intriguing door and seemed eager to see what was on the other side.

Tulip's nanny, however, seemed skeptical. "What's this?" she snapped, looking at the door with confusion and wonder. But Lumiere urged them on.

"Go inside and see for yourself!"

Tulip opened the giant gift-wrapped door to find a winter wonderland within. There was an enormous oak tree stretching to the very height of the golden domed ceiling. It was covered in magnificent lights and beautifully ornate finery that sparkled in their glow. Under the tree was an abundance of gifts, and standing among them was the prince his arms stretched out as he waited to greet her. The poor girl's heart was filled with joy, unaware the smile on the prince's face was forced.

"My love! I am so happy to see you!" she said, wrapping her arms around him. We Odd Sisters watched as the prince looked at her with disgust. It was the same look he gave our Circe when he saw her covered in mud with the pigs. No matter how hard he tried, he couldn't keep himself from showing who he truly was. It didn't matter what Gaston said or did, the prince was far too gone. He was in the curse's grip, and we couldn't have been happier he was going to get what he deserved.

"Hello, my dearest. You are in quite the state from

traveling, aren't you? I'm surprised you didn't insist to be taken to your rooms to make yourself more presentable before showing yourself."

"I'm sorry, dear, you're right, of course."

Lumiere, always the gentleman and eager to please, jumped in. "It's my fault, my lord. I insisted she follow me at once. I knew you were excited to show the princess the decorations."

"I see. Well, Tulip dear, soon you will be queen in this house, and you must learn to decide for yourself what is right and insist upon it. I am sure next time you will make the right choice." With that, he motioned for her to go upstairs.

Tulip was in tears as Lumiere showed her and Nanny to their rooms.

"As I said when you arrived, dear princess, you look beautiful, as always," Lumiere said kindly as he led her away. "Do not heed the master's words. He has been rather distracted of late."

The rest of Tulip's visit drifted further into nightmare as the curse tormented the prince and everyone in the castle. More of the staff were disappearing, disturbing statues were appearing in strange places like the observatory, places he knew they hadn't been before, and the prince was haunted by our words of warning when we uttered the second part of the curse.

"Your castle and its grounds will also be cursed then, and everyone within will be forced to share your burden. Nothing but horrors will surround you, from when you look into the mirror, or sit in your beloved rose garden."

It rang in his ears with each disappearance and with each new statue that appeared, and he knew the horrors he had created. Yet at any time the prince could have tried to change his ways, he could have been tender to Tulip, but his constant mistreatment of her pulled him—and everyone in the castle—further into a vortex of hopelessness. They wondered if they would be trapped forever in this misery. And Gaston was angry.

"What's this I hear of you making Tulip cry? What is wrong with you, Kingsley?"

"You should have seen her, Gaston! She wasn't fit to be in my company!"

"Have you seen yourself in the mirror lately? Look

338

at yourself. You're lucky Tulip still wants to marry you. You're lucky what's left of the household hasn't deserted you. Get yourself together, man, and make it up to her! Do you understand me? Make it up to her and break this damn curse. We have lost almost everyone we love, and how soon before the rest are gone, too? How long before you lose yourself completely?"

"That's enough, Gaston. I understand."

"Do you, though? You'd better. Now go; she is waiting for you."

After that, the prince seemed determined to break the curse. But he made a mockery of love, falling all over himself trying to make Tulip happy.

"Tulip, do you really love me? Would you love me even if I were somehow disfigured?"

"What a question. Of course I would! You know I love you, more than anything in this world!"

"I do now, my love, I do now." And that was all he needed. She loved him. Truly loved him. She would help him break this curse.

As far as he was concerned, he was halfway there. All he had to do was convince us, the evil Odd Sisters, that he loved her, too. Of course, there were things about Tulip he loved. He loved her beauty, her coyness, and that she kept her opinions to herself. He loved that she showed no interest in books, and that she didn't prattle on about her pastimes. In fact, he had no idea how she spent her time when she wasn't in his company. It was as if she didn't exist when she wasn't with him. He imagined her sitting in a little chair in her father's castle, just waiting for him to send for her.

He loved how she never gave him a cross look or scorned him, even when he was in the foulest of moods, and how very easy she was to manage. Surely that counted for something. Surely that was a form of love. So he decided the sweeter he was to her, the quicker he would break the curse. All that was left was sealing the deal with a kiss, and the curse would be broken. Everything would go back to the way it was.

It was quite comical, really, watching him pretend to love Tulip. Putting on a show for us. But we saw into his heart. Unfortunately for Tulip, she did not.

Lumiere was given the tasks of spiriting Nanny downstairs to have tea with Mrs. Potts and taking the hamper Mrs. Potts had packed for the prince and princess for their romantic interlude, as Lumiere called it. It was all planned. This would be the moment they would declare their love for each other and kiss! And bam, the curse would be broken. Just like that.

We watched as the prince led the princess to the edge of the hedge maze. Her eyes were covered with a long white silk scarf. Her heart raced because she was afraid of the dark and filled with nervous excitement about the surprise the prince had arranged for her. He asked her to count to fifty and then take off the blindfold, assuring her that the path to her surprise would be quite clear.

She ripped off the sash from her eyes the moment she got to fifty, needing a moment to let her eyes adjust before she saw the path laid before her. The tips of her shoes touched the pink rose petals that had been strewn across the courtyard, creating a path that led into the hedge maze. Her fears fluttered away as she quickly walked the petal path, eager to enter the maze of animal topiaries.

The petals led her past a stunningly crafted topiary

of an exceptionally large serpent, its mouth gaping wide and bearing long, deadly fangs. It twisted its way around the corner, revealing a part of the maze she had never seen. A replica of the castle, almost exact in every way except without the griffins and many gargoyles perched on almost every corner and turret. The petals led out of the maze and into a small enclosed garden that was filled with brightly colored flowers. It felt as if she had somehow stumbled upon springtide in the midst of this winter landscape. It was such a remarkable sight, so bright and full of life. She couldn't imagine how the flowers thrived in such bitter cold. Among the flowers were beautiful statues from various stories, characters from legends and myths. She recognized them from eavesdropping on her brother's lessons before she was ushered away to learn how to walk like a lady. It was no wonder men didn't take women seriously. They had classes in walking while the men learned ancient languages.

The garden was stunning, and every bit like a fairy tale in the cold blue light of the winter afternoon.

Nestled in the center of the enchanted garden, all pink and gold, was a stone bench, where the prince was waiting for her.

"I arranged flowers from the hothouse to be moved here so you might experience the joy of spring."

"You're amazing, my dearest! Thank you."

The prince decided this was the moment when he would kiss her and break the curse.

"May I kiss you, my love?"

And they kissed. And it was magical. For Tulip, anyway. She was blissfully happy—if only for a moment, before everything went terribly wrong.

As they walked back to the castle through the maze, the prince was sure he had broken the curse with the kiss. But then he heard something stirring and growling in the hedge maze. Tulip joked that perhaps one of the animal topiaries had come to life, but the prince sensed they were in real danger. He knew there was truth to Tulip's words, even if she didn't. So he dashed off to see what manner of beast was in the maze, leaving Tulip alone and defenseless. When he finally returned, he looked stricken and angry as he stood there staring at Tulip as if in a daze, bleeding from the deep gashes in his arm.

"My love! You're hurt!"

"Brilliant of you to have surmised that, my dear." It was his usual cruel and bitter tone, full of venom, as if he, too, were one of the topiary creatures that had sprung to life in the hedge maze. Little did she know he was becoming more beastly by the moment.

Chapter XVII

From the Book of Fairy Tales

The Mystery of the Servants

To our delight, the castle was in a panic. We couldn't have been more pleased everything was going according to our plan. Gaston had been in the servants' hall when Lumiere came bounding downstairs to give them the news. The prince had been attacked. Gaston had just been consoling Mrs. Potts because Mr. Cogsworth had been missing all day, and she was in a heap of tears. He suggested she have her tea with Nanny to try to get her mind off things, suggesting also having Chip search the castle for Mr. Cogsworth. But Gaston feared they wouldn't find him. They hadn't found any of the servants who had disappeared, only the strange statues that seemed to be appearing in odd places around the castle. Statues that you would swear you saw moving out of the corner of your eye, and when you turned around, their position had changed. It was no wonder Kingsley was losing his wits. Everyone was afraid, including Gaston, who knew this was due to the curse. If they didn't stop it, everyone within the castle would turn into these wretched statues. The only thing that gave Gaston hope was that the prince finally believed that Princess Tulip loved him, and they were at that very moment in the garden, where the prince planned to give her the kiss that would break this curse.

At least, that is what Gaston thought, until Lumiere came downstairs in a state of fear and dismay.

"Gaston! The prince was attacked!" Lumiere was out of breath, having run all the way. "Where's Francis? Someone needs to fetch the doctor."

"I haven't seen Francis all day, and what do you mean, attacked? By who?" Gaston stood from the table and went straight to his blunderbuss, propped up in the corner of the room. This was the last thing they needed. Cogsworth was missing, and now an attack? He felt like he was going mad.

"Some sort of beast in the hedge maze, I don't know. But don't go running after it and disappearing on me as well." Gaston had never seen Lumiere so frazzled.

"Then what do you suppose I do, Lumiere?"

"I don't know, see to the prince? He is in rare form. He's angry and insisting we find Cogsworth, and I have a feeling his surprise for Tulip didn't turn out as he would have liked," he said.

"I should think not! He was attacked!"

"No, there's something else. He was being very impatient with her. I don't think things went as planned."

Gaston sighed. "For goodness' sake!" he said as Nanny came padding down the stairs. What she was doing down there he didn't know, but he didn't have time for this.

"Can we help you, Nanny?" he asked, trying to be calm. It wasn't her fault the castle was falling down around them and soon everyone would succumb to the curse. He had to try to play it off. The last thing he needed was Tulip's nanny getting into a fit.

"I'm sorry to bother you gentlemen, but have you seen Mrs. Potts?" she asked.

"No, we thought she was with you." Gaston felt his stomach and chest tighten. Was Mrs. Potts missing now? What would they do without Mrs. Potts? This was too much. He was struggling to breathe. It was all he could do to maintain his composure, but what he wanted to do in that moment was pick up the closest thing and hurl it against the wall.

"She was with me, but I slipped away just for a moment to get us more hot water for our tea, and when I came back, she wasn't there. It's the strangest thing. She was just gone, but in her place was a teapot."

"A teapot? Not a statue?" asked Gaston.

"A statue? What do you mean? What in the Many Kingdoms do you mean, a statue? It was a teapot! A teapot that hadn't been there before."

"I mean a statue, woman! Haven't you seen them? They're everywhere!" Gaston could see she didn't know what he was talking about.

348

Gaston felt the anger and panic within him rising. Kingsley must have done something horrible to Tulip. It was becoming clear that every time he did something nasty, someone they loved disappeared. Did he see it, too? Gaston didn't know what to do. He and Lumiere just stood there looking at each other, not saying a word, overcome by fear.

"What's going on?" Nanny asked, eyeing them both with suspicion. "Something is going on. I may be an old woman, but I can tell when something foul is afoot." Thankfully, Lumiere jumped in and took over.

"It's nothing. Nothing to trouble you with, anyway. Go upstairs to see to Tulip. I daresay she needs you just now. There was some sort of mishap in the garden, and I need to call the doctor to look at the prince."

"Call the doctor? Is Tulip all right?"

"She's fine, but in need of consoling I fear," said Lumiere with a weak smile.

"Mark my words. Something's not right here, I feel it in my bones. This castle is cursed, I tell you, and I am going to tell Tulip we should leave at once." Nanny padded away and went quickly up the stairs, but not before turning back to give Gaston and Lumiere a seething look.

"I guess it's just down to us, then," Gaston said. "I'll fetch the doctor, you go console Tulip and her nanny."

Gaston took care of the prince while Lumiere looked after Tulip and Nanny. Despite the evidence against this likelihood, Gaston hoped once Kingsley recovered they would start making plans for the wedding. Maybe Kingsley had broken the curse by kissing Tulip in the garden before the attack. Perhaps it wouldn't be long until they started to see evidence of the curse reversing. Maybe Kingsley hadn't messed things up. So Gaston sat at Kingsley's bedside and watched as he slept fretfully, tossing and turning, muttering in his sleep about curses, kisses, and witches. He held his friend's hand and assured him Lumiere would not let Tulip leave the castle until they were certain the curse was broken.

Meanwhile, Tulip and Nanny wondered what could have become of Mrs. Potts and Mr. Cogsworth. Lumiere did his best to try to hide that most of the servants had already disappeared before Tulip's recent arrival to the castle, but there was no hiding this. There was no hiding that Mrs. Potts and Mr. Cogsworth were gone. Lumiere had his hands full trying to make things look as if they weren't in the middle of a crisis, especially with Nanny trying to talk Tulip into leaving.

"I assure you, ladies, the prince is resting comfortably. The doctor just left, and Gaston is with him now. There is no need to fret, or to go rushing off into the night. Dinner will be served in the dining hall at the usual time."

"You needn't fuss over us this evening, Lumiere. You can just bring us something on a tray. We can eat in our rooms, or perhaps next to the fire in the sitting room. I am sure everyone is in a tizzy downstairs with Mrs. Potts and Cogsworth missing. I don't want you worrying about us," Tulip said, but the flirty Frenchman wouldn't hear of serving guests on trays in the sitting room, or any other room, for that matter.

"Oh no! That will not do! If Mrs. Potts were here,

she would blow her lid at the thought of you two eating off trays. And as for the menu this evening, never fear, we have something special planned for you," he said with his magical grin that always charmed the ladies. Later that night, in the main dining hall, you would have never known almost the entire household staff was missing, let alone two of the most important figures. The room was lovely, decorated with the hothouse flowers from Tulip's earlier surprise, and the candles were sparkling brightly in crystal votive bowls, casting an unearthly light.

The two ladies were enjoying their dessert when the prince stumbled into the room, looking haggard and half crazed.

"I'm happy you ladies are savoring your meal while the household is falling to shambles around you!" He appeared as if he had aged several years since earlier that afternoon. He looked exhausted and unwell, with a wild look in his eye.

Nanny and Tulip didn't know what to say. They just stared at him, at a complete loss.

The Mystery of the Servants

"Have you nothing to say for yourself, Tulip? Sitting here stuffing yourself while my childhood companions are suffering such a terrible fate?" His face turned into something inhuman, something wicked and cruel, making both women recoil in fear.

"Don't you look at me like that, old woman! I won't have you casting the evil eye at me!" And you . . ." He turned his anger on Tulip. "You lying strumpet, playing with my emotions, pretending you love me when clearly you do not!"

Tulip gasped and melted into tears at once, hardly able to speak.

"That's not true! I do love you!" The prince's face was ashen, his eyes sunken and dark with illness, his anger growing with every word.

"If you loved me, truly loved me, then none of this would be happening. Mrs. Potts and Cogsworth would be here. The animals in the maze wouldn't have attacked me. And I wouldn't look like this! Look at me! Every day I grow uglier, more wretched."

Nanny put a protective arm around Tulip. The

princess was crying so hard she could hardly breathe properly, let alone say anything in her own defense.

"I can't stand the sight of you! I want you out of the castle this moment, don't bother packing your things." He rushed toward them, grabbed Tulip by the hair, and violently dragged her to the door, knocking Nanny over in the process.

"I won't have you in this castle for one more moment, do you understand? You disgust me!" he said, spitting at her. Tulip cried harder than ever, screaming for the prince to let go when Gaston came into the room.

"What on earth is going on here, man?" Gaston wrenched Tulip from the prince's clutches and then helped Nanny to her feet.

"What are you playing at, sir? Are you deranged?" Gaston had never been so angry with Kingsley, not since the night his father died. He couldn't believe what he was seeing. Had he somehow never truly seen who Kingsley was before, or had the strain of the curse pushed him to this? Either way, it was all Gaston could do not to strike the prince right then and there, seeing him manhandle a woman in this way. It was vile and beneath contempt.

"Quickly, go to your rooms, ladies. I will take care of this," Gaston said, leading the two women to the door, where Lumiere met them. "Lumiere, see to Nanny, and take her and the princess upstairs." The moment Lumiere closed the door behind them, Gaston punched the prince in the face, hitting him across the jaw and knocking him to the floor.

"What in blazes is going on?" Gaston was looming over the prince, his face full of fury. He longed to kick him in the stomach but stopped himself. "How dare you lay your hands on Tulip like that?" Gaston was ready to leave, ready to leave the castle and his friend for good. He expected Kingsley to get up and defend himself, to rail at him for striking him, to throw him out of the castle, but he just wept.

"She lied to me, Gaston. She didn't love me. She never did."

Gaston was shocked by how changed his friend

was. He didn't look entirely human. But Gaston could sense there was still something of his old friend lurking behind his hideous form and angry heart.

"What are you talking about, man? She did love you."

"Then why isn't the curse broken? Why have all the servants been turned to stone? Why was I attacked by the animals in the hedge maze?"

"Perhaps it's because you don't love *her*. It's not her fault, Kingsley. She doesn't deserve this."

"And I do?" Kingsley said, his face transforming into something monstrous. His voice grew deep and growling. It sounded more like a wild animal than a man's voice.

"I deserve to be turned into a monster? I deserve to be cursed? This is your fault! I blame you! You're the one who pushed me into that dimwit's arms. Now you deal with it!" Kingsley's voice was as loud as thunder, and he looked as if he was going to strike at any moment. "Get those women out of the castle before I kill them. And don't bother coming back."

Gaston shut his eyes against his friend's snarling

face. He had no intention of going anywhere. Kingsley needed him. He had never seen such rage, such bitterness. He was afraid for his friend, and for them all. How could Kingsley come to love anyone, such as he was? And who would love such a beast?

Chapter XVIII

From the Book of Fairy Tales

The Descent

Princess Tulip Morningstar never heard from the prince again. And it seemed Kingsley had stopped raving about spells and evil curses at last, but he refused to go out of the castle. He never left his room and didn't allow Lumiere or Gaston to open the drapes. And he allowed them to light just one candle in the evenings. The only visitor he allowed was Gaston.

"Are you sure this is how you want to handle this, Kingsley?" Gaston asked him one morning, shortly after Tulip and Nanny had left in the night. The prince looked at Gaston as if he was trying his best not to slip into one of the fits of rage that seized him so easily these days. And Gaston didn't want to do anything that would bring one of them on.

"I am quite sure. You are to ride out to Morningstar Castle and to officially call off the engagement."

"And what of the marriage settlement? The king will be destitute without your promised arrangement."

The prince smiled. "I'm sure he will. But that is what he gets for flinging his stupid daughter at me! She never loved me, Gaston. Never! It was all lies! All a means to get my money, for herself and for her father's kingdom."

Gaston shook his head. It seemed all Kingsley's anger was now leveled at the Morningstars. His friend wasn't content to destroy the princess's heart; he wanted to destroy her kingdom as well. Gaston didn't bother arguing with him. He saw that his friend was getting worked up again, and he had already tried convincing him Tulip loved him. Gaston was at a loss for how to help. Nothing he said would convince the prince he had been wrong about Tulip, and that whatever had happened in the hedge maze wasn't her fault. Kingsley's conviction was so strong, however, that even Gaston began to wonder if his friend might be right. Or was he just losing himself and his reason to this curse? Was Tulip really playing them for fools all along? Was she smart enough to pull off such a clever trick, making Kingsley believe she loved him when she did not? Gaston wasn't sure. He had thought he had chosen wisely when he made the match, and he was sure Tulip loved the prince, but now he just felt sorry for the trouble it had caused, for his friend and for the Morningstars.

"I will ride out this day, my good friend. You just rest."

The prince's smile was wicked, distorting his face in the vague candlelight, casting villainous shadows. It almost made Gaston frightened of his friend.

As Gaston made his journey back from Morningstar Castle, he began to forget why he had been there, and what it was he had done while he was there. By the time he got back to Kingsley's kingdom, he had forgotten he was ever in Morningstar at all, and the devastation it caused. He would never know that Tulip was so distraught she would fling herself off the rocky cliffs, hoping to end her suffering—only to find herself making a bargain with Ursula in the watery depths below. And from that point, Tulip decided she would live only for herself. She would do everything she ever wished, say what she felt, give herself the education she had always longed for, and live her life exactly as she pleased. You already know how Tulip's heartbreak and travails shaped Princess Tulip Morningstar into the woman she eventually became, the woman she is now, despite how the prince tried to ruin her and destroy her kingdom. She is Queen Morningstar, with her legion of Tree Lords and Cyclopean Giants, ruling one of the most powerful realms in the Many Kingdoms. Friend and ally to the queens of the Dead Woods, and therefore a friend an ally to us, the Odd Sisters, and under our protection. But we get ahead of ourselves. That part of Tulip's story is still being written.

There were many things Gaston would never know, the first of which was how entrenched in this curse he and his friend had become with this final act of cruelty. They might as well have pushed Tulip off the cliff themselves. Because the moment she decided she could no longer live in the world, the moment she jumped off that cliff, the curse was all but sealed. The prince became the beast we knew he was. He had shown himself to be a monster, and that is how everyone would see him. And in succumbing fully to the darkness, it caused Gaston to forget. And eventually the prince would forget his friend.

Gaston didn't go to the castle upon his return from Morningstar. He went to his estate, leaving his friend alone to languish in the clutches of the curse.

Gaston forgot about his friend, and all of the adventures they had together. He forgot they had killed the Beast of Gévaudan. He forgot he had grown up in the castle, and about all his friends, and people he thought of as family. He forgot Mrs. Potts, Mr. Cogsworth, Lumiere, all of them. All he remembered was growing up with his father, and how his father and mother were killed by a beast. A beast Gaston vowed to kill. He didn't remember the day he and his best friend killed that beast together, saving each other's lives. All he remembered was a deep abiding hatred for the creature who took his family from him, and his vow to keep the village safe, which made him, in the eyes of everyone in his small town, a hero.

CHAPTER XIX

FROM THE BOOK OF FAIRY TALES

The Hunter in the Woods

It had been several months since the prince had sent Gaston on his dastardly errand, and the prince hadn't left his room since, held captive by fear and anger. Gaston was gone, and the prince was exactly where we wanted him: his misery mounting by the day, and his fate closer to being sealed. The only servant the prince saw was Lumiere, and he was oblique on matters of the household staff when the prince inquired. Gaston was now free of the horrors of being trapped within the cursed castle.

We watched Lumiere in his master's room holding

his small candelabrum, afraid to cast light on the prince's face, or his own, for fear the prince would see how desperately he was trying to conceal his terror. We delighted to see the prince so ghastly, pale, and worn. His eyes dark pits and his features more animal than human. Lumiere didn't have the heart to say everyone in the castle, one by one, had been transformed after each foul act the prince committed, and now, after what the prince had done to Tulip and her family, Lumiere was the only servant left in his human form. But it seemed this had already become clear to the prince, what was left of him, anyway, going on about servants disappearing, afraid of the statues moving about the castle, casting their eyes in his direction when he wasn't looking.

But this was not the way the servants saw themselves. They did not see horrors lurking in the shadows or moving statues. They saw nothing of the sort. That horror was reserved for the prince alone, now that his friend Gaston had escaped the horrors of their childhood friends vanishing, of fearing they were trapped within stone. In fact, they had been turned into household objects and were doing their best to help the prince try to break the curse.

Lumiere knew it was only a matter of time before he, too, would transform into some household object like the others had, and the prince would be left alone with only the horrors that were conjured in his mind. Until then, Lumiere would do what he could to comfort him.

Late one evening, Lumiere talked the prince into going for a walk in the woods. It was twilight, the prince's favorite time, the in-between time when anything was possible. When everything looked perfect. The darkening sky was lilac, making the moon all the more striking by its contrast. Lumiere was right, the prince thought, a walk in the woods was what he needed after being cooped up in his room for so long. As it got darker, he was more at ease, the canopy of tree branches overhead obscuring the light except for little patches revealing a star-filled blanket of night. We watched the prince as he became more comfortable, his eyes adjusting to the dark like a forest animal, and we saw that he was now enjoying his new form, feeling quite beastly and prowling the forest. Stalking, looking for something to kill. He was home; everything felt right and perfect in the woods. He was where he belonged.

Something—he wasn't sure what, maybe instinct—made him quickly hide behind a large, moss-covered tree stump. Someone was coming. A hunter stalking through the forest holding a blunderbuss. But before the beast prince could react, shots rained upon him, penetrating the tree trunk, splintering the wood, and sending his heart into a manic rhythm he thought would kill him.

We were delighted; this couldn't have been more perfect. Would this be the moment Gaston would kill his friend, thinking at last he had killed the beast that had taken his family from him? The moment Circe had predicted? Or would the beast prince kill the hunter, not knowing it was his friend Gaston? It was all too delicious. And we watched as something terrible and dark grew inside the beast prince. It obscured everything, making him forget Gaston. He felt like he was slipping into a deep dark ocean, he was drowning in it, losing himself and his memory of his friend completely while something else took over, something that felt alien yet familiar and comfortable at the same time.

Everything in his periphery narrowed, and the only thing he could focus on was Gaston. Nothing else existed, nothing else mattered but the sound of blood rushing to Gaston's beating heart. The sound enveloped him, matching his own heartbeat.

He wanted Gaston's blood. He wasn't even aware he had rushed forward and knocked Gaston over and pinned him to the ground until he found himself looking at this man he had taken down so easily, this man he had rendered defenseless. This man with fear in his eyes.

All he wanted was to taste his blood. He licked his lips, imagining what it would taste like: warm, salty, and thick. But then he looked into the man's eyes and saw fear, and he saw his friend. This man, this hunter, was Gaston. He'd never seen Gaston look so afraid, not since they were young boys. The prince had almost taken the life of his best friend. A man who had saved his life. So he snatched Gaston's gun from his shaking hands and flung it far into the woods, running away as quickly as he could, leaving Gaston alone and confused in the woods, wondering what manner of beast attacked him. The beast prince could only hope Gaston didn't know it was his old friend who tried to kill him.

After that moment, if Gaston had had any lingering half memories of the prince, their friendship, or his previous life in the castle, they were now entirely forgotten. And Gaston's previous life forgot him, too. Lumiere did not know him when he showed up in the servants' courtyard, battered, bruised, and bloodied, needing assistance. He was just a man who stumbled in needing their help, and who forgot he had even been there after he left.

It seemed to us that Gaston would finally have his happily ever. He was free. Free from his obligation to the prince, and his memories of him.

As far as Gaston knew, he was attacked by the Beast of Gévaudan in the woods, not by the man who had once called him brother. The man who said he had no room in his heart for anyone but him. So after he was patched up and sent on his way, he went back to the only life he had known. The hero of the town. The only man brave enough to hunt the Beast of Gévaudan.

Gaston had a new life, living on his estate, forgetting it was the prince who gave it to him. He was free to live as he wanted. Free to be the best at everything, make his own choices, and do everything he could to protect the people of the town, who did not forget him like they had everyone who lived within the castle once the curse was sealed. The castle that was now regarded as an old, abandoned relic left over from obscurity, a haunted, ghostly place no one had reason to visit.

And for a time, Gaston was living his best life. It seemed at last he would be able to live on his own terms. But little did Gaston know we still had plans for him. We saw deep into his heart, and we saw that he still loved the prince even if he didn't remember him.

And we didn't want this brotherhood between them to spark his memories, causing Gaston to help the beast. To venture back to his old home, seeking answers to foggy half memories or strange dreams about another life. We wanted him to be self-possessed, to focus almost entirely on himself. To be the man he was meant to be. To be the best.

We needed something to distract him. Belle felt like the perfect choice. She loved books almost as much as Gaston once had, even if he didn't remember those days of sneaking into the castle library or the prince reading to him. Even if he didn't remember loving stories, even if he started to share the same closed-minded notions as the other people in the village about having to fit in, that women had no business having their noses stuck in a book and they were peculiar for daydreaming. As far as he knew, he was like everyone else in town, and had always been so. As far as he knew, he grew up with these people, and he shared their values. He was exactly what the town thought they needed. And Gaston was happy to belong.

Our curse changed Gaston, but at least he fit in.

And he was loved by everyone in the town. But we needed assurances. So we did what witches do best. We cast a spell. One that made him switch his focus to Belle.

One that made Belle Gaston's greatest desire.

Chapter XX

The Beast

Late into the night and early hours of the morning after Gaston was attacked by the beast, he and his estate manager, LeFou, were in the tavern, surrounded by all the usual revelers who frequented Mr. Higgins's establishment. This was Gaston's favorite place to be, surrounded by his admirers. The walls were filled with the trophies he had been collecting for years. There wasn't a stuffed or mounted animal head on that wall anyone but him could claim to be their own. As far as everyone knew, he was proud of that, and in a way, it did give him a certain sort of pride, but it was also a reminder there was one trophy missing. The head of the beast who killed his parents. And on this day, he'd had the chance to kill it, but the beast had gotten the better of him, and got away.

Everyone's gaze was fixed on Gaston, rapt with attention as they listened to his harrowing story. He had been spending more time in the village and at his estate, even before the prince had fully transformed. He and the prince had already been slowly starting to forget each other before that fateful night when they would forget what they meant to each other forever.

"And out of nowhere the beast pounced on me, pinning me to the ground! I thought I was done for. You should have seen his snarling face, his massive, razor-sharp teeth, ready to rip my throat out."

What Gaston didn't say was that he had just taken a shot at it and missed. And how truly frightened he was when the beast had gotten the better of him. It was like lightning! He hadn't even seen it happen; one moment he was standing there, and the next he was on the ground fearing for his life. He didn't tell them he was afraid he was going to die, that he felt like he had failed his mother and father, or how powerless he was while pinned to the ground. The beast was too strong. But something strange happened when he was lying in the dirt looking into the eyes of the beast: for one flashing moment, he thought he knew who the beast was. He thought he recognized it. And in that fleeting moment, the beast grabbed Gaston's blunderbuss and tossed it away, running deep into the woods. But how was that possible? How could a beast do that? It was all so confused in mind. All he could remember then was finding his gun and making his way to the tavern, feeling that there was only one thing he wanted more than to kill the beast. He wanted to tell Belle all about it.

"What happened next? Did you kill it, Gaston? Where is the monster now?"

"I would have, but the damnable thing took me by surprise and managed to knock my gun from my hand," said Gaston. "And it ran off. I can't explain it."

"You'll be ready next time, won't you, Gaston?" said LeFou, always there to bolster Gaston's spirits.

"Sure he will!" said Mr. Higgins "The beast won't know what hit it!"

"I will! Don't you fear. I will kill the beast! You can be sure of that!" he said, distracted by the clock on the wall. LeFou, look, the sun is up! It's already morning. I think it's about time for Belle to make her way home from the bookshop. Come on, I want to impress her with my story about the beast. No woman alive can resist a good hunter, especially if that hunter is handsome like me!"

LeFou seemed confused but tagged along anyway. "Since when do you care about impressing Belle?"

"Since I decided I am going to marry her, that's when!" Gaston said, opening the tavern door and stepping outside. And just his luck—a flock of geese was flying overhead. This was his chance to show Belle his hunting skills. "Quick, LeFou, grab your bag! Make yourself ready!"

LeFou had been with him for as long as Gaston could remember. In fact, he wasn't even sure how he came to be his land agent. Neither of them could, but it didn't matter. Gaston assumed it was something his father had arranged. He wasn't sure. What he did know was LeFou was loyal and always by his side. By all accounts, LeFou seemed to worship Gaston more than anyone else in the village, and that was saying something. Gaston didn't mind. He liked having him around. Always ready to do his bidding. Always reminding him of how handsome he was, and how he was the best at everything. But it wasn't as if Gaston needed reminding. He knew he was best. He knew he was everyone's favorite guy.

Gaston raised his blunderbuss and shot at the geese overhead, causing one of them to come plummeting to the ground. Gaston liked to imagine LeFou was unable to catch the bird when it fell from the sky because he was so distracted by how impressed he was by Gaston's shot.

"Wow! You didn't miss a shot, Gaston!" LeFou seemed gobsmacked by Gaston's talent. "You're the greatest hunter in the whole world!" Gaston knew his sidekick was easy to impress. And he also knew he was trying to make him feel better about letting the beast get away. LeFou was perfect that way. Though apparently not perfect at catching geese.

"I know," said Gaston.

"Huh. No beast alive stands a chance against you . . . and no girl, for that matter!" said LeFou.

"It's true, LeFou, and I've got my sights set on that one!" said Gaston, wrapping one of his arms around LeFou's neck and lifting him up, using his blunderbuss to point at Belle so LeFou could see who he was talking about.

"The inventor's daughter?" LeFou sounded confused. As if somehow Belle was unworthy of Gaston's affections. It was true, she didn't seem like the obvious choice for Gaston, but there was something about her he liked. Something different. Something special. And there was something that kept telling him she was the girl for him. The woman he was meant to marry. So why fight it? Why not ask her to marry him? He was, after all, the most handsome man in town. Why wouldn't she want to marry him? All he had to do was ask.

And that was exactly what he planned to do.

"She's the one! The lucky girl I'm going to marry,"

said Gaston, setting his sights on Belle like she was one of his prey. As if he planned to make her one of his trophies.

"But she's . . ."

"The most beautiful girl in town," he said, getting annoyed with his friend.

"I know . . ." said LeFou.

"And that makes her the best. And don't I deserve the best?" Gaston said, dropping his blunderbuss on LeFou's head.

"Well, of course, I mean you do, but I mean . . ."

Gaston snatched his gun from LeFou and set off on his pursuit, he was determined to catch up with Belle, but that did not stop him from admiring himself in a mirror before pursuing her down the busy thorough-fare. She continued to read her book as she walked, blissfully unaware of what was going on around her.

Gaston dodged carts and swooning admirers as he pushed past gossiping villagers, all the while keeping his eye on Belle, who was several yards ahead of him. He could hear people talking about her as he passed them, saying how peculiar Belle was for reading so much, how strange they thought she was, but that didn't matter to him. He declared his intentions to everyone within earshot that he was going to make Belle his wife.

Gaston had to agree with everyone in town. Belle was strange, with her love of books, and faraway looks, always daydreaming. She was the oddest girl he had ever met. She wasn't like anyone else in town, but that might have been why he was so infatuated with her. Gaston didn't care; even if Belle didn't fit in, he was still going to marry her. He had to! Something was driving him toward this. He was going to ask her that day. And gods help anyone who spoke out against her once they were married.

Gaston gave up trying to reach Belle by making his way through the throngs of people gathered in the thoroughfare and decided to go into one of the houses at the end of the street. He ran up to the attic as fast as he could, climbed out the window onto the roof, and slid down so he could surprise Belle on the other side. He had timed it perfectly.

How he felt about Belle that day was almost as strange as she was. He had never really thought of her like this before. At least, he didn't think he had. He had never really given her a second thought. Sure, he had seen her in the village since she and her father moved there. But it wasn't what one could call love at first sight. It was more like an unexpected bolt of lightning. A jolt that hit him after he was attacked by the beast—suddenly he was in love with Belle. He couldn't explain it. And he didn't care.

At last he caught up to her. He knew she would be overjoyed to learn he had feelings for her. What woman wouldn't be? She had probably been pining for him since she and her kooky father moved to town, and only walked up and the down the street reading her books to get his attention. And somehow he had never noticed her, not really, not like this, not until that day. The day he decided he had to marry her.

He hopped down from the roof, landing right in her path, and struck one of his best poses: hands on his hips, showing off his muscles. He knew in that moment he looked more handsome than ever, if that was even possible.

"Hello, Belle," he said, sure she would be surprised and pleased he was striking up both poses and conversation with her. He'd have her swooning in no time.

"Bonjour, Gaston," she said as Gaston snatched her book from her hands playfully. He was even good at flirting! "Gaston, may I have my book, please?"

"How can you read this? There's no pictures!" he said, turning the book sideways and then upside down.

"Well, some people use their imaginations."

"Belle, it's about time you got your head out of those books and paid attention to more important things . . . like *me!*" He tossed the book into the air with a flourish, letting it fall into a puddle of mud. She didn't look impressed. She wasn't overjoyed he was talking to her. What could be the problem? Any other girl would be swooning now. In fact, Claudette, Laurette, and Paulette, the three blond beauties who worked at the tavern, were standing in the street, swooning over him that very moment. What was wrong with this girl?

"The whole town's talking about it. It's not right for a woman to read. Soon she starts getting ideas . . . and thinking," Gaston said with the upmost sincerity as Belle fetched her book from the mud. It never occurred to him that he once loved books as much as she did; he had forgotten all about those days. And if he had remembered he'd be happy to spend his life with someone who loved to read, someone so sweet and kind, who would happily take the time to teach him to read books for himself, if he didn't act like such a prig . . . But all he knew was that he loved this woman, and he didn't know why. He didn't remember wishing he had the opportunity to court her after their conversation at the ball, how he longed to spirit her away from the ballroom to the library and show her all his favorite books. He didn't remember how on some level he was protecting Belle when he steered Kingsley in Tulip's direction. He didn't remember any of it.

He wasn't even the same person he was before the curse. He was more like the people in the town, narrow-minded, with antiquated ideas. He fit in. And he was obsessed with a handful of things: being the hero the town wanted, being the best, killing the beast, and wooing Belle. Everything else was obscured by the curse, even if it was lingering under the surface, shadowy and indistinct. These new obsessions distracted and inspired him. Even if this obsession with himself made him insufferable, there was no chance of him remembering.

"Gaston, you are positively primeval." Belle gave him a dirty look as she cleaned her book off with her apron. This wasn't going well, and Gaston didn't understand why. She should have been over the moon to have such a handsome man strike up a conversation with her. Was she immune to his extreme good looks? Was she not impressed with his superior hunting skills? His reputation for being the bravest man in the village? Impossible! There must be something else at work, he thought, and he decided to take her comment as a compliment. He took everything as a compliment; life was so much more enjoyable that way. He put his arm around her and smiled.

"Why, thank you, Belle. Hey, whaddaya say you and me take a walk over to the tavern and have a look at my hunting trophies?" Surely if she saw all of his achievements, she'd realize what a catch he was.

"Maybe some other time," she said. Claudette, Laurette, and Paulette gasped audibly, and Gaston knew how they felt. Belle was turning him down. How was it that everyone in town loved him except for Belle?

"Please, Gaston. I can't. I have to get home and help my father. Goodbye." And just like that, she was walking away from him. How was it possible? He stood there in disbelief as LeFou arrived on the scene, and the two stood next to each other, watching Belle walk toward her house.

"Ha-ha-ha, that crazy old loon, he needs all the help he can get!" LeFou always knew what to say to make him laugh. Belle's father was a bit of a kook. There was no denying it.

"Don't you talk about my father that way!" She whipped around and gave them a stern look. This was the first time Belle had let her anger show. And Gaston knew if he was going to win this girl's heart, making fun of her father wasn't the way of going about it.

"Yeah, don't talk about her father that way!" Gaston said, knocking LeFou on the head. But Belle was still angry. She stood there glaring at them.

"My father's not crazy! He's a genius!" she said as something exploded in the basement of her home, causing smoke to billow out. More than likely one of crazy old Maurice's contraptions.

As she ran off, Gaston said, "I don't care what anyone says about her, LeFou! I am going to marry that girl, and you're going to help me do it!"

And Gaston meant it. Everything else was melting away. There was nothing else that mattered. He had to marry Belle. It was a feeling in the pit of his stomach, an inexplicable urgency pushing him, almost as if his life depended upon it.

CHAPTER XXI

FROM THE BOOK OF FAIRY TALES

The Odd Sisters' Spy

The Odd Sisters here. Don't worry, dears, we'll get back to Gaston's baboonery soon enough. It's not as if you don't already know what's going to happen. What a disaster his surprise wedding turned out to be, but far be it for us to spoil the story for you. I am sure by now you have surmised all these stories are intertwined, an intricate web, woven together like the strings of fate. So be patient with us, dears, while we share some pages of the Book of Fairy Tales.

At the top of a grassy hill was a dark green gingerbread-style mansion trimmed in gold with black shutters. Its roof stretched skyward, the shape resembling a witch's cap. We were nestled within, having our morning tea. Martha was bringing in the blueberry scones when she heard me squeal with delight.

"She's here! She's here!"

Ruby and Martha ran to the window, tripping over themselves to see *who* was here. We watched her walking up the dirt path as her beautiful golden eyes lined in black shined with little specks of green in the morning light. We were so happy to have her home at last.

"Pflanze, hello! We've seen everything! We've seen it all! You've done well, our beloved."

Perhaps you wondered how we saw everything that was going on in the castle. Maybe you thought it was through one of our many magical mirrors, and in some cases it was, but it was also Pflanze. Yes, Pflanze, Gaston's old cat, the cat Tulip loved so dearly when she was at the castle.

And everything would have gone as we planned if Circe hadn't realized we were meddling, after we promised her we would not. We tried to make her think we were just spying, just keeping an eye on the prince.

"And what did you see?" she asked, coming into the room. And just like that, our words rained down on her like a storm. We couldn't help ourselves. And poor Circe was caught in the flurry of our fragmented stories. I am so thankful we don't speak that way anymore. When we look at ourselves, how we were then, it's like we were entirely different witches. And I suppose we were.

"Oh, we've seen everything!"

"Nasty, terrible things!"

"Worse than we imagined!"

"Murder!"

"Lies!"

"Ugly, nasty, horrible beast!"

"Broken hearts, romancing tarts!"

"Ah, are we rhyming now? Lovely!"

Circe put an end to it before the rhyming continued. "No, no, you're not! No rhyming! Now calm down and tell me everything, in a straight line. I know you can do it."

And that's what we did: We told her everything. Everything that had happened since the curse—and of course she felt responsible, especially for what happened to Tulip.

"The prince did that to her, Circe, not you!"

"I know, but he destroyed her and her family in order to break the curse! My curse!" We knew it was a mistake to tell her the moment we opened our mouths. We knew she would feel like she had to do something, and there was nothing we could say to sway her conviction. But we tried.

"The Old Queen Grimhilde blighted the land and left a trail of disaster and death in her wake. Should we blame ourselves?"

We didn't want Circe blaming herself for Tulip jumping off the cliff, just as we couldn't blame ourselves for Grimhilde doing the same so many years before. As much as we tried, we couldn't control everything. Besides, Tulip was saved by the Sea Witch Ursula. She was fine. There was nothing for Circe to worry about.

"What did the Sea Witch demand in return?"

"You think so little of the company we keep?" Ruby was hurt by the question. We all were.

"And how are we to know what Ursula took from her? We are not privy to the goings-on in every kingdom." But Circe knew that was a lie. Of course we knew. We knew more than Circe could have fathomed at the time. But she had an inkling. She was far more powerful than she realized then. She wasn't the queen then as she is now, but she was taking the first steps that would lead her to her destiny.

"She took nothing Tulip actually needed." Circe was not convinced. She had no reason to trust us; she knew our ways. Even if we were only trying to protect her.

"I want you to make things right with Ursula! You give her something in exchange for whatever she took from Tulip! And I am going to sort out Morningstar Kingdom's affairs!"

Ruby and Martha flew into a panic, as they often did in those days, reluctant and anxious at the idea of giving away any of our cherished possessions.

"But what will we give her? Nothing too precious. Nothing from the vault."

"Circe would have us give away all our treasures! First one of our enchanted mirrors, now what?"

But I knew exactly what we would give her. And it wasn't too precious. My addlebrained sisters had forgotten about it, tucked away in the back of the pantry. It was in a little velvet drawstring pouch. I gave it to Circe to take with her to Morningstar.

"When you get to Morningstar, go to the cliffs and give Ursula this. She will be there waiting for you."

And that was the last time we saw our dearest Circe for more time than we'd like to acknowledge.

Sometimes a simple act can cause reverberations throughout your life you don't expect. And giving Circe Ursula's seashell necklace that day set us down paths we never fathomed. But we didn't see that then. All we knew was Circe was determined to help Tulip, and quite possibly the prince. We knew our daughter, and we knew her heart. And if you've read the beast's story, you know in the end it was Circe who stepped in and helped Belle and the beast, and she is the reason they are together today.

But we didn't know this at the time, so our aim was to make sure the prince didn't break the curse. We saw in the Book of Fairy Tales it was Belle who could help him break it, and we had to do everything in our power to make sure that didn't happen.

Even if it meant taking Gaston down in the process. Even if it meant driving him mad with desire for Belle, and with bloodlust for the beast. So we did what witches do best.

CHAPTER XXII

THE SURPRISE

Gaston had LeFou running errands all morning preparing for the big surprise. He was dashing all over town making the arrangements, and everyone was happy to help. This was for Gaston, after all, and there was nothing the people in that village wouldn't do for him. The baker was happy to make the wedding cake, and the preacher didn't mind a last-minute wedding. LeFou had no trouble assembling the band, or finding volunteers to make the wedding feast, or gathering men to build a dais and set up the banquet tables and chairs. And of course, everyone was happy to attend. All LeFou had to do was make an announcement in the tavern that Gaston was getting married, and everyone was ready to join in the celebration.

Everything was prepared for Gaston and Belle's wedding. All set up and arranged, right outside Belle's house but on the other side of a tall hedge so she wouldn't see what they were up to. The only thing missing was the bride.

"Heh! Oh boy! Belle's gonna get the surprise of her life, huh, Gaston?" LeFou said as Gaston pulled back a branch from the hedge, revealing Belle's house.

"Yep. This is her lucky day!" Gaston said, letting go of the branch, which smacked LeFou right in the face.

As he stood there looking at all his guests, he thought to himself how this would be the highlight of Belle's life. A dream come true. The day she would marry the bravest, most handsome man in town. He couldn't wait to show her his surprise.

"I'd like to thank you all for coming to my wedding. But first, I better go in there and . . . propose to the girl!" Everyone laughed heartily, except for Claudette, Laurette, and Paulette, who were in tears at the thought of Gaston getting married to someone who wasn't one of them. Gaston supposed there wasn't a woman in town who didn't wish she could marry him. And Belle would no doubt feel honored he chose her. This was going to be a snap!

"Now, you, LeFou. When Belle and I come out that door—"

But LeFou didn't let Gaston finish. "Oh, I know, I know! I strike up the band." He was so excited to show Gaston he had it all under control, he started directing the band to play at once. Gaston rolled his eyes. Clearly the band had been in the tavern when LeFou found them. No matter. Everything would be perfect as long as LeFou didn't mess it up.

"Not yet!" Gaston slammed the tuba on the fool's head. What a dolt LeFou could be sometimes. No matter. The time was at hand. He knocked on the door and waited for Belle to answer. It felt like he was standing on the front stoop for ages. What was she doing in there? What was taking so long? How long must he wait to marry this girl? It was maddening.

What's wrong with you, man? Calm down, he told himself. Why was he in such a panic? Why had this suddenly become so urgent?

When she finally opened the door, she was wearing the same blue dress and white apron she had been wearing earlier. No matter. She was beautiful whatever she wore. She would make the perfect bride. His bride. The luckiest bride in the world.

"Gaston, what a pleasant . . . surprise." Gaston let himself into the house and struck one of his best poses, putting his hands on his belt to show off his fancy new outfit. There was no way she could resist him in his new gold waistcoat and long red coat. He couldn't remember ever feeling more handsome than he did that day. Which was quite the thing, since he always felt handsome.

"Isn't it, though? I'm just full of surprises. You know, Belle, there's not a girl in town who wouldn't love to be in your shoes. This is the day . . ." he said, getting distracted by his own reflection in a mirror and taking a moment to admire it. Yep, he was more handsome than ever. No doubt about it. "This is the day your dreams come true." And he meant it. He believed it. He felt it in his very core.

"What do you know about my dreams, Gaston?"

"Plenty. Here, picture this." He plopped into a chair and slammed his mud-covered boots on Belle's book, which was sitting open on the table. He could get used to this, he thought, and he kicked off his boots, revealing his threadbare, hole-laden socks. It felt good to take his boots off, to wiggle his toes, and imagine his future life with Belle.

"A rustic hunting lodge, my latest kill roasting on the fire, and my little wife, massaging my feet, while the little ones play with the dogs." What was that look on her face? Revulsion? Maybe she wasn't fond of dogs.

"We'll have six or seven," he said, flashing his best smile.

"Dogs?"

"No, Belle! Strapping boys, like me!"

"Imagine that." He could tell she was nervous as she occupied herself around the house, picking up her book, placing her bookmark in the pages, and putting the book back on the shelf. Was she so overcome by his proposal, and the life he had planned for them, she didn't know what to say? Or did she not understand? And here he thought Belle was smart.

"And do you know who that wife will be?"

"Let me think," she said, pretending she didn't know it was her. Or was she pretending? Was she just playing hard to get, or did she truly not understand? He had a feeling she was teasing him. Well, he'd had enough of these games. He couldn't have been clearer. Perhaps it was time to be more direct.

"You, Belle!" He moved in close and cornered her, but she quickly ducked out from under his arm and made her way to the other end of the room. Playing hard to get was one thing, but this was going too far. Everyone knew she was going to marry him. Everyone, it seemed, except for her.

"Gaston, I'm speechless. I really don't know what to say," she said as Gaston flung chairs and anything else that stood between him and his future wife out of his way. Then at last he reached her. She was standing with her back against the door, facing him. Finally, they would have their moment.

"Say you'll marry me."

"I'm very sorry, Gaston, but I just don't deserve you," she said, opening the door and making him fall off the porch and into a giant puddle of mud.

As he sat there, mortified, covered in mud, he saw his boots being flung out before she slammed the door closed.

Gaston felt like a fool, and he looked like one. But as the band played "Here Comes the Bride," he realized something. She hadn't turned him down. Not really. She simply didn't believe she deserved him, and while that was most likely true, it didn't matter. He wanted her. Heck, he could have anyone he wanted. But he wanted Belle, although he wasn't even sure why. So how was he going to prove to her she was worthy? How would he be able to allay her fears that she didn't deserve him? And what woman didn't like a surprise wedding, anyway? And to the most handsome man in town? Was she as addled as her father? Was she trying to make Gaston look like a fool? He didn't know, but what he did know was that he didn't like being made a fool of, by mistake of happenstance. And he would do anything to make her marry him.

"I'll have Belle as my wife, make no mistake about that!"

Chapter XXIII

No One Fights Like Gaston

Later that night, Gaston found himself back in the tavern with LeFou, licking his wounds. He wasn't sure how to feel: angry, hurt, or confused? Maybe it was all of them. Even if Belle didn't feel worthy of him, how could she publicly humiliate him like that? There wasn't a person in town who hadn't heard about how she turned him down and threw him out of the house. And how did that make him look? No. How did that make *her* look? No doubt they all wondered how she could resist his charms and such a romantic proposal of marriage.

He couldn't think straight. His mind was racing,

it was like a maelstrom, swirling. He heard the same words being chanted over and over in his mind: *You must marry Belle.* He didn't know who was saying the words. Was it him? Were those his own thoughts? It didn't sound like him. Was it someone else? There were moments when he thought it was the voices of women, three, in fact. Voices he thought he knew but couldn't place. It was driving him mad. Did he even want to marry Belle? Of course he did. He had to. There was no turning back now.

"Who does she think she is? That girl has tangled with the wrong man. No one says no to Gaston!" The last thing he desired was to feel weak in front of the other men, least of all LeFou. He needed to save face. He needed to get his head straight.

"Darn right!"

"Dismissed. Rejected. Publicly humiliated. Why, it's more than I can bear." He turned his chair away so the others would not see him acting like a child.

"More beer?" It was just like LeFou to try to cheer him up, but even beer wasn't helping. There wasn't anything anyone could do.

"What for? Nothing helps. I'm disgraced."

"Who, you? Never. Gaston, you've got to pull yourself together." And it was true, Gaston had never been so down in the dumps, and it was just like LeFou to try to cheer him up. And without even knowing how it happened, everyone in the tavern started swaying back and forth, singing Gaston's praises. The maelstrom of voices that had been driving him mad was replaced with his friends' song. Oh yes, this was what he needed to raise his spirits. This was what life was about, being in the company of good men who saw his quality. People who loved him. Loved him for who he was.

And just as Gaston's friends cheered him with their song, just as he was feeling better, and more like himself again, or maybe an even better version than he had been before, Belle's father Maurice came stumbling into the tavern from the freezing cold. Gaston was sure the man was there to ask him what happened with Belle. If anyone could talk sense into Belle, it was her father, so for a moment Gaston was pleased to see him. But it didn't look like Maurice was in any condition to do much at all, shivering and panicked as he was.

"Help! Someone help me."

"Maurice?"

"Please! Please, I need your help! He's got her. He's got her locked in the dungeon." Maurice was making less sense than usual. None of them knew what he was talking about.

"Who?" asked LeFou.

"Belle. We must go. Not a minute to lose!" said Maurice.

"Whoa! Slow down, Maurice. Who's got Belle locked in a dungeon?" Gaston was going to get to the bottom of this. There was no way he was going to stand for anyone locking up his future bride in a dungeon.

"A beast! A horrible, monstrous beast!" Maurice was running from man to man, pleading with them for help. But they just laughed. This hadn't been the first time Maurice came into the tavern saying strange things, and the men were all worked up after a long day. They thought they'd have a bit of fun with the poor old man.

"Is it a big beast?"

"Huge!"

"With a long, ugly snout?"

"Hideously ugly!"

"And sharp, cruel fangs?"

"Yes, yes. Will you help me?"

"All right, old man. We'll help you out," said Gaston.

"You will? Oh, thank you, thank you!" said Maurice. And three of the men picked him up and threw him out the tavern door.

"Crazy old Maurice."

"He's always good for a laugh!"

"Crazy old Maurice, hmm? Crazy old Maurice. Hmmm?" Gaston had an idea.

He knew if Maurice had really been face-to-face with the beast, he would not have lived to tell the story. If a skilled hunter like Gaston had barely escaped with his own life, there was no way Maurice could have. Besides, the Beast of Gévaudan was a wild animal. It didn't go around putting people in dungeons. It devoured them. No, this was just one of Maurice's stories.

Everyone knew he was an eccentric old coot, always going on about one thing or another. Wasn't this the same man who came into the tavern claiming the owls were not what they seemed? What did that even mean? And on that same night, he said he was actually building a contraption that could chop wood into logs. Whoever heard of such a thing? And why would anyone want or need it? Everyone was tired of listening to his stories, contraptions, and wild notions about things. And this was just another example.

No, Maurice was just spouting nonsense, as usual. But Gaston had an idea how that would work to his advantage. He just needed a way to convince Monsieur D'Arque, the man who ran the sanatorium, to go along with his plan.

CHAPTER XXIV

KILL THE BEAST

D'Arque was more than happy to comply with Gaston's request to put Maurice in the sanatorium if Belle did not agree to marry him. It was clear D'Arque knew very well that Maurice was just an odd little man who loved only one thing more than his clanking apparatuses, and that was his daughter, Belle. And Belle loved no one more than her father. Gaston almost felt bad going to these lengths, but there was something that kept pushing him, as if some strange power had a hold on him. And it wasn't just Belle's beauty; it was something else. Maybe it was fate, he didn't know. All he knew was he had to marry her, and he would do anything to convince her to say yes. Since he was attacked in the woods, it felt like there was something missing, something he couldn't explain. He had a strange, hollow feeling, like he'd lost something important, or someone important, like he wasn't whole, but he didn't know what it was. Once he'd realized he had feelings for Belle, he had started to feel like maybe once she was his wife, he would feel right and whole again.

It's seemed D'Arque was content with their arrangement, and why wouldn't he be? Gaston made sure his coffers were filled, and D'Arque was happy to have made a new alliance with Gaston. Together, they were about to partake in some good old-fashioned skullduggery.

Even Gaston had to admit how intimidating D'Arque now appeared, illuminated in the torchlight as they stood in front of Belle's home. It seemed to Gaston this man loved nothing more than causing fear. And that was a trait Gaston admired.

Gaston and his mob were gathered in full force in front of Belle and Maurice's home. They stood near

D'Arque's wagon, which was ready to take Maurice away should Belle refuse to marry Gaston. They were a rowdy bunch Gaston had collected at the tavern. There was nothing quite as menacing as a group of hooligans after a long night of drinking, with gold in their pockets and hate in their hearts. All of which, in this case, was supplied by Gaston.

There was little doubt Belle would marry him now. She couldn't possibly resist, nor do better. Who else in town would have her, with all her strange ways? And how could she say no under the circumstances? He'd make it up to her after they were married. She would be the happiest woman alive. Who wouldn't be? After all, she would be married to him.

And with that, he knocked on her door.

Belle answered the knock tentatively, with eyes full of fear. "May I help you?"

"I've come to collect your father," said D'Arque. His withered, skull-like face looked horrid and menacing in the torchlight.

"My father?" She looked confused.

"Don't worry, Mademoiselle. We'll take good care

of him," said D'Arque, with a face like death itself.

Gaston could see Belle was seized with fear. She understood what was happening at once. She saw D'Arque's wagon in the distance. She knew they were taking her father to the asylum.

"No, you can't do this!" she said, hopelessly trying to stop them. She was afraid, and desperate, and her look of betrayal and loathing almost made Gaston call it all off. Something about the fear in her eyes reminded him of someone, a woman who was hurt—not by him, but by his complicity. What was he doing? But his head started to swirl again, the voices were back, urging him on, telling him he would be a laughingstock if Belle didn't marry him, that he would be alone. That he would die if he didn't marry Belle. So he shook his head, freeing himself of his doubts, and went on with his plan. And it should have worked.

It was a simple, straightforward plan. If Belle agreed to marry him, he would talk D'Arque out of taking her father away. Belle was headstrong. He expected that, and in a way admired her for it, but what he didn't expect was proof her father had actually seen a beast. She raised up a hand mirror and revealed the monster for all of them to see. And he was shocked. Shook to his very core.

Gaston couldn't believe what he was seeing; it was the same beast that attacked him in the woods. The same beast that killed his parents. He didn't understand why he hadn't believed Maurice from the moment he asked for help. Gaston couldn't figure out what was wrong with him lately. It was almost as if he had forgotten he was attacked at all. His head had been so muddled, and all he seemed to think or care about was Belle. But seeing that monster in Belle's mirror triggered something, a spark, and he knew he had seen that beast before. And what was wrong with Belle, defending this monster? Did he just hear her say it was gentle and kind? Had the beast cast some sort of love spell on her, binding her to him forever? This was insanity.

"If I didn't know better, I'd think you had feelings for this monster," he said, looking at Belle.

"He's no monster, Gaston. You are!" Gaston was

sure Belle was under some wicked enchantment. Clearly this beast had some kind of magic. How else would she have gotten this magic mirror if not from the beast? This was madness. She was delusional.

"She's as crazy as the old man," he said as he snatched the mirror from her hand. He had to do something. He had to break this evil curse the beast put on Belle. It all made sense now, why she didn't want to marry him. Why she never paid him any attention. It must have been the beast's influence all along. Enchanting her somehow from afar, luring her to its lair, where it could have her all to himself. Well, he wasn't going to let Belle be locked away forever. He wasn't going to let it stalk the countryside, killing more innocent people. He was going to put an end to this creature and break the evil spell it put on his darling Belle. Once the spell was broken, she would see, and she would forgive what he'd had to do to protect her and everyone else in town.

He would kill the beast.

CHAPTER XXV

BROTHERS IN BLOOD

Fueled by fear and anger, Gaston and the other villagers ventured toward a nightmare through the mists and the woods, through the darkness and shadows until they reached the castle. It was a terrifying place, shrouded in monstrous gloom. Everywhere they looked were statues of gargoyles and other foul creatures, looming in the darkness, peering at them. Gaston could feel their eyes on him and hear whispers within the walls. He couldn't hear what they were saying, or if anyone was saying anything at all. But he couldn't let the atmosphere distract him from his

414

purpose. He was there to save Belle by putting an end to this beast, once and for all.

As the mob stormed the castle, Gaston stalked his prey, quietly searching every room for the beast. He wasn't sure how, but something about the castle felt familiar. It was the strangest feeling; as he went from room to room, he felt as if he had been there before. He came upon a room that looked different from the others, decorated as he would decorate a room for himself. On the dressing table were two objects that looked out of place: a spindly gold candelabra and a peevish-looking wind-up clock. On the bedside table were a squat, cheerful teapot and a small chipped teacup on a saucer. His mind began to shift as images of faces he didn't recognize appeared in his mind. And again, he wondered what he was doing. Why he was there.

He cleared his head and remembered. He was there to save Belle. To kill the beast. He wasn't going to lose someone else he loved to this monster. So he shook off his confusion and tried to ignore the whispers, and kept searching, until at last he saw the beast.

The beast was alone, looking as if it had been waiting for Gaston to get there. For a brief moment, he felt sorry for it. As if the creature knew its fate. As if it had already been defeated before Gaston arrived. There was something about its demeanor that told Gaston the beast knew it was about to die. Gaston took his aim as the beast slowly looked up at him. And just as Gaston released his arrow, he saw sadness in its eyes. For a fleeting moment, Gaston felt the beast's pain as the arrow struck its shoulder. He wanted to scream in pain, too, as the beast roared.

Before Gaston knew what he was doing, before the beast could retaliate, Gaston rushed the creature. It was pure instinct, and it caused them both to careen out the window onto the balcony. They scuffled, until Gaston had the beast cornered at the edge of the roof. The beast just sat there in self-loathing and despair as Gaston mocked the creature, laughing at it. Wondering how he was ever afraid of this monster. How could this weak, pathetic creature be the Beast of Gévaudan? How did it kill his father, the bravest, strongest, best man he had ever known?

"Get up! Get up! What's the matter, Beast? Too kind and gentle to fight back?"

But the beast wouldn't even look at him. It deserved its fate. It knew one day Gaston would come for it. How could he not, after everything the beast had done?

As it just sat there, it gave Gaston a moment to snap off a jagged piece of the roof that he could use like a club. He raised it into the air, ready to smash the beast's skull wide open, when he heard Belle's voice below, screaming out in terror.

"No!"

With one word, she broke his heart. Belle wasn't afraid *for* Gaston. She was afraid *of* him. Afraid Gaston would kill the beast. He heard the beast mutter Belle's name as he snatched Gaston's weapon out of his hand. The creature found his strength and rose up, roaring in Gaston's face.

It was a terrible battle, the two scuffling perilously on the rooftop, until the beast managed to escape Gaston's clutches and hide himself among the shadows. Gaston couldn't find it. He couldn't believe he had let the beast escape again. But it hadn't gotten away, had it? He would have seen it flee. No, it was hiding like the coward it was.

"Come on out and fight! Were you in love with her, Beast? Did you honestly think she'd want you when she had someone like me?"

The beast sprang out from his hiding place among the gargoyles. Something about what Gaston had just said felt familiar to him. Like he had said the words before. No, that wasn't it. Words like those had been spoken *to* him, but by whom? He shook off the flurry of half memories and images swirling in his mind. He couldn't let himself be distracted. He had to focus. He needed to save himself and Belle from this monster.

"It's over, Beast! Belle is mine!" he said, but the beast wrapped his monstrous hand around Gaston's neck and squeezed it as he held him out over the edge of the roof. As he dangled there, Gaston felt the world drop away from under his feet. He knew death waited for him below. His mind was flooded again with veiled memories, most of which he didn't understand, but which somehow he knew belonged to him. With things he had forgotten.

"Put me down. Put me down. Please, don't hurt me! I'll do anything! Anything!" Gaston said, pleading with the beast for his life, and then he saw the beast's anger melt away, and in its eyes he saw something he recognized as the beast pulled Gaston back onto the roof. The memories were beginning to come into focus now. Strong, wretched, horrible memories filled with sorrow, pain, and revulsion.

"Get out!" the beast roared, shoving Gaston to the ground, turning his attention to Belle, who was running out onto the balcony.

Gaston watched as the beast climbed the balcony to reach Belle. His mind was a whirlwind of half memories and fear. And then it clicked. He knew this beast, and not because he had been attacked by it. Gaston's memories were jumbled and confused. Only flashing images were flooding his mind. Partial memories and half-truths. He didn't see their entire story. He didn't see the whole truth. He only saw the horrible things the prince had done, the pain he caused Gaston. He remembered Mrs. Potts, and the night she told Gaston how his mother had died. He saw the pain in her eyes when she described the beast eating his mother alive. He remembered the night the prince insisted they disobey Gaston's father and hunt the beast, causing his father's ghastly, gruesome death. And he remembered having to send Princess Tulip away to keep her safe from the prince.

How could he have forgotten all this? As he stood there watching Belle and the beast looking at each other with love, he knew he had to save her, too, from this horrible creature. This horrible man. He had to kill the beast to protect Belle. He had to kill him to avenge his family.

He was sickened by the thought of Belle being with this monster, and he had to do whatever he could to protect her. He crept up on them as slowly and as quietly as he could, and he took the beast by surprise! Using all his strength, he buried his knife as deep as he could in the beast's back. The beast roared out in pain as Gaston quickly pulled out the knife and swung at him with it, this time going for the kill. He missed, and the two teetered at the edge of the balcony, losing their footing. Both of them perilously close to falling to their deaths. In that moment, Gaston was ready to die. At least he would take the beast with him. And Belle would be free of them both.

But then he saw it, Belle's hand reaching out, but not to him. It reminded him of the statue of his mother in front of her mausoleum, reaching out her hand to him, as if beckoning Gaston to join her on the other side. And in a flash Gaston remembered. He saw the truth. He saw everything. His mind was no longer obscured in a thick fog. And all his thoughts were his own. He saw everything clearly. He saw his and the prince's story, almost like one of the books he and Kingsley had read together. He remembered his best friend, the man he loved. Like a brother. More than a brother. The man who said he had no room in his heart for anyone but him.

And with the few moments he had left, before he fell to his death, Gaston hoped his friend had truly made space in his heart for someone else, and with Belle he would break the curse at last.

A CALL FROM THE DEAD WOODS

Lucinda, Ruby, and Martha were in the Underworld library eating cake under the glow of dancing blue flames. They read while they waited for Hades, who was at the ferry dock ready to usher in the recently departed souls. Pflanze was curled up between Martha and Ruby on the love seat, and Lucinda was sitting across from them, smiling. She couldn't remember the last time she was so happy. Any moment Hades would be home, and they would have their nightly feast with the newly dead.

Their afterlife was good. Better than good. It was delicious. And she knew Circe, Primrose, and Hazel could handle anything that came their way. They were far more powerful than she and her sisters had ever been, not that she would ever admit it. Not to anyone but Hades, that is, because there is no sense in lying to a god.

As she sat there, waiting for the bell to chime to let her know it was time to make their way to the dining room to greet Hades and their guests, she heard Circe's voice from her enchanted mirror on the wall. She assumed it had something to do with Snow White. Snow had written the queens of the dead, afraid there was something wrong with Grimhilde's mirror, and asked for their help. Lucinda didn't detest Snow as she once had, but her hatred for Snow had once been so bitter it was hard to lose the taste completely. She sighed, got up, and went to the mirror, and there in the glass was her sweet Circe.

"Mother, I need your help. Princess Tulip Morningstar has asked for our assistance. She plans to attack the beast prince's castle."

"And I suppose she has the Tree Lords and Cyclopean Giants at her side. I wondered when this would happen."

"*What do you mean? You saw this coming and never told me?*"

"How did you *not* see it coming? Besides, if I told you everything I saw coming, I would never stop talking."

This made Ruby and Martha laugh. "You never stop talking anyway," they said in the background, waving to Circe from across the room. Lucinda sighed. She feared the new queens of the dead would be cleaning up after the messes she and her sisters had left behind. But she also knew Circe would be able to face it, especially with Hazel and Primrose at her side.

"*She has a right to declare war on him, of course. But after all this time? And we are sworn to come to her aid as her ally. Mother, what do we do?*"

"My sweet girl, you know time means nothing. It sounds like you have no other choice but to join your army with hers and march into battle."

"*But is there no other way?*"

"If there is, my sweet, I am sure you will find it."

THE END